£1·00

A

The nurse said, 'Mr Campbell ... How long you here for?'

'A year.'

'Like it?'

'It's very interesting.'

'Mah forebears came from England.'

'Really?'

'Yeah. Glasgow. Mah grandpa's uncle was hung there for stealing sheep.'

'Really?'

'But we love it. Like, we always watch Masterpiece Theater. It's so cute. . . . Bedpan twelve, Cindy. Looks urgent. You with Family Practice, Dave?'

'Yes.'

'Like it?'

'Just started.'

'D'you have stuff like this in England, huh?'

'No,' said Campbell.

Also in Arrow by Colin Douglas

Wellies from the Queen

A CURE
FOR LIVING

Colin Douglas

ARROW BOOKS

Arrow Books Limited
17-21 Conway Street, London W1P 6JD

An imprint of the Hutchinson Publishing Group

London Melbourne Sydney Auckland
Johannesburg and agencies throughout
the world

First published by Hutchinson 1983
Arrow edition 1984

Printed and bound in Great Britain by
Anchor Brendon Limited, Tiptree, Essex

ISBN 0 09 934700 8

PART ONE

'You'll find a whole lot of things here different than in England.' The man in the white coat opened a door for Campbell and ushered him into a large office lined with framed certificates. He indicated an armchair opposite the desk. Campbell sat down.

'Tea, I guess?' Campbell hesitated. The man smiled. 'Dr Campbell, we have a whole lot of English visitors here, and I believe mah secretary makes an excellent cup of tea . . . Oh. Coffee? Yes, certainly. No trouble at all.' He leaned down to a hatch in the wall by his desk, opened it and said, 'Uh, Debbie. One coffee and one tea.'

He settled behind his desk. Campbell checked the name on one of the larger certificates: Philip Z. Drucker. Dr Drucker, his new head of department, or possibly division, squared off a sheaf of typescript and laid it to one side. 'Flight all right?'

'Yes, thanks.'

With that he seemed to have run out of conversation. There was a pause then he said, 'We're very glad to see you.'

'Thank you,' said Campbell. 'I'm very glad to be here.'

'Give yourself a couple of days. Find your way round and settle in to your apartment. Get over your jet lag and meet a few people. Your first time in the States?'

'Yes, actually.'

'You'll find things here plenty different than in England.' There was another short mystical silence. 'And I guess there are more differences in health care than in anything else. . . .' Dr Drucker seemed to be getting nearer what he wanted to say. 'I've travelled some and looked around, and you're from England, Dr Campbell, and I don't mind telling you that there are some things on the delivery of service side here that we can't rightly be proud of. . . . An' you may find yourself comparing things with your National Health. But you have to remember, Dr Campbell, that we're a young country and we set great store by freedom . . . an' the role of market forces. I suppose what I'm saying is. . . . Well, you'll get the idea.'

Campbell felt obliged to say something. 'I've read a bit about it.'

'Fact is . . .' Dr Drucker lowered his voice. '. . . you might say, to put it kinda strongly. . . . Well, to put it very strongly but it's the way some people put it. You might say that medicine here in the United States has been, uh, corrupted by fee for service. That's putting it very strongly indeed.' He glanced nervously at a certificate headed 'West Carolina State License', leaned forward and lowered his voice further. 'Though that's not something that's widely discussed in medical circles generally. . . . Here in academic Primary Care, naturally, we're free to say pretty well what we want, at least within these four walls, but generally speaking you'll find that there's not a whole lot of discussion about the way we run things.'

'I see,' said Campbell, who took all that as some sort of fairly strong warning. 'It'll be interesting to see how things are run here.'

'I guess you're maybe the twelfth or fourteenth Albert Memorial Fund Fellow we've had the privilege of accommodating here, and I think I can say that most of the folks seem to have enjoyed their year with us. For our part we value the link with the British. Those guys at Memorial Fund seem to be able to keep everybody happy.'

'So I gather,' said Campbell.

'Uh?'

2

'I rang a couple of former Fellows a little while ago.'

'I'm glad they didn't put you off us.'

'On the contrary.'

Dr Drucker smiled and moved the sheaf of typescript back to the centre of his desk. 'This year, for a variety of reasons, the arrangements will be . . . improved a little. If you agree. . . . Oh, nothing radical. Just a partial reallocation of some of your clinical contact time into a field that's, well, part of Primary Care, and expanding rapidly.'

'Oh?'

'Yes. We've recently been developing an aspect of Primary Care. In response to need of course, and partly in response to a Federal funding incentive. MacHardy University Medical Center is, uh, proud to have attracted a major Federal award in what you British call terminal care. A big step forward for the Medical Center and an opportunity for all of us to develop our skills and serve, indeed, as a centre of excellence. . . . As head of the Division sponsoring your fellowship award, I've been asked by the Dean to talk with you about this development.'

'Development?'

'Well, Dr Campbell, uh, David, I think we could certainly call it a development. It's well within the guidelines for the Albert Memorial Fund Fellowship. And I'd like you to know there's certainly no financial penalty. As a matter of fact we might have had a problem if the Agency for Life Ending Americans money hadn't turned up. The departmental matching funds element of your fellowship was soft money which terminated. The new grant covers this shortfall. We've written you into the Life Ending money for fifty percent funding.'

'Sorry,' said Campbell. 'You've written me. . . .'

Dr Drucker took off his spectacles, polished the lenses on the lapel of his white coat, put them back on, glanced at a scroll headed 'Golden Apple Award for Excellence in Teaching', and began again. 'Let me put it the other way around. From MacHardy's point of view, from the point of view of MacHardy University Medical Center, it would be highly satisfactory if you agree to participate in a program

3

we're improving. In what you call terminal care. In what we for fund-attracting purposes call Life Ending.'

'I see. And the bit about funds? Soft something. . . .'

'A very generous Federal grant permits us to substitute the lost element in your fellowship finance dollar for dollar.'

'Lost?'

'The soft money ran out.'

'Oh?'

'But the Federal Life Ending money covers you completely for that. Of course only if you'd be interested in this, uh, challenging new area.'

It was clear that resistance would be churlish. 'And this would be . . . half time?'

'The funded commitment as of now is fifty percent.'

'I see. Well. . . .'

'Good.' Dr Drucker smiled. 'But your affiliation is still very much to the Division of Primary Care in general and the Department of Family Practice in particular. You'll find our Family Practice residents warm and caring people and our faculty only too willing to help. And by meeting the challenge I just told you of you'll be doing a great favour to us here in Primary Care. It's an area of great potential, David, and I believe it's one in which British clinical skills have an important part to play.'

The hatch opened and two cups and saucers were passed through. 'Cream?' said a soft female voice. Dr Drucker glanced at Campbell.

'Yes please.'

A hand reached through and emptied a little packet of yellowish dust into Campbell's coffee.

'Sugar?'

'No thanks.'

Dr Drucker handed Campbell a cup of streaky brown liquid. The hatch closed. Host and guest stirred their respective beverages. Campbell sipped his coffee. 'If the job's so . . . important . . . why doesn't someone here. . . ?'

'Overcommitted, unfortunately.' Dr Drucker smiled. 'Our Primary Care physicians here are stretched to the limit. We're just a small division and we have contracts, service,

4

teaching, career development, and major research commitments to cover. Unfortunately. And naturally, David, as a visiting Fellow you'll be expected to go where you can contribute most. And of course you'll have the Family Practice resident on the new four-week rotation in Life Ending to help you. So we can look forward to seeing you make a major contribution to service and teaching and the ongoing research program in Life Ending. Our Center, you'll find, has a thriving thanatologic tradition. There's a major reference library and a whole lot of expertise around the campus. The clinical skills of a British physician will be welcome on the program and in turn I'm confident you'll gain a lot from contact with the various professions that come together in an inter-disciplinary activity like thanatology. It's a very interesting field.' Dr Drucker smiled and half stood up. Campbell, happy enough to leave the rest of his coffee, rose to go. 'We appreciate it,' said Dr Drucker, 'Call round at eight-fifteen tomorrow. I'll take you over to the Thanatology Center myself. You'll meet some interesting people.'

Campbell turned towards the door. Dr Drucker put a hand on his shoulder. 'And not just around the Center. Some very fine people across the State are written into the Life Ending money. Some very fine people indeed.' He paused. 'Down in Split Rock, the physicians in Family Practice operate a very high quality facility. They have shown what can be done for Life Ending Americans even in a rural environment. . . . Dr Totenberg is a wonderful physician, David, and deeply committed to the program.' Dr Drucker followed Campbell out into the corridor, still smiling. 'Oh, yes. We have one or two items we can be a little proud of here at MacHardy. . . . Tomorrow then, David. A quarter after eight. Have a nice day.'

That was unlikely. For Campbell it was around eight in the evening on a hungover day after a sleepless night spent getting from Edinburgh, Scotland, to Crimond, West Carolina, USA, where it was now three in the afternoon. Out in the open again, he found the sun high and hot, and the campus swarming with young people presumably changing classes. They carried textbooks, notebooks and disposable

5

containers, full of popcorn or iced drinks and ranging in size from ordinary cup to half-gallon bucket. Most were dressed casually, as for an informal game of tennis, and many wore red tee-shirts or running-shorts with the word 'MacHardy', in bold white Gothic script, emblazoned over breast or buttock.

Uncomfortable and self-conscious in his tweed jacket, Campbell strove against the stream of summery pedestrians, edged from the path by the weight of numbers and the faint menace of spilt Coca-Cola. He tried to listen to their conversation as they ambled past, and found only that they said 'huh' a lot and that most of the other words were indistinct.

When the worst of the rush was over, he realized that, in addition to being hot and tired, he was lost again. He looked round for landmarks, found the big church-like building and the white tower block and took out the map headed 'MacHardy University Welcomes You to Crimond and the Campus' which had been laid out along with a Gideon bible and three bank advertisements in his campus apartment. If the church, the tower block and the presumably now westering sun were to be believed, he was somewhere north of the John Sloop MacHardy Institute for Social Policy and heading in the wrong direction. He took off his jacket and sat down on a low wall in the shade of the Social Policy place and tried to sort things out.

The church to the right, a newish building on traditional lines, was the MacHardy Chapel. The white tower block was MacHardy East, a part of the MacHardy University Medical Center. The gleaming bronze figure seated high over a flower garden at the central intersection of the campus was, it turned out, a statue of someone called MacHardy.

Two months previously, Campbell had known little about the Albert Memorial Fund, less about the American South and nothing at all about MacHardy University Medical Center. Three years out of medical school, with a short and undistinguished spell in his teaching hospital and two years of service with the Royal Navy behind him, he had been looking around for a job rather than a career, and had run into someone in a pub who had, for family reasons, returned early from an Albert Memorial Fund Fellowship at MacHardy.

The previous incumbent had been enthusiastic about the job and reticent about the precise circumstances of his leaving it. In his view, MacHardy offered decent weather, cheap liquor and a rich social life, though he had not put it quite like that. He described the Albert Memorial Fund selection process: one interview by an agreeably eccentric board which included the chairman's dog. In Campbell's case the dog had growled but the views of a retired admiral, who had been quite taken by Campbell's time at sea, had presumably carried more weight. His application succeeded. Now, having undergone due process at the hands of visa authorities, airlines, customs, immigration officials and taxi drivers, he had reported for duty.

Next morning, having lain awake for three hours or so, Campbell got up and made his way back to Dr Drucker's office in the Division of Primary Care for ten past eight. Debbie, the secretary, fluttered her eyelashes at him, gave him a cup of coffee and an enormous doughnut, then told him that 'Phil' had been called away suddenly to a meeting in Altamont. When Campbell had finished the doughnut she took him over to a wall map of the campus and explained slowly and carefully to him the way from Primary Care to the Thanatology Center.

It was somewhere inside a large old-fashioned hospital called MacHardy West. He made his way along a corridor labelled 'Traumatology Radiation Oncology Environmental Services' and found an elevator. He went up two floors and got out into a long unlabelled corridor. It was deserted apart from a black lady with a mop and bucket. Campbell asked her the way to the Thanatology Center. She looked at him then said 'Wa'?' Campbell asked again and she erupted in kindly laughter. 'Hey! You fum England? How abou' dat? Hey!' Campbell, who in the previous corridor had wondered what Environmental Services were, was surprised to find

7

from a label on her vast bosom that it meant cleaning ladies. When he had made himself understood she laid aside her mop and demonstrated with both hands the remainder of the way to the Thanatology Center. Campbell thanked her and soon found a door marked 'DeeAnn Plotkin, Secretary to Dr J. Calbert Pulver Director Thanatology Center'. He knocked. A voice called him in.

A slim middle-aged lady got up from her desk and welcomed Campbell, invited him to sit in an armchair and offered him coffee and a doughnut. Uncertain on the finer points of Southern etiquette, he accepted, and was given coffee and a doughnut even larger than the first. The lady smiled and said, 'Dr Pulver has a prior appointment presently but will be with you directly.' Campbell took that to mean he would have plenty of time to finish his doughnut.

The outer office in which he was waiting was also a library. There were several shelves of bound volumes labelled *MacHardy Thanatology Reports*, going back for twenty years or so, and some cheerfully coloured modern books with titles like *Dying Alive*, *How to Lose Your Life and Love It*, and *Ending Up Good*. On the coffee table there was a selection of pamphlets. Campbell picked up one called *Current Topics in Pediatric Thanatology*, started to read an abstract about the application of behaviour modification techniques to children with leukaemia and laid aside the remains of his doughnut.

In the next room voices were being raised. One was male, one female. The male noises, a sort of booming bay, predominated, and gradually the female noises became shorter and more high-pitched. Campbell wondered if that meant the interview was drawing to its close. DeeAnn Plotkin smiled from across the room and offered him more coffee, presumably to indicate that it was not. He declined and wondered whether he should ask her now where the nearest gents' loo was, or possibly even how long the forthcoming interview with Dr Pulver was likely to be.

The noise from the inner office subsided somewhat but continued. Campbell waited. The first abstract in *Current Topics in Pediatric Thanatology* failed to convince him of any benefits accruing from behaviour modification techniques in leukaemic children. The second, devoted to the psychodynamics of pre-teen bereavement, was imcomprehensible, and the third, a review of something called 'alternative modalities' in the management of childhood cancers of bone origin, sounded like malpractice.

After about a quarter of an hour the door of the inner office opened and a tall ungainly girl with acne came out. She hurried to the outer door, her eyes moist and pink. A small loudspeaker on the Plotkin desk barked 'Who's next?' The secretary smiled down at the instrument and said 'Dr David Campbell, MD, from Edenburg, England.' The loudspeaker grunted. DeeAnn Plotkin got up and Campbell was shown into the office of the Director of the MacHardy Thanatology Center.

The office was a large one with windows in two of its walls. In the shaded corner between the windows a man stood behind a desk: he was of medium height, broad and powerfully built, with legs too short in relation to the rest of him. He leaned forward over his desk, resting the knuckles of both hands on it, rather as though deciding between doing a few push-ups and leaping up over it. In the end he did neither, but walked round towards Campbell with a hand extended.

'Pulver. Thanatology.' He ground Campbell's hand in his and smiled, baring large yellow teeth. 'Great to have you on board.' He advanced further, backing Campbell wordlessly towards a waiting armchair. 'Great to see you.' He ambled back round his desk, his legs looking smaller than ever from behind, sat down and barked at a device similar to that on the desk of the secretary outside. 'Two coffees.' Campbell settled uneasily into the armchair.

'First off. . . .' The Director leaned over his desk and jabbed a menacing finger at Campbell. 'First off . . . I don't like Brits coming over here and telling us how to run our health services. . . . I know a lot of Brits. Hell, I even like some of 'em. But I will not stand for their loose talk and their . . . sneering at the American way of doing things. It's our way, it's the way we do things, and it suits us. . . . You might think things, I suppose, but I . . . don't . . . wanna know! Okay?' He narrowed his eyes. 'I've seen enough of the thing you call your system to know that it just about gets by over there. Maybe so. But it wouldn't work here. So don't go round telling people that *you* think it *might*. O.K?'

Campbell nodded. The Director returned to his theme. 'I *know* about your way of doing things. I spent two years in a British colony and all I can say is those guys in 1776 sure did the right thing. So that's it. Just leave us alone. O.K?' Campbell nodded again. 'And another thing. If you see something here you don't like, that's *your* problem. Got it?'

When the Director wanted to stress something he stuck out his jaw and furled his brow. Much later, when Campbell recalled this interview, it seemed that at the same time he had raised one hand high above his head and beaten his chest vigorously with a clenched fist. Most probably he had not, but as the weeks went by that idea became more and more part of his recollection. 'What was I saying. . . ? Yes. Brits. Comin' here and tellin' us how to run things. I won't have it. No way. Not before they got their own house in order. And not even then.'

There was a knock at the door. The secretary came in with two cups of coffee and glanced solicitously at Campbell. The Director ignored her, leaning towards him. 'Now tell me how you like your coffee. We gotta know. You're one of us now. . . .' He leaned back without waiting for an answer. 'Yes, Brits. Did a coupla years in the old Gold Coast. Got to know a lot of Brits. Liked them a lot. Did my field work in the Northern Territories of the old Gold Coast. Bolgatanga. You know, with the Kassena and the Fra-fra. Fine buncha folks. Specially the Kassena. Yessir, Bolgatanga. That's where thanatology first gotta hold of me. You might think it's a long way from Crimond, West Carolina, but those folks knew it all. Never saw funerals like it. Some old guy would die, then all the other old guys would get together for his funeral and drink themselves silly. Then some other old guy would die. Wonderful field work. What was I sayin'? Yes. Thanatology. One thing I won't stand for is you coming here and telling us how to run our Thanatology Center. This Center is probably the most respected Center of its kind in the world. Bar none. You musta heard that. That why you're here?'

10

Campbell nodded. 'We are ahead,' the Director said quietly. 'And we will keep on bein' ahead.' His voice rose. 'MacHardy thanatologists are to be found in every significant thanatologic center in the world. *Because we're good!*' he shouted. Then he dropped his voice to a whisper. 'Lemme tell you something about it. You saw old MacHardy sittin' out there on the campus. A great American. A great man. A man of vision, a man of wealth, a man of high ideals. And above all a man who took thanatology seriously.' He was shouting again. 'D'you know this university exists *only because Ephraim MacHardy believed in thanatology*? And that's why MacHardy leads. . . .' His voice was once more a dramatic whisper. '. . . and why it will go on leading.' There was a silence. Campbell smiled and pretended to sip his coffee.

'Doncha *like* coffee?' The jaw protruded. 'Too *strong* for ya. . . ? What was I sayin'. . . ? Thanatology. . . . And now we got *Federal recognition*. We have a Federal Life Ending Americans Program Evaluation and Resource Study. This Center has. We are the *leaders*, see? Opportunity brings opportunity. Greatness breeds greatness. We *are* ahead, so we *stay* ahead. Yessir. Ole Mac was a thanatology man, an' Ole Mac's school is a thanatology school, and don't let anybody tell ya different. O.K?' Campbell nodded. 'And it's great to have you on board. . . .'

'Thank you.'

'But you know it's a *favour*, huh?'

'Oh.'

'Your money ran out. And old Phil, a good man ole Phil, he said, "Cal, I got this Brit comin', and his money's run out. An' *can you help*? Can you help, Cal," he said. An' I said, "I can, but I also wanna talk strategy, see? We got Federal dollars. You got a spare Brit. We can talk. But we can also talk strategy." ' He paused, raising his chin in a statesman-like gesture. 'David. A whole helluva lot has happened in thanatology since the Title Twenty-Five money came on stream. Suddenly everybody, *but everybody*, wants to be a thanatologist. Geddit? So we can choose, and Phil knows that, and Phil's got one of his boys in here. And he's got his

11

money. So he doesn't have a spare Brit with no money any more. . . . He's got a guy in thanatology. Strategy. . . ? Yeah. . . . Strategy. And what *you* don't unnerstan' is that half a dozen guys, big guys, heads of departments, heads of *divisions* even, would give their right arms to be in on this Title Twenty-Five money. No, sir, Phil and I didn't just talk. We talked strategy. . . . So it's great to have you on board. You gonna finish that coffee? O.K. to leave it.'

Campbell murmured appreciatively and got up feeling far more uncomfortable than he would have dared imagine and turned towards the door. Dr Pulver advanced on him, slapping him on the back and saying, 'If there's anything I can do. . . .' Then he interrupted himself and said 'Wait' and went back to his desk. 'Stump!' he roared into his intercom. 'Stump!' Campbell waited, uncertain what was going to happen next, and Dr Pulver paced back across the room towards him and held his elbow. 'You need to meet Stump, my head honcho. He'll take you round, so you meet the folks. Give you deep background. Five minutes and he'll be over here. Cuppa coffee? Some hot in that? Did DeeAnn give you the newsletter? DeeAnn!'

With Dr Pulver pawing his arm all the way across the room and saying things like 'Great to have you on board' and 'If there's anything you want. . . .', Campbell was finally ushered from the presence to the outer office.

'Mr Stump will be here directly,' said DeeAnn Plotkin. 'Please sit down, Dr Campbell. I know Dr Pulver would be pleased for you to have the Center Newsletter and I'd be delighted to give you this month's and the last one and the one before that too. Okay?'

With great care Campbell sat down, which helped a bit. 'Thank you,' he said in a faint, strained voice.

'Would you also like a list of recent publications from the Center?'

'Yes, please.'

'We also publish our own Thanatologic Abstracts. And of course there's the "What's New" listings prepared by our own librarian.' From a shelf near her desk the secretary scooped a handful of leaflets and brochures and held them out to Campbell, who had to get up very carefully and reach out for them. She smiled again. 'Dr Pulver likes to know that people have what he calls the big picture. . . . We also have a prospectus of forthcoming workshops that will interest you. . . . And since you have talked with Dr Pulver your name is automatically added to our mailing list. Dr Pulver likes for people to be kept in touch.' Campbell crossed his legs and tried breathing very slowly, which helped.

Painful minutes later the door opened. 'Hi, DeeAnn. Uh, hi, Dave. . . . Yeah, Stump. Randy Stump.' Mr Stump was tall and fit-looking, in his middle thirties and neatly blazered. He shook hands with Campbell. 'Boss tell ya I'd take ya round? Yeah. He usually does. . . . You feelin' O.K.?'

'Not quite.'

'Jet lag, hey?'

'A bit.' Campbell moved towards the door.

'You need to be out in the fresh air,' Stump asked. 'Sick on your stomach?'

When they were out in the corridor Campbell said, 'I wonder. . . . Where's . . . ?'

'The jahn?'

That sounded promising. 'Yes, please.' The large man smiled and winked. 'You need the second door on the right.'

A short while later Campbell reappeared, feeling much better. Stump was still grinning and winked again. 'Had a hangover myself once. Feel like a beer? We could go down my office.' Campbell smiled uncertainly. 'Nothing like it,' said Stump. 'Walk across the campus. Some fresh air, a quick beer then maybe some coffee. We'll fix you up.' He laughed. 'Must be the change of whisky.' Campbell smiled.

They went downstairs and out onto the campus again. Stump walked quickly and asked questions which sometimes needed complicated answers.

'How long have you bin in Thanatology?'

'Well,' said Campbell, striving to keep pace. 'I'm not really in it yet. But Dr Drucker thought it might be a good idea. . . .'

'Phil.'

'Yes.'

'Smart guy.'

'Is he?'

'Sure is. Who else outside the Center is in on the Title Twenty-Five money for salary. . . ? Only the shrinks. So Phil's a smart guy gettin' you in there. . . . How come you heard about MacHardy?'

'A chap in my year came here on an Albert Memorial Fund Fellowship quite recently.'

'Gus?'

'Yes.'

'You tail-crazy like him?'

'I'm sorry. . . .'

'He had a problem . . . that he shoulda kept strapped to his leg.'

'So I gathered.'

'Wife quit?'

'Sorry?'

'Heather. Did she finally leave him?'

'I think so.'

'He had one fantastic time here while he lasted. And you two were at school together?'

'Yes. Medical school. Edinburgh.'

'So. It's got a reputation.' Stump winked again. 'You could have yourself a real good time here in Crimond.'

They had slowed down and were crossing the main intersection of the campus, with its statue in the flower-bed. 'I don't know much about MacHardy,' Campbell ventured.

'O.K. school. Strong in thanatology. I guess Cal mentioned that.'

'Yes, he did. I meant the chap.'

'Ole Mac?'

'Yes.'

'Cal usually talks about him.'

'Yes. "Great man and great American".'

'That's him. "Industrialist, Philanthropist, Educationalist".' Stump read from the bronze statue's pedestal. 'Yup. Moonshine millionaire.'

'Really?'

'Sure was. Did for Carolina booze what J. P. Morgan did for Pennsylvania oil.'

'And all this philanthropist and great American stuff?'

'Yup. Like, with his moonshine millions.'

They stopped and looked up. The statue was of a man in middle life clad in an old-fashioned suit rather than the bath-towel arrangement favoured for comparable British worthies. The hands were ranged conventionally on the knees and a kindly smile braved the pigeon droppings. 'He was an old bastard,' said Stump. 'But it's only trustees can say that in public.'

'Dr Pulver said something about his interest in thanatology.'

'Yup. His fear of Hell 'n' damnation.'

'Oh.'

'Presbyterian,' said Stump. 'Scotch, like you and that tail-crazy other bastard. Our founder was born in Glasgow, Scotland.' As they stood there something connected for Campbell: the church on the right was a whiter cleaner replica, life-size or near it, of Glasgow cathedral. He mentioned this to Stump, who said, 'Replica of what? Jeeze, maybe. He was a crazy old bastard.' They walked on.

'Cal tell you much about the Center?'

'Only in general terms.'

'Yeah, well, he's the boss. On hard money and the only one with tenure. The rest of us work our butts off hopin' they'll like us enough to want us to work our butts off next year too. It's all soft money.'

'Someone mentioned that.'

'Money that runs out. But this Title Twenty-Five stuff looks good. For a start there's plenty of it. Like a million bucks over three years, so most of us think we'll be around for another coupla years anyway. But it's kinda complicated. I'm fifty percent Thanatology and fifty percent Social Policy, but the way it works out it's more like eighty percent to both. Sorta depends who's shouting loudest, so mainly I'm with Cal.'

'What did he start in? Psychiatry?'

Stumped laughed. 'Nope. Dr Pulver ain't no medical

doctor. Kinda anthropologist. Story is he went out a missionary and came back an anthropologist, with another
missionary's wife.'

'He mentioned the Gold Coast.'

'Yup. Funeral rites. So, thanatology. So, Life Ending. So,
a million Federal bucks.'

'Clever.'

'Beats preachin' Sunday School.'

'So who actually looks after the dying people?'

'You do.'

'*I* do?'

'Yup. That's the deal with Phil. Soon as you can start. We
gotta run you by the State Licensing Board, put you through
the MacHardy people processor, find you a stethoscope and
let you get on with it.'

'But who. . . ? Who else? I mean, who's doing it now?
And are there wards or what?'

'So far it's been mainly counselling, Attitude Adjustment
and Peer Support Groups. And for the relatives there's
Thanatologic Family Dynamics and the Pre-Bereavement
Counselling Package. But right now we're into trying to beef
up the medical component. The Feds are real keen on that.
Like, not psychiatrists.'

'Psychiatrists? What do they do?'

'Not a lot,' said Stump. 'They're kinda negative about
death, so we get a buncha half-assed dago residents plus a lot
of excuse-me's from the big guys we're actually payin'.'

'What?'

'The shrinks we pay prefer to send FMGs.'

'Sorry. . . .'

'I shoulda said. We're also gonna send you for some language credits. An FMG is a foreign medical graduate.'

For the first time Campbell saw himself as a foreign medical graduate, and said so.

'These guys ain't from Edinburgh,' said Stump. 'Not most
of 'em.'

'I see.'

'So the deal is you go sort things out.'

'Oh.'

'So now we're goin' over to Lee-ack.'

'What?'

'After our beer. We're goin' to LEAC. The Life Ending Americans Clinic. You gotta meet the folks. After all, you're gonna be workin' with them.'

Like all the MacHardy buildings Campbell had visited so far, the John Sloop MacHardy Institute for Social Policy was airconditioned and rather chilly inside. Stump had a third-floor office looking out over the back entrance of the hospital, a small cluttered room which had the air of housing a man who lived for his work. There was a couch, a refrigerator and a small cassette recorder. Stump closed the door, switched on some rather suprising Bach and opened the fridge. 'Regular or light?'

'Hm?'

'Hell, we'll have the regular.' Stump opened two cans at once, tossing their rip-tops expertly into the wastepaper basket. 'Light's no good for hangovers.'

'Cheers.'

'Cheers.' Stump smiled. 'Cheeyahs, as the British say.' It was not yet ten o'clock and Campbell, who had never previously drunk beer so early, realized he was acting as if he did it all the time.

'How's the apartment, Dave?'

'Fine.'

'On your own?'

'Yes.'

'We hired you a double bed anyway.' Stump winked again. 'Jeeze, that guy.'

'It's quite comfortable.' Campbell wondered if he was already labelled both a lecher and a drunk. 'You said something about the State Licensing Board.'

'Yeah, we'll get Phil's lovely secretary to fix an appointment with the Board. Just a formality for guys like you. Meets in Bear Fork every coupla months, you go down there and say you never committed any felonies and they license you. Quicker the better. We get no work out of you till you're licensed.'

The beer was cold but welcome. Campbell finished his

first. Stump noticed and said 'We better stop at one for now. Feelin' better?'

'Yes, thanks.'

On the way out Campbell inquired about the Institute for Social Policy. 'We're a kinda right-wing think tank,' Stump explained, 'when we're thinkin'.'

By now it was hot outside. They made their way across to a low building between the campus proper and the hospital and entered a doorway marked 'MacHardy Thanatology Center Life Ending Americans Program Evaluation and Resource Study Life Ending Americans Clinic'. A smaller sign just above the handle on the glass door read 'We take Visa Mastercharge American Express and Diners Club'.

At the reception desk of the Life Ending Americans Clinic sat one of the most beautiful girls Campbell had ever seen, apart from girls who were, so to speak, professionally beautiful. She was blonde, in an undecided natural way that was either natural or had taken a great deal of time, and she was going through a box of file cards as though it had never occurred to her that she could be doing so and looking beautiful as well. She had long, neat hands, greenish eyes and a beauty spot on her right cheek. She looked up only when Campbell and Stump were quite close to her.

'Candy.'

'Hi, Randy.'

'Candy, I want you to meet Dave. Dave, Candy Konopka is our office manager.'

'Hi, Dave.'

'Dave's comin' on the LEAC team real soon, from Primary Care. He's from Scotland.'

'From Scotland?' The office manager's voice was tiny and whining, and she gawped crassly at Campbell. Perhaps she *was* professionally decorative.

'Candy, who's around just now?'

She looked up at Stump as if he had asked her for the square root of a large prime number. 'Couldn't rightly say. . . . Uh, maybe Gary. An' Sharron, I guess. An' I think I did see Dr Mikoyan a while ago, but maybe he's gone right now. But Dr Kazirasta, you know, fum India, maybe he's someplace.'

'How about Patti?'

'Oh, Patti, uh, she's *supposed* to be here. . . . You could try her office.'

'Thanks,' Stump led briskly past the desk and down a corridor. 'Shoulda warned ya. She only does the job to pay her shrink's bills, but the work upsets her. So. . . .' He shrugged. They stopped at a door marked 'Patti Love Coordinator of Clinical Thanatology Life Ending Americans Clinic'. Stump knocked. There was no reply. They stood in the corridor. Stump looked sour.

'What's she?' Campbell asked. 'A shrink?'

'Counsellor.'

'Oh.'

'Spent fifteen years in analysis. Hell, let's go find Gary, Gary Ascue, our clinical psychologist.'

They walked a few yards more to a door marked 'Clinical Psychometry' with a 'Do Not Disturb' notice on the handle. Stump pulled a face. 'He'll be with a client. That's somethin'. . . . Dave, how about a cuppa coffee?'

'All right.'

They went back to the reception desk. Stump smiled and said slowly, 'Candy, any chance of some coffee?'

The office manager smiled brightly. 'Oh, yes, Mr Stump. Be a real pleasure.'

'Can we take room three?'

'If you think Dr Mikoyan's through with seein' folk this morning, Mr Stump.'

'We'll risk it. Thanks, Candy. Sugar, Dave? Cream?'

'Just black, thank you.'

Stump relaxed again, nudged Campbell and winked. 'C'mon, let's go talk strategy. Give you the picture. Aw, Hell, gimme a coupla minutes. I need to fetch something. . . . You have a seat in there.'

Campbell went into room three, which was furnished with a desk, an easy chair and a couch along the wall opposite the window. By the head of the couch stood a little table with an economy size box of paper handkerchiefs. On the wall above was a poster with two kittens, fluffy and wide-eyed, peeking out from a pair of old-fashioned, highly polished ankle boots against a background of soft-focus daffodils. The caption asserted that 'Every Morning Is A Wonderful New Beginning'. The air in the room was sour with stale cigar smoke. Campbell decided to wait standing up.

A voice called him away from the window. 'Excuse me. . . .' A girl in her early twenties, pale and tired looking, stood in the doorway. She carried a handbag in one hand and a credit card in the other. On the right of her neck was a large irregular lump, reddish and blotchy and lined in a faint grid by some indelible marker.

Hodgkin's, thought Campbell. And if she's thin and having radiotherapy it's the bad kind. It took him a moment to realize that he had just set eyes on his first Life Ending American.

'Excuse me,' she said. 'Is that girl gonna come back?'

'I should think so,' said Campbell. 'Probably fairly soon.' The girl looked curiously at him, thanked him and went away. Campbell returned to the window and looked out, wondering in what way, and how much, the Life Ending Americans Clinic helped dying people. Outside an old woman in a wheelchair was being propelled towards the door by a uniformed black, followed by a little old man in a dark suit.

Stump reappeared, breathless and carrying a folder of documents and a red-covered book the size of the Edinburgh telephone directory. 'Sorry,' he said. 'Had to go right the way back to mah office. Where's that coffee? Candy!'

'Yes, Mr Stump, I'm right here.'

'Thanks, Candy.'

'It's a pleasure, Mr Stump.'

'Candy. . . .' Campbell remembered the girl with Hodgkin's. 'A patient, a girl, was looking for you.'

'Huh? O.K. That'd be Belle Yount, Gary's nine-fifteen Transitional Acceptance Counselling.' She left them, and as Stump got up to close the door Campbell heard her say, 'Oh, hi, Miz Yount. Yeah, Visa's fine.'

Stump settled into the armchair. 'Where do you want me to begin?'

'Hm?'

'You were looking a bit lost. Where would you like me to begin?'

'I was wondering about this clinic. I mean, who's actually looking after the patients. . . . Drugs, X-rays and all that. And what about beds, for later on?'

'Their own physicians. And we gotta huge hospital complex here. A lot of our referrals come from the Rose G. MacHardy Cancer Center just up the street. They got physicians and beds.'

'So why does everybody think I'm needed here in the Clinic. . . ? If it's just counselling.'

'Because it's part of what we said we'd do.' Stump held up the red book and smiled like someone in a commercial. 'The LEAPERS grant money. The Life Ending Americans Program Evaluation and Resource Study. Remember? A million bucks, and we said we'd have a hands-on physician input in the LEAC in Phase One.' He laid the book on his knee and began to look through its pages. 'Yeah, fact is we shoulda had a hands-on doc for a year already. But that's O.K. I mean, we can only do our best, and now we really do have one.'

'When that license thing. . . .'

Stump shrugged. 'Yeah, yeah. And the other thing we need you for. This clinic's supposed to be self-supporting. Financially.' Campbell may have looked surprised. 'That's right, doc. When you see those guys, even a quick look before their Counselling or Peer Support Groups, that's a physician's assessment. Fifty bucks minimum.'

'Oh.'

'More, if you ask them to put out their tongue.'

'What?'

'That's a joke, but you got the idea. That's Phase One.'

'And Phase Two?'

'Phase Two. . . .' Stump raised the red book in a preacher's grip. 'Phase Two is the really big bucks. Do you know about Medicare?'

'Not much.'

'Kinda government subsidy for health care, Great Society

21

stuff from nearly twenty years ago. If you're old and sick the Feds pay your doctor's bill. Sometimes. But not all the time. There's these rules, see, which can be real tough. You only get so much. So, like, if some old lady gets sick too often and her Medicare runs out, the old guy, her husband, has to divorce her if he wants to stay rich or even half rich or keep things together for the kids. Some guys in Washington say that's life, but some other guys think it's tough, say, if you're dying, and you have to decide about divorce and poverty an' all on top of that. So they say, let's make a law that says when you're dyin' you don't have to spend down after your Medicare runs out. At least not all the way. Basically they want to waive the Medicare rules if they're sure you're dyin'. So some bleeding heart Democrat from the Northeast makes it his own great mission in life for a few years. Goes all around sellin' it to everybody on the Hill. The lawyers don't like it and you can't blame them, but the doctors, eventually the doctors get to see the point of this humanitarian piece of legislation. The mortician lobby is all for anything that leaves more for them. . . . Little things like that, the congressman gets it all together, and a couple of dozen deals later the House sets up this Agency for Life Ending Americans, called that on account of dying having a kinda negative image, and they decide to try it out in the pilot studies. They put one in the congressman's home state, one in the President's and one in the South. That's us. They needed one in the South, and with a Thanatology Center we already got an interest. An' ole Cal's pretty good with contacts. So me and him and some shrinks and some guys from Social Policy wrote this. . . .' He held up the red book again. 'It's called a grant application. Successful, as it happens, so at today's prices you're lookin' at a million bucks.'

'I see. And Phase Two?'

'Well, we gotta finish Phase One, which is planning and initial evaluation kinda stuff. Pilot clinic at the Center, where you work. It all looks good, so we hit the big time. We apply the lessons learned in Phase One and we expand. And in this Phase all medical bills will be fully and Federally met, regardless. So there isn't a physican in the whole Medical

22

Center that aint been makin' up sweet to Thanatology. We start August first.'

'You nearly got it, Gary. Nearly but not quite. You gotta understand that for a kid like this death is just sex. The fear of death's just plain old fear of sex. They're scared because Big Daddy up there's gonna screw 'em for sure. So. . . . Uptight, huh? The incest vibrations make it kinda worse. So they gotta be scared.'

The chairman of the meeting, a large untidy man with a string tie and a moist cigar twitching in a smoky semaphore as he talked, looked round the room. The man who had just presented the case coughed and looked round the room too. Most of the people in the room were looking at their hands, or their notes, or their disposable coffee cups or the remains of their doughnuts. A young man in an open-necked check shirt coughed and looked meekly up at the chairman and smiled. He coughed again and said, 'An' given that . . . that *ordeal* of a psycho-sexual history, with her losin' no less than three successive significant father substitutes. . . . In the epoch of maximum Oedipality. . . .'

There was a shocked silence. The speaker blushed and smiled said, 'Uh-oh. . . . I'm sorry. *Electrality*. . . . Forgive me. Right across maximum Electrality. . . . Sure, she's gonna be uptight as hell about the whole thing. . . . She's gotta be. No way she can't be.' He stopped speaking and looked towards the chairman who, after a moment's thought, returned his gaze. The younger man beamed across the table at the older, who then abruptly turned his attention to the woman on his left. 'Whaddya say, Patti?'

The woman smiled and said, 'I'd go right along with you, Dr Mikoyan.'

Dr Mikoyan's cigar rolled suavely from the right of his mouth to the left, strewing a little ash over his shirt on the way. He looked round the table once more. This time a small sleek Asian raised his head.

'Kazi?'

'Dr Mikoyan, whaddabou' de womitting up?'

23

'Yeah? Whaddabout the vomiting. . . ?' The Asian opened his mouth to speak but Dr Mikoyan ignored him.

'Bob?'

The man in the check shirt flashed his teeth at the cigar. 'Rejection. . . ? The anorexia model? A classic pattern of father-oriented acting-out?'

Dr Mikoyan smiled at a point six or eight feet above the centre of the table. 'Next case.'

Campbell sat at a corner fairly far from the chairman wondering if he had made a mistake. Stump had recommended the Life Ending Americans Clinic Wednesday Teaching Conference, but little had happened so far that had anything to do with looking after dying patients. It was then tempting to wonder if the whole unexpected involvement in terminal care was to be regretted, and if so, whether it had been a mistake to have come to MacHardy at all. Whatever else, the glossy pink doughnut had been an undoubted error of judgement: it sat sourly in his stomach as Campbell, bored by the inconsequence of the proceedings, swept the remaining pink crumbs together with his fingertips, making a nasty little pyramid in the shadow of his coffee cup. The conference was now listening to a trainee social worker who had introduced herself by saying she was majoring in thanatologic social work and now completing her practicum at the Clinic. She described the plight of an old black man with cancer of the prostate, dwelling at length on a side effect of his drug therapy and how the old man was coping with his new breasts. Campbell razed his little pink pyramid and quartered the resultant disc with the point of his pencil.

The girl had stopped talking. No one was talking. The effect was oddly liturgical, as though those present had been exhorted to contemplate something in the silence of their hearts. Campbell looked up and to his surprise met the searchingly professional gaze of Dr Mikoyan, who then bared his teeth and twitched his cigar in a small admonitory smile and signalled to the social worker to carry on, the undivided attention of her audience restored.

'So we have this, uh, elderly black married male with, uh, breasts . . . and a one hundred percent wiped-out libido. An'

24

it's really gettin' in the way of his transition to Acceptance. . . . So he's a kinda hung-up KR Four, with transition problems secondary to a gender problem. I gave him thirteen.'

Dr Mikoyan listened impassively. Patti Love raised an eyebrow at the last statement, lifted a pencil and jotted something on a notepad. The trainee social worker looked round the table. Only Patti Love and Mikoyan were still looking up.

'Patti?' said Mikoyan.

'Louella, I jes' cain't see how Mr Prendergraft comes to thirteen.'

The girl who had presented the case bit her lip and looked thoughtful, flicked through her notes then said, 'Miz Love, with a lousy Transition to Acceptance he's just gotta be marked down on Development. No way more than a two, and we agreed everything else at the Tuesday conference Tuesday. So his eleven from Tuesday and a two. So thirteen.'

'Lucky for some,' said Mikoyan. There was a duteous snicker. 'Maself I'd go along with Louella. He's a two on Development. He's stuck in a bad place and he's gotta be helped on through with Acceptance. . . .' He paused and took the cigar out of his mouth. 'Maybe a bra. . . . But seriously, folks, poor Washington Prendergraft's havin' trouble, an' this mornin' we gotta try to help him on his way ahead. Uh, Gary, you got any places comin' up on the Metastatic Prostate Cancer Peer Support Group?'

The man with the beard who had presented the first case said, 'Uh, maybe. Clancy Harrap is headin' for Final Acceptance real soon. Like, he quit showin' up. Yeah. I guess so.'

The meeting droned on. A man with lung cancer and a youth with what sounded like a very nasty malignant melanoma were presented, but the details that Campbell would have found interesting and helpful, such as the symptoms and the main points of medical management, were little in evidence, probably because the cases were presented by a trainee Methodist minister and a behavioural psychologist respectively. Dr Mikoyan and the man in the open-necked check shirt dominated the discussion, juggling with a jargon in the general area of family dynamics. Twice more there was talk of KR stages and a pondering of mysterious numbers. To Campbell it was new but not interesting. He wondered how long it would take him to dislike an approach which he already found suspect, but sat quietly with all the appearances of rapt attention.

When the Life Ending Americans Clinic Wednesday Teaching Conference finally broke up, half an hour beyond schedule, Stump was waiting outside to collect Campbell, who apologized for being late.

'Only just got here,' Stump replied. 'They generally quit around this time. . . . Coupla guys you gotta meet now, and you're remembering you gotta check in with Family Practice this afternoon. I'll take y' over there as soon as we get through with lunch. And Cal says hi, and hopes you're doin' fine and you're gonna like LEAC.'

'Oh. Did he?'

'Then he went to San Diego. Be there till Thursday night. An' he said can you come to dinner Friday.'

'Yes, thanks.' Campbell was still rather nervous about supermarkets but already bored with fast food.

'Dean's Dining Room. Seven-thiry. Some other guys from LEAC and LEAPERS'll be there. Great chance to meet folks. I'll come around for you seven-fifteen. The Dean's Diner's kinda hard to find.'

'Thank you.'

'Now let's go meet some more of the guys on the team.'

'Hi there. Well, terrific. Sharron Sneed, head of Education and Evaluation. Great. . . . So you've come from Scotland? Wonderful. First time here. . . ? and how do you like the States? Wonderful. But you only just got here. . . . Terrific. Just great luck they found someone so quickly after Gus went home. Randy was sayin' the other day you knew Gus. Yes . . . . Our former Albert Memorial Fund Fellow. From Edenburg. And you're from Edenburg too, huh? Wonderful. A great city, I hear, and of course a world respected

26

medical school. . . . I mean, it's the only English school anybody's ever heard of. And it's so wonderful. Great. . . . And how's Gus?'

The girl in the babyish pink dress stopped talking, which presumably meant that Campbell was now expected to reply. 'I think he's all right.'

'Terrific. Gee, he's a wonderful guy. Doncha think so? I mean energy, charisma, everything. And his wonderful wife. . . . Heather, wasn't it?'

There was another inviting pause. Campbell said, 'I don't know her.'

'Such wonderful people. And how are you settling in? Randy said you got Gus and Heather's old apartment. Yes, he loved it. Really loved it. And so did Heather. You can sure see why. That patio. . . . And the wonderful view of MacHardy Chapel. Just wait till spring, that's real lovely here, with the dogwood in flower. . . . Outa this world.'

She had stopped again. Campbell asked her what she did. She beamed and leaned forward, her hands spread theatrically. 'Well. . . . More or less anything I'm asked. So you understand, my background's in health care sciences, majoring in speech pathology of course. I guess you all call that speech therapy. But my doctorate work has all been in education. Gotta doctorate in Infrastructures of Brainstorming. So you could say my heart is in health care, even if my head's in education. . . .' She touched Campbell's forearm with her right hand. 'Wonderful. Wonderful to meet you. And I want you to know that if there's anything you need. . . . Anything at all, but especially to do with education 'n' evaluation, you only have to ask. . . . I mean it.' She took her hand away slowly.

Campbell said, 'Thank you, Miss Sneed,' which proved to be a serious error.

She clutched his hand in hers, which was warm and moist, and said, 'Sharron, David. . . . Call me Sharron.'

Stump stood watching, which was somehow helpful. They were in the Education and Evaluation Unit of the Life Ending Americans Program Evaluation and Resource Study, a surprisingly modest office: low and cramped and in

27

the worst sense feminine. Fluffy toys sat on filing cabinet, desk and window sill. There were many more scatter cushions than the place could reasonably ever need, and a lurid embroidered sampler advised 'Be Good and Let Who Can Be Clever'. There were many books, mostly about how to do something, few of which looked as if they had been opened.

Though she had stopped talking and Campbell himself had no inclination to prolong their conversation, Miss Sneed continued to stand very close to him. In her late twenties or early thirties, tallish by European standards, she was not exactly pretty but had about her either something that reminded Campbell of someone he had known who was pretty, or the sort of near good looks that improve with familiarity: or was it simply that once, a few years ago perhaps, she had been briefly attractive? Her features were small and regular and her hair was decidedly blonde. She had blue, rather cold eyes and a high forehead. Her teeth were regular and very white, in the American fashion. Perhaps aware of Campbell's scrutiny, she smiled with her mouth and examined him with her eyes. Behind her, Stump was making time-we-were-off gestures, beamed at Campbell, which Miss Sneed appeared somehow to perceive, for she touched Campbell's arm again and said, 'Are you guys going for lunch?' Stump made a face, which she did not appear to perceive, combining distaste and resignation. 'Yeah,' he said. 'Come on and join us.'

Miss Sneed smiled as though indebted to Campbell for an unexpected good idea. 'Luckily, I can. Teddy Totenberg's secretary just called and cancelled me. I had been lined up to report to the LEAPERS Steering Group.'

That information displeased Stump, and may have been intended to.

'Seems they had to cancel,' she said, looking at Stump.

'Cal's outa town.'

'Maybe that was it. So's Bottger of course.' Again Stump appeared displeased. 'Yeah,' said Miss Sneed. 'So we cancelled. . . . Where are we goin', you guys? David, you been to the Oxford Room yet. . . ?' Campbell indicated that he had not. 'You'll love it. It's, uh, real old-world, you know? Kinda cute.'

The three went out into the corridor. Miss Sneed locked her door and fiddled with a home-made cardboard device until it read 'Working Lunch'. On the way across the campus Campbell walked between Miss Sneed and Stump. From time to time each addressed him as if the other were not present.

The Oxford Room was a long wood-panelled restaurant one floor up in a thirties Gothic building. It looked out, through leaded double-glazed windows fringed with ivy, on to the centre of campus and its statue. And old black man dressed as a Beefeater met them at the door and limped ahead of them to a corner table and when they had sat down threw them two menus and said, 'Make up yo' mind quick, hey? Kitchen's closin' real soon.'

Miss Sneed threw him a dazzling smile but already he had turned and was limping away. 'He's a real character, ole Jake,' she remarked to Campbell. 'Treats everybody just the same. . . . Seafood's wonderful here. Really terrific.' A fat black waitress appeared even before Campbell had found his way through a column of tightly antique script headed 'Starters'.

'Yes?' The waitress glared at Stump.

'Oliver Twist steak, please. Medium rare with a Garden of England salad and a light beer.'

'No light. . . . Reg'lar.' The waitress turned to Campbell, who for simplicity's sake ordered the same. The waitress eyed him suspiciously. 'You, miss?' She glowered at Miss Sneed, who smiled back at her.

'Uh, I'll have the Drake's Delight Seafood Platter. And a ladylike side of fries.'

'Drake's off. Nelson Touch is the same without pompano. You gonna take that? And' wha' kinda dressin' you all want, huh? French, Italian or house Olde English, regular or low calorie? Huh?' They decided quickly, and she hobbled away muttering to herself.

'How did you make out at the Wednesday Conference, Dave?' Stump asked.

'Interesting.'

'Hey,' said Miss Sneed, smiling fiercely. 'You took in a Wednesday Conference? Already?'

'Yes,' said Campbell. 'This morning. It was interesting.'

'Great.' She leaned over towards him. 'So you're really gettin' into Thanatology? That's wonderful.'

Stump picked up a roll and looked out of the window. Miss Sneed leaned closer still. 'Are they showin' you patients already? You really gettin' in there?'

'Shortly, I expect,' said Campbell. A glimpse of the girl with the credit card hardly counted. 'I still have to go and see about my license.'

'They have inneresting cases this morning, huh?'

'Oh, yes. Most interesting.'

'It's a wonderful forum for awareness development and personal growth. I mean, the learners really get to inneract. And didn't you just love Stef? He's a truly wonderful clinician and preceptor. Sharp as a tack. Just gets straight to the key issue. And you know he hardly ever sees any of the patients himself, but he's just so perceptive about the cases these kids present, just from hearin' about them, huh? And his research is truly significant.'

Stump reached for a second roll. Campbell asked politely about the research.

'Well,' said Miss Sneed, baring her teeth and talking at the same time. 'It's real significant, you know. He goes just about everywhere talking about the miles data.'

'Miles?'

'Miles. MILES. You know, the MacHardy Index of Life Ending Satisfaction.' She smiled at Campbell as though he were an idiot child spilling his orange juice. 'You bin here three days and took in a Wednesday Conference and din't get to hear about MILES?'

'I'm afraid not.' The rolls looked good and there were only two left.

'Gus didn't tell ya?'

'No. We really didn't spend much time on that sort of thing. I don't think he mentioned it.'

'It's wonderful.'

'You two the Garden of Englands?'

'Oh, yes, thanks.' The waitress put down two small tired salads.

'It's the single most significant contribution of MacHardy to Thanatology worldwide.' Miss Sneed was reverent and emphatic.

'Pepper, David? Salt?'

'Thanks, Randy. Is it?'

'Beers here and here, please, miss.' Stump lifted his right away. Campbell followed.

'Cheers.'

'Cheeyahs.'

'And MILES technology will guide and shape the Life Ending Program nationwide.'

'Can I pour you some water, Miss Sneed?'

'Huh, no thanks, David.' Miss Sneed touched his arm again and smiled fiercely. 'Call me Sharron, David. Sharron. Like I was sayin', David. . . . The MILES technology is just terrific. It's MacHardy's biggest chance yet to really influence Life Ending nationwide. Do you know what I'm sayin'? Like, it's a, huh, really comprehensive multi-phasic bias-free instrument. I mean, it's good for the whole schtick, from infancy through advanced senility. Clinically, you know, for individual Life Enders, but also for epidemiological applications to, uh, populations. That's why we pulled a LEAPERS with only three going. A million bucks came here because here at MacHardy we already had an ongoing thanatology program with evaluation as one of its leading modalities. So our application just creamed through, see? We're tops in Life Ending situational and symptomatologic quantitation.'

She stopped talking but left her hand resting on Campbell's arm and gazed up into his eyes. He put down his beer. She waited.

'I see,' said Campbell. 'Evaluation.'

'You got it.' She beamed. 'Evaluation. That's why we're out front. We got full MILES documentation and data on upwards of seven thousand Life Endings with anything up to five hundred in process at any point in time. We got 'em from eight months to ninety-seven. We got plenty caucasians, but we also got blacks and hispanics and the economically disadvantaged. We got the only native American thanatologic

31

series in the literature. We got retirement communities, we got prisons, we got migrant labour, we even got half the faculty here covenanted to participate on an eventuality basis. That's just wonderful. Last fall Cal went on campus TV signin' himself up and then we had a sign-in on the steps of MacHardy Chapel. You shoulda seen it. And we got the whole lot on a computer. I wanna take you over there, David. I wanna take you over to the LEAPERS Data Storage System and Information Center so you can see what we do with MILES data and what can be done with it. We got real time input from every floor of MacHardy East, we got computer terminals in all the nursing homes in the county and we just got funded for a new section with abrupt Life Ending input from the State Troopers Major Incident and Natural Disaster Unit. They might not come in often, but, boy, when they do. . . .'

'Sharron,' Stump said. 'Sharron, David just got here. He's still just meetin' the folks.'

'He's gotta meet Ben. David, you booked for this afternoon? You gotta meet Ben. Ben is just wonderful with data.'

Campbell was about to say something. Stump put down his beer and said slowly, 'This afternoon we gotta check in over at Family Practice. Is that O.K.?' In the pause that followed Campbell picked up his beer. After that, lunch was a subdued affair. It seemed that Campbell's suspicions that Stump and Miss Sneed did not get on had some justification.

The Department of Family Practice was off campus, and consisted of three or four frame houses on an old-fashioned street canopied by trees.

'He'll be roun' here somewhere,' said Stump. 'That's the yellow peril.' A long low sports car of menacing design stood outside one of the houses. 'But he's never where you look first.' They got out and walked up a cinder path. An old black man was cutting grass.

In a room which must once have been a front parlour the Director's secretary was expecting them. She smiled and said, 'He's roun' here somewhere, Mr Stump. I'll ring down to eleven oh six, you might just be lucky. . . . Oh. Oh, O.K. I'll try ten ninety-three. Thanks, Mary Jane. Oh, hi, Belle. Is doctor. . . . Oh. Great. You tell him Mr Stump from Life Ending's here with the noo Scotch doctor, O.K.? Thanks, Belle. . . . Mr Stump, Dr Kidd's sewin' up a li'l girl's foot right now an' won't be more'n two minutes. Would you two like a cuppa coffee?'

'I won't, thanks, Jo,' said Stump. 'Cal's outa town and I gotta go mind the store. Be O.K.? Seeya, Dave. Remember Friday.' He left.

Campbell waited, until suddenly the door burst open and a tall, lean man loped into the room. His face was deeply tanned and his eyes were blue. He smiled and waved his hands a lot as he talked. 'Hey there. Howdy. Billy Kidd. Yeah, Director over here. Great. You got here at last. Come on in, we gotta talk.' He hustled Campbell into a smaller office, perhaps once a dining room. 'And no calls, Jo. Nothin'. For ten minutes minimum. From nobody, you hear? Then me'n Dave's goin' off to Split Rock, O.K.?'

The secretary smiled fondly as Dr Kidd closed the door. Campbell sat as indicated on an old sofa. Dr Kidd sprawled backwards in his chair and began to talk. Peering round a pair of elaborately tooled highly polished brown leather boots with biggish heels, Campbell listened.

Dr Kidd related the brief history of the Department of Family Practice, and made it sound like an epic of pioneer survival. To hear him was to hear of small beginnings and a long struggle against the odds, in a tale of perseverance and sometimes guile, wherein a small enlightened band had braved harsh terrain and the hostility of dark and powerful forces, clung on for three or four precarious seasons more in faith than in prosperity, but succeeded at last in bringing something new and better to a raw and hungry land. Campbell, who had no particular reason to regard family practice as innovative, was nevertheless impressed: the tale as told, and the cowboy boots, brought to his mind wagon trains and flaming arrows, in a sort of medical rerun of archetypal frontier life, with proud tribes of savages such as the internists and the neurosurgeons menacing this tiny outpost of enlightened health care delivery. After eight minutes or so a treaty or two was being signed and a pipe of peace being nervously passed around.

'So we came to an arrangement with the MacHardy orthopedists an' we even got a couple of them to come over here sometimes 'n teach, and then the radiologists started thinkin' straight, an' ole Hank still comes over twice a week. And, y'know, they got to like us. Even though we were family docs, and that's mainly because our residents here are not just fine physicians but are also just a great buncha kids. You'll meet 'em, Dave. You'll love 'em too.'

Somewhere, the titles rolled against a clean brave frontier sky and Dr Kidd looked piously upward, then got up, hitched up his waistband, shook the legs of his pants down over his boots, narrowed his eyes and said, 'C'mawn, Dave. We gotta head out to Split Rock,' rather as if there were rustlers in someone's gulch there.

'Teddy Totenberg is a horse's ass.' The sports car snarled at a red traffic light. 'Ya gotta understan' that, Dave. An' he's a horse's ass who's out to screw us, and the way he does it is to pretend he ain't doin' it. But he does.' The light changed and the car leapt forward. Dr Kidd changed gear five times in four seconds then slowed for another red light. 'Yessir, Teddy Totenberg is somethin', and Amy Totenberg, down in Split Rock, is somethin' else. An' maybe that's why ole Teddy's got it in fer us. Amy's a MacHardy graduate, AOA and all that. . . . That's like a summa cum laude, I guess you'd call it. So she coulda done anythin' she wanted. She decided to stick around MacHardy because the pediatric neuro-oncology program here's tops, then after two years of it she says "The Hell with this" and quits. She goes off and gets herself on a Family Practice program somewhere in the Northeast, for Chrissake, an' ole Teddy, her father, is Dean of Medicine, like, in a leading Southern school. So he makes like she's dropped out, and it's all our fault. He didn't like us before. Now he can't stand us.'

They roared into a curving freeway marked 'Downtown

Loop Get in Lane' then round a traffic island presided over by a lone figure on a war memorial marked 'To Our Confederate Dead'.

The name Totenberg was familiar. 'Dr Drucker mentioned a Dr Totenberg.'

'The horse's ass?'

'He didn't say. Something about Life Ending in rural America.'

'That's Amy. The daughter. Phil's kinda torn about Teddy. He used to work with him on splanchnic afferents, which is big stuff if you're into that kinda thing, then he quit for Primary Care. An' Teddy isn't sure ole Phil didn't have a kinda chat with Amy before she quit pediatric neuro-oncology. So Teddy makes like he loves us on account of Amy bein' in Family Practice, an' screws us up any time he gets the chance on account of her promising career she gave up. See?'

They stopped at a level crossing and waited as a goods train clanked past. The lights stopped flashing and the yellow car snorted and jerked over the tracks into a tumbledown street where the houses were small and decrepit and black children played in the dirt.

'West Crimond,' Dr Kidd explained. 'Poortown. We head south on thirty-six and go west by Pittsville and Split Rock's only another twenty down the river. Be there in an hour.'

Out of Crimond there were pinewoods and small farms. The road undulated up a series of hills then topped a ridge looking out over a patchily cultivated plain fading to a hazy skyline in the east, then twisted down a scarp. Dr Kidd drove for fun, with engine howling merrily and tyres squealing. Dense pine forests slewed past feet away on the curves and sometimes only a low wall separated the road from a long rocky drop. Twice they crossed a steeply falling stream, then the slope eased and the corners became less nauseating. Dr Kidd, who had not yet explained why they were going there, talked about Split Rock and its Health Care Center.

'I guess it's kinda rural-industrial. They got a noo plant that makes things for missiles and they got a sawmill. An' there's farming like everywhere else roun' here. So Split

Rock Health Care's got it made. Small town, no big-deal specialists around, and lotsa contracts. They got the missile place, an' the sawmill's great for minor trauma, an' they do the county jail, which ain't worth much but looks good, like civic responsibility.'

'Dr Drucker mentioned something about Life Ending down there. . . .'

'Hey, you're really lit up 'bout this Life Ending shit, huh?'

Campbell had not intended to give that impression: it was simply the only thing that he knew about Split Rock and it seemed polite to keep the conversation going.

'Yeah,' said Dr Kidd. 'They gotta flea.'

'Sorry?'

'A FLEA. A Facility for Life Ending Americans. Split Rock Health Care Inc. owns the nursing home and Cal from Life Ending talked 'em into some kinda Pilot Project in the LEAPERS grant application. An' the money came through, enough so they couldn't change their minds. They got about half a dozen beds. You could take a look.'

'Thank you.'

'Amy runs it. How long have you bin interested in Life Ending, Dave?'

'Well. . . . We got a little about it at medical school.'

'Is that British for you gotta whole buncha Thanatology credits?'

'Oh, no. People talked about it sometimes.' In Edinburgh old-fashioned physicians sometimes murmured about 'letting Nature take its course', eased perhaps by 'the poppy and plenty of it', but there had been no very systematic teaching. One of the more accident-prone surgeons, perhaps making a virtue of necessity, had declared an interest and once a hospital chaplain had arranged a showing of a film about hospices, but as an undergraduate in medical school Campbell had noted a general tendency on the part of his teachers to minimize the problems of those patients so tactless and ungrateful for their efforts as to appear to be dying, though nurses didn't seem to mind so much.

'You use a whole lotta heroin over there, doncha?'

'It seems quite good, for some things.'

'Malpractice here. Street drug used by addicts.'

'So I've heard. But I was sort of wondering about all the terminal care people here. I mean the people in Life Ending. You know, most of the people I've met weren't doctors. I mean physicians.'

'That might change.' Dr Kidd narrowed his eyes and overtook a truck with a dozen black farm labourers in the back. 'The way things are goin', that might change a whole lot.'

'Oh?'

'Yup.'

'I see.'

'Yup,' said Dr Kidd again. 'That might not go on forever.' The sports car drummed over a wooden bridge from which an urchin was fishing. 'The way things are shapin' up, that could change real quick.'

This time Campbell said nothing and waited. Dr Kidd shifted in his seat and looked down the empty road ahead. 'Come Phase Two,' he said after a long pause.

'Oh?'

'Yup. . . . Phase Two is when the big LEAPERS bucks come on stream. And a lotta guys aroun' MacHardy might get to thinkin' that Life Ending is too important to be left to a buncha social workers and shrinks.'

'I see.'

'Didn't Cal tell ya?'

'No. We didn't discuss that.'

'I guess not,' said Dr Kidd. 'So hang in there, doc. I guess you're our stake in the system. Great to hear you're enjoyin' it. Look, I'll get Amy to take ya round the FLEA while I see the guy I gotta see. . . . If you're really into that sorta thing.'

'Thank you.'

'It's O.K., buddy. . . . Anybody tell ya about the Injuns?'

'Sorry?'

'We got Injuns down here.'

Campbell's mind went back to the interview earlier. 'Really?'

'Sure do. Real live Federally subsidized native Americans. 'Bout half the folks in town. Buncha them works in the missile factory and the rest's drunks. Yeah, we gotta tribe. You heard about the Lost Colony?'

'No.'

'Some folks think the Injuns we got down here's some of you guys that came over in a colony'n got lost somewhere aroun' sixteen somethin'. Maybe there's that in 'em, but there's plenty else besides. Like, some of 'em's black. But the paler ones, they could be some kinda breed. Lotta goitre and a helluva lotta diabetes. Anyhow, as far as Uncle Sam's concerned they qualify for Indian Money. . . . When the money started, though, that's maybe when some of the funny ones joined.'

Campbell found a lot of that strange and some of it unlikely. Dr Kidd was evidently being serious. 'The tribe's got a contract with Split Rock Health Care Inc. And they even got themselves signed up for some LEAPERS bucks. Seems native Americans gotta die like everybody else, and Cal's outfit was interested.'

'I'd heard that,' said Campbell.

'Jeeze, so you're really into this Life Ending stuff? Good luck, kiddo.'

The yellow sports car slithered to a halt beside a rambling single-storeyed building on the edge of a small town. Dr Kidd switched off the engine and said, 'We got half an hour, Dave, then it's back to the ranch, O.K.?'

'O.K.'

As they got out of the car a tall girl appeared and welcomed Dr Kidd. They both smiled and laughed.

'Dave, c'mon meet Amy. . . . Amy, I want you to meet Dave Campbell from Scotland. He's half with Life Ending and half with us.'

The girl wore a white coat. She was tall and lithe with skin much paler than most of the people Campbell had met so far in West Carolina. She smiled and they shook hands. She had a large cool grip, and looked at Campbell and said, 'We must talk,' then let go his hand. Dr Kidd was shaking the legs of his pants down over his boots again. Stiff from the journey, he hobbled around a little then said, 'Amy, I gotta talk to Don. Is he around somewhere? Does he know?'

'Don's around. He knows you're dropping by.'

'And George?'

'George would like to meet with you first.'

'Fine,' said Dr Kidd. 'Amy. . . .' He laid a hand on her shoulder. 'While me and George and Don's sortin' things out, howsabout you takin' Dave here round your place. Y'know, the Facility.'

Dr Totenberg smiled. 'Be happy to.'

'Dr Campbell knows a whole lot about Life Ending.'

Dr Totenberg smiled wider, with perfect teeth. 'A whole lot of the early terminal care work was British, wasn't it. . . ? That hospice physician? Sir Saunders? I read some of his stuff. Oh, I'd love to show you our service here, but I got one more patient to see over this side. But if you don't mind waiting some, maybe we could go make rounds on the Life Enders. That be O.K.? And I'd love for you maybe to help us with one poor old guy we're havin' trouble with.'

Before Campbell had time to disclaim expert status Dr Kidd said, 'Half an hour maximum, Dave,' and went off.

Five minutes later Campbell and Dr Totenberg were on their way across a patchy lawn to the Facility for Life Ending Americans.

'Is this O.K., Dr Campbell. . . . Dave? Would you mind taking a look at one particular guy? I mean, if you'd rather not. . . .'

'What's wrong with him?'

'It's a hydration and alimentation problem.'

'Oh.'

'Ninety-six-year-old black married male with a pulmonary primary and widespread secondaries. Painfree and alert until Monday, an' now he's got an acute change of mental status. Won't eat, won't drink and tears out his I V lines, so we have to restrain him. Oh, and he's blind. It's real sad. He's an old preacher, an' all his family come around and talk with him. It's so sad he's outa touch, 'cause they're real neat people. Sometimes they sing, you know, gospel songs, and he joins in, but mainly he's outa it.'

They went in. 'Did Billy explain about our Facility?'

'A little.'

'We got twelve beds for the Life Ending Pilot Project. We do the medical care and the MacHardy guys, mainly Dr Sneed and Dr Ascue, keep track on how they're doin'. You know, all that MILES stuff. I guess you know all about that.'

'Yes.'

'Kinda flaky, some of it.'

'Sorry?'

Dr Totenberg stopped and so did Campbell. She looked at him earnestly across the language barrier. 'Flaky means . . . oddball, kinda weird.'

'Oh yes,' said Campbell. 'I see what you mean. Yes, it seems fairly flaky, from what I've seen of it.' She laughed and touched his arm.

'How long are you gonna be here?'

'Half an hour. Oh. In West Carolina? A year. It's a sort of Fellowship.'

She smiled again. Some black people were sitting in the corridor. 'That's Mr Barbee's family, well, some of 'em. Excuse me.' She left Campbell and sat down next to a fat middle-aged lady who asked, 'How's mah daddy? How's pappy, Dr Totenberg?'

'We're just goin' to see him, Miz Harper. How's he bin with you?'

'He still ain't et nothin'. Pore ole pappy.'

'Lawdy Lawdy. Oh Lawd. Oh Lawd, strike off mah bonds. Oh Lawdy, set me free. Oh Lawdy Lawdy Lawdy. Oh Lawd. . . .'

A thin and ancient black man was struggling on a bed with cot sides. His hands were tied to its rails by strips of padded cloth.

'Reverend Barbee. Reverend Barbee, are you O.K.?'

'Oh Lawdy Lawdy, set me free o' mah bonds. . . .'

'Reverend Barbee, I've got another doctor here to see if he can help you.'

'Who's there?'

'I'm sorry, Reverend Barbee. It's Dr Totenberg. And

Dr Campbell. David, you wanna take a look at him?'

'We could look at him together.' Campbell had not yet acquired a state license. 'Mr Barbee? Mr Barbee. Hello.'

'Oh Lawdy.' The old man's mouth was cracked and dry and when he cried aloud to his Maker his tongue was raw and patchy, with dull creamy-white blotches extending on to his gums and cheeks. That could be cured.

'Mr Barbee, is your mouth sore?'

'What's that?'

'Reverend Barbee,' Dr Totenberg asked, 'you hurtin' in yo' mouth?'

'Lady, I am.'

'Open your mouth, Reverend Barbee.' He did so. His breath was foul.

'He's got candida.' Campbell laid a hand on the old man's arm. 'Mr Barbee, does it hurt when you eat?'

'Lawdy, yessir.'

'Have you any other pain?'

'You hurtin' anyplace else?' Dr Totenberg asked.

'Sure am, miss. Mah belly. . . . An' mah feet some.'

Campbell turned down the sheet. The old man's abdomen was distended but soft under his hand. He percussed it with one finger on another. It sounded hollow. A long diminuendo gurgle, the sound of intestinal action against obstruction, arose and Campbell turned to Dr Totenberg, who looked thoughtful. A few years previously Campbell had spent some time in Gastro-enterology: not much, but enough to learn how to diagnose constipation. He asked for a rectal examination tray and Dr Totenberg went off to get it. As they waited, the old man asked Campbell why he had been tied up.

'Because of that thing in your arm. Maybe you were trying to pull it out.'

'It's hurtin' bad.'

Campbell looked at the IV line. It was leaking uselessly and painfully into the skin of the old man's forearm. Dr Totenberg came back. 'I guess I should do the rectal,' she said, pulling on a glove.

'O.K. to untie him?'

'I guess so, for a little while. God, his I V's wrecked again.'

Dr Totenberg confirmed Campbell's diagnosis. They went out of the room to discuss the case. 'I guess I shoulda thought of that,' she said. 'And his mouth.'

'What about the nurses? Don't they keep an eye on that sort of thing?' They did, sometimes, at home.

'I can't blame them. And his mouth, you reckon candida? Swab for mycology? Down here it's a coupla weeks.'

'Treat it, it's candida.'

'No lab work?'

'If you want, but treat it now. Help his mouth.'

'So he can eat?'

'And drink.'

'So I guess then we could take down his IV.'

'Yes.'

'That's awful. . . . I mean, I shoulda thought of both these things.'

Campbell felt rather sorry for her. 'How long's he been like this . . . ? How long d'you think he's got?'

'He was doin' fine, doin' real well till Monday. We thought he'd have weeks. Well, maybe a couple anyway. Yeah, if we sort out his mouth. . . . And his rectum. Gee, that's awful, David.'

They went back to the old man and Dr Totenberg said, 'Reverend Barbee, we're gonna fix your mouth, so's it won't hurt and you can eat. An' we're gonna sort out your bowels.'

'Praise the Lawd,' said the old man. 'An' now, brothers an' sisters, we're gonna sing. . . .' He lifted both hands in broad, conducting gestures. '. . . "Shall we gather by the ri . . . ver. . ." ' Dr Totenberg looked a little sad. Then they examined the old man's feet and found that he had infected pressure sores on both heels, which made her sadder still.

'Well, doc,' said Dr Kidd as they moved out on to the highway again, 'How's Life Ending in Split Rock?'

'Seems all right.' Prior to meeting Mr Barbee, Campbell had had grave doubts about his ability to contribute anything

42

to the medicine of Life Ending in West Carolina. Now there were possibilities. 'We looked at an old man,' he said.

Dr Kidd was thinking of other things. Eventually he said, 'We got a guy down here who's havin' problems.'

'Oh?'

'Yup. A resident. Could be tough.'

'Really?'

'Yup. . . . What d'ya think of the nursing home? You know, the Facility.'

'Seems all right. We looked at an old man.'

'What had he got?'

'Bronchogenic primary. Lot of spread.'

'He O.K.?'

'Should be, for a little while anyway. A nice old man. A preacher. He was singing hymns.'

'The guy I saw wasn't.'

'Oh?'

'Jeeze, it could be tough. Second year resident. Young guy, good school, good record, but for the last coupla weeks actin' like he didn't care. And that's new. Old George, the guy in charge down here, had to talk with him, then he got onto me. Odd kinda story, with nothin' big but just a whole lotta li'l things that'd make you think something big's gonna happen soon.'

'What sort of things?'

'Late showin' up, which he never was before. Kinda slow makin' up his mind, which is also new. An' just . . . well, it's kinda hard to explain. He used to be a real tidy guy, and now there's some days he shows up he ain't shaved.'

'What was he like before all this?'

'Reg'lar kinda guy. Well, maybe a bit of a loner, but sharp, a smart young physician. He had a kinda tough time as an intern, but he made it.'

'And now you think he might. . . ?'

'Might be. Kinda borderline for a characterologic disorder.'

'Family?'

'This guy's single.'

'I meant family history.'

43

'Yup. As a matter of fact his old man's in a state bin in the mid-west. He was a physician too.'

'With. . . ?'

'Yup.'

'Schizophrenia?'

'Yup. It's real tough. So we're gonna give young Don Kravitz a week, an' if he's worse, we get him seen. Even if he's the same we get him seen. Hell, he's gotta be seen.'

'Does he know?'

'Hard to tell. Like, he just comes on like a guy who's havin' a tough time on a rural rotation. They work 'em hard in Split Rock. . . . It's all kinda worryin'. You got schizophrenic physicians in Scotland?'

Campbell thought of a popular television psychiatrist, then of a man in his own year who had read the Bible when everyone else had been preparing more conventionally for Finals. 'I suppose so.'

There was no further conversation for some time. Campbell watched the unfamiliar landscape flash past and from time to time experienced recurrences of disquiet about being in the wrong side of a car on the wrong side of the road. He also thought about the old man whom he now saw as his first American patient. If the MacHardy Life Ending Program were solely concerned with the sort of shallow-end, cocktail-party psycho-social analyses on display at the Teaching Conference, then he could always get out, giving MacHardy, probably in the person of the mild and reasonable Dr Drucker, the option of sending him home or permitting him to limit his activities to the perhaps more agreeable Family Practice scene. On the other hand, if he were duly licensed and encouraged to continue with the sort of simple but potentially rewarding medicine he had just been practising, it might be more interesting to stay with the Life Ending Program, put up with its flakiness and do a little good, by stealth if necessary. That, in retrospect, was probably what Dr Drucker had had in mind, and if Dr Totenberg was representative of the local state of the clinical arts he might be able to help quite a lot.

Then Campbell thought of Dr Totenberg, and decided

she was quite interesting as a potential colleague. By the time the yellow car had reached the foot of the scarp he had made up his mind to ring her in a couple of days to find out how the Reverend Barbee was getting on.

As Dr Kidd drove up the hill a convoy of huge timber-laden trucks descended, faster than seemed safe and all the more alarming to Campbell through being on the unexpected side of the road. They took the corners wide, and after each one Campbell wondered how many more there would be.

Near the top the ascending traffic slowed to a crawl then stopped. A state trooper, grey-uniformed and wearing a wide-brimmed hat, stood by a car with its blue light flashing. One of the timber trucks was slanted across the road, its front off-side corner propped up. As the trooper signalled cars past one by one, Campbell saw what had happened; the huge front wheel was embedded in the crushed remains of a small open car, from which a hand and forearm protruded at an awkward angle. As the trooper waved them on, Campbell took several deep breaths.

'Gee,' said Dr Kidd as they cleared the summit, 'that coulda been us. D'ya see how far out that truck was. But quick, I guess, for the guy on the other end of that arm.'

'I suppose so.'

'How d'you rate that for quality of death, Dave?'

Campbell did not answer.

'Most likely cause of death in our age group. Well, yours.'

'I could do without it.'

'Jeeze, so could I.' Dr Kidd wound his window down and raised his voice. 'How d'you make out with Amy, doc?'

'Seems a nice girl.'

'Beats me how she does it. I mean, when you look at her father. Kinda sad about her marriage.'

'Oh?'

'A shrink.'

Campbell did not wish to seem too interested in the matter. Dr Kidd continued anyway. 'Yup, a skunk of a shrink, and mean with it. I mean real mean. Took all her old jazz seventy-eights when he quit.' Among other things, Campbell

45

made a mental note of the rural physician's interest in jazz.

Nearer Crimond, Dr Kidd talked once more about the Family Practice resident down at Split Rock, so that Campbell wondered why he was being told so much. Then the Director of the Family Practice Program explained the arrangements for the new month-long rotation in Life Ending. Dr Campbell, as visiting Fellow, would supervise the first resident, Dr Kravitz. It seemed an unpromising start.

'Iranians or Afghanistanians, who cares. We shoulda bombed them weeks ago.' The Dean spoke more in sorrow than in anger. Round the table there was a respectful silence. 'You gotta show these guys, an' you cain't start by quittin'. When you start quittin' you keep on quittin', so you gotta show 'em. Right, Cal?'

The Head of Thanatology and Director of the Thanatology Program was sitting next to the Dean. 'Right, Teddy, it's a lesson of history. Look at the guys that quit.'

'An' it's not only the Iranians and the Afghanistanians.' The Dean paused and gazed slowly round the room. 'What about the Panamanians?' The question hung in the air and he nodded his head in statesmanlike gloom. 'Are we gonna give it to 'em?' the Dean asked. 'That canal? On a plate? No, sir. We dug it, we use it and now we gotta hang onto it. With them Iranians and Afghanistanians about, we gotta hang onto it.'

Campbell, slow on geopolitics, pondered that point but it was not elucidated. Dr Pulver spoke once more. 'You're right again, Teddy. Canals are things you gotta hang onto. That's another lesson of history.'

If you looked at the Dean rather than listened to him, he was quite impressive. More ancient Roman than Southern gentleman, Dr Teddy Totenberg had a head and face that would have looked well in bronze. His eyes misted in contemplation of the lessons of history then he turned to Dr Pulver again. 'Whassaname of that canal, Cal? The one the British quit in Egypt.'

'Good point, Teddy,' said Pulver. 'Yeah, that canal Attlee

46

handed over. . . . An' givin' away that canal really kinda finished the Brits.'

'Nineteen. . . .' the Dean growled. 'Nineteen somethin'. Yeah, I remember. Despite everythin' Dulles 'n' Ike could do. Nineteen . . .'

'Campbell. . . ?' Dr Pulver barked, looking down the table.

'Fifty-six, sir.'

'Yeah. Fifty-six. I was just finishin' up in the old Gold Coast.'

'An' they quit their canal,' said Dr Totenberg. 'They quit.'

The Dean's Dining Room was high in the mock Gothic building at the centre of the campus. It was panelled in wood, with small leaded windows and a series of portraits of people with ruddy complexions and long noses who, paint-erly tact allowed for, must all have been rather ugly.

The dinner was an unexpectedly weighty occasion. Of the ten present, six were senior figures, it seemed, in the MacHardy University Medical Center. Over drinks beforehand, Campbell had been introduced to them all, but now had some trouble sorting them out. Dr Drucker, the head of Primary Care, sat on the Dean's left, opposite Dr Pulver of Thanatology. The man at the end opposite the Dean was Dr Bottger, the Chairman of Psychiatry, who was small and round and said little, but, to judge from the way he was being cultivated by Bob Nance, the junior lead psy-chiatrist from the Wednesday Conference and now sitting by him, was a man of considerable influence.

Campbell sat somewhat below the salt, between Sharron Sneed and a man called Abey Schlepp, a dermatologist, the need for whom at an otherwise essentially Life Ending occa-sion was not obvious. Conversation had now become general and Campbell, who could think of nothing to say to a der-matologist, turned to Miss Sneed, who was sitting on his right and was the only woman present. Before he could say anything she smiled and touched his arm and said, 'David, I heard you were down at Split Rock. Wonderful. Really terrific. And Reverend Barbee's MILES score is up to seventeen, and that's just wonderful. A seventeen at KR

Five was his projected maximum, because his blindness has just gotta bring him down, but he's a wonderful Life Ender. Straight fours on Spirituality.'

Campbell said he was glad the old man was feeling better, and asked how Miss Sneed had come to hear of it.

'Well, a Director of Education 'n' Evaluation's gotta be most everywhere sometime.' She laughed and smiled. 'I take the LEAC learners out for their practical experience of Transition Management. Reverend Barbee's one of Rick Allen's cases, and we went down to Split Rock yesterday for his mid-semester assessment. Rick's real cute, and wonderful with his wheelchair, so you forget about his paraplegia problem. And so sincere. . . . Oh, by the way, David, Amy Totenberg says hi and thanks. I guess you helped with Reverend Barbee's latest Transition, huh?'

'Dr Totenberg did most of it,' said Campbell. 'She seems very good.'

'You don't have to tell me.' Miss Sneed's manner altered as she talked of the physician rather than of the patient.

'D'you know her well?'

'I guess I do. We shared a house for a while, a while back. Just after. . . . David, you settlin' in O.K.? I mean, you gettin' to know folks, findin' your way round town and all that stuff? I know it took Gus a coupla weeks, but he always knew he could call me, about anythin'. . . . So I want you to call me, huh? In fact, David, you booked for brunch Sunday. . . ? You come on round maybe ten-thirty, O.K.? Eleven twenty-one MacHardy Boulevard East. It's a little white house. I'll write it down for ya. Ten-thirty? That'll be terrific. O.K. Ten-thirty.'

Campbell, who had simply been listening politely, realized that all options in the matter of Sunday brunch were now gone and smiled and nodded his thanks with as much visible good feeling as he could muster.

'And terrific! Here's ole Jake. Aren't you *hungry*?'

The old black man from the Oxford Room, dressed on this occasion in a black tail coat and grey striped pants, limped in and bowed to the Dean, departed, and returned at the head of a bevy of standard corn-fed campus belles, functioning for the time being as waitresses. The Dean and his guests each received a portion of melon which, in relation to everything else about the proceedings so far, was really rather small. When all were served, the Dean said 'Cal,' and the head of Thanatology bowed his head and growled, 'Bless this food to our use and thus to Thy service, O Lord our strength and our redeemer.'

The portions of melon were not only small but tough and only sketchily prepared, so that Campbell was concerned that nothing he did with spoon or fork would inconvenience those around him. As he ate a fragment of melon from somewhere on his left darted across his field of vision.

'D'ja mind?' said a harsh male voice. 'D'ja mind fielding that bit o' my starter?' Campbell spooned the stray fragment back from somewhere in front of Miss Sneed's plate and returned it to the man on his left. 'Gee thanks,' he said. 'This is a real fightin' melon. Thanks. I'm Schlepp, by the way. I dunno if we were introodooced out there before.'

Campbell smiled politely and re-introduced himself to Dr Schlepp. 'Call me Abey,' said Schlepp. 'Everybody else does.' The dermatologist had receding reddish hair and a selection of facial features which together with a pair of remarkable ears somehow made him look like a fox and a rabbit at the same time. 'How long ya been here, uh, Dave?' He talked with his mouth full and was already gouging out more melon.

'About a week,' Campbell said.

'Different than socialized medicine, huh?'

Campbell agreed.

'Gonna try an' stay?'

Campbell thought it was too early to say.

'We got clinical freedom,' said Schlepp. 'And tax shelters.' He attacked his melon again. 'Give freedom a chance.'

Across the table from Campbell, Stump was listening politely while Stef Mikoyan, the fat psychiatrist from LEAC, explained what Eastern Airlines had done to his baggage on the way back from a Life Ending workshop in Chattanooga. Further down the table Dr Nance had succeeded in engaging the attention of Dr Bottger but had not yet managed to elicit any verbal response.

The waitresses returned and took away the plates and remains of the first course. This broke up the various conversations around the table. The Dean turned to Dr Drucker and said, 'It's kinda nice, Phil, ain't it, how this noo program's gotten all these different people all together.'

Dr Drucker smiled, took off his glasses to polish them and looked as if he were about to speak. Before he could do so Dr Pulver had protruded his jaw and lowered his eyebrows, contriving somehow to smile and at the same time say, 'Yessir. That's what Thanatology's all about. We at the Center are always delighted when we can bring people and resources together from across the whole of the MacHardy scene. Twenty-seven disciplines have contributed or at this point in time are contributing to programs sponsored by the Thanatology Center.'

Dr Drucker put on his glasses again and smiled in agreement. Dr Mikoyan smiled and chortled. 'How else would us poor shrinks ever get to meet a dermatologist?' That amused people, Schlepp most of all. 'Yeah,' he said. 'It's kinda nice. I think the last time I saw a shrink was when the Dodgers bottomed out in sixty-three.'

Dr Pulver was not amused. 'We can joke about it, but the only way we're gonna hang on to a LEAPERS program is by working together and making it work. . . . We in Thanatology are committed to the multi-disciplinary model. We pioneered it and now we're gonna expand it. A meeting like this, Mr Dean, sir, can only strengthen our commitment to each other and the cause of bettering the Life Endings of our fellow Americans.'

'That's what I kinda like about dinners like this,' said the Dean. 'We may have our differences, but while we can eat and drink and joke together MacHardy's in good shape. An' I kinda like the idea of gettin' into Life Ending. Maybe we didn't get it right all the time before, but a million dollars of Federal money makes me think we'll get it right most of the time real soon. An' from what I hear from Cal here the Life Ending money's gonna be good for a good few years. Remember how cancer money was fine, for a while. And Ageing money's O.K., but it ain't gonna last forever. But this stuff I guess I kinda trust, because I know it'll do good, even just makin' us think a bit more about the way people die.'

'There are so many ways. . . .' said Dr Pulver, having drawn a deep breath.

'One's gonna be plenty for me,' Schlepp interjected. 'A nice one, I hope.'

'That's what we all hope.' Pulver spoke louder. 'And the unique contribution of the MILES technology. . . .'

'I kinda like,' said the Dean, softly but very firmly, 'I kinda like the story about the man hoein' his garden, and some guy asks him what he'd do if he knew he was gonna die that evenin'. St Thomas, wasn't it? An' he says, "I guess I'd finish hoein' mah garden".'

'Yessir,' Pulver barked. 'St Thomas Aquinas.'

'You sure o' that, Cal?' Dr Drucker asked. 'Sounds more like St Thomas à Kempis.'

The girls reappeared with the main course and there were long periods of silence while each diner addressed his spinach, cornbread, black-eyed peas and whole roasted spring chicken. Interrupted sometimes by stray fragments of chicken bone from the left, Campbell wondered about this dinner party and the future at MacHardy of Life Ending which, as Dr Kidd had pointed out only a few days before, might now have become too important to be left to social workers and psychiatrists.

As he ate his chicken Campbell wondered also about the man at the head of the table, who, when not talking grand strategy, had been mild and conciliatory, saying nothing that could have been interpreted as hostile to the interests of Primary Care or Family Practice. He had Dr Drucker right next to him, and had been polite to him, far more so than had Dr Pulver. Was he simply a quiet man nearing the end of his career and seeking only to avoid trouble for himself and others?

His appearance too was interesting: though an old and large man he had certain things in his face, mainly around the eyes, that brought to mind the tall pale girl at Split Rock who, Campbell realized, had brought off the perhaps remarkable feat of both resembling her father and being

51

quite pretty. Campbell made a mental note to ring Split Rock Health Care Inc. on Monday morning to find out how old Mr Barbee was getting on.

No wine had been served with the meal, but as the waitresses took away the main course plates the old black man went around the table distributing small glasses, then disappeared and returned with a decanter of port on a silver tray. He bowed and left it on the table at the Dean's elbow. Two waitresses tidied up, concentrating discreetly on a semi-circle of avian debris centred on Dr Schlepp and extending three feet or so across the table. Two more girls brought in things for coffee and left, whispering to each other.

The Dean passed the port and watched it circle slowly from Dr Drucker round to Dr Pulver. As Dr Pulver put down the decanter Dr Totenberg leaned forward and began to speak. 'In case any of you are scared this is goin' to turn into a long, speechifyin' kinda dinner, let me set your minds at rest. But I thought that you would not wish to let this, uh, occasion pass without at least one little toast. We're here tonight to recognize the, uh, very substantial award that has come to MacHardy, and that's somethin' to celebrate. But we're here also to roll up our sleeves, so to speak, for a whole lotta hard work that that award will bring. As Dean, it's been mah pleasure to invite you here and tell you I look forward to further meetings, when we'll be able to look back and say how we, an' by that I mean you, worked together for better Life Ending and achieved something.

'This is neither the time nor the place for, uh, fine print details. There will be other meetings in other places for that. I just wanna say to all of you from all your different departments and interests that MacHardy expects a lot from you guys, and I'm sure we're gonna get it. Gentlemen. . . .'

An untidy shuffle brought the diners to their feet, except for one. On the Dean's right Dr Calbert Pulver sat still and pale, his face greyish and sweating. His eyes glazed over and he fell forward, spilling his port. He coughed and gurgled and vomited, spluttering half-digested dinner between his cheek and the table, then groaned and lay still.

There was a shocked silence and for a moment no one moved, then the Dean looked over and put a hand on Dr Pulver's shoulder. 'Cal. . . . Cal. . . . You O.K.?' He was not. As he lay there the Dean stared round. 'Somebody better get a doctor,' he said. 'Real quick. . . . Cal ain't well. Git help. Phil. . . . Stef. . . . For Chrissake get a doctor, someone!'

The first person to do anything useful was Nance, the junior psychiatrist. He ran from the room shouting, 'I'll go dial the rescue squad!' The next was Campbell. He ran round to the top of the table and hauled Dr Pulver from his chair and laid him out on the floor, semi-prone so that no further vomit would enter his airway. Then he knelt by him and felt for a pulse in his neck. There was none, so he rolled Dr Pulver on to his back and thumped him once in the middle of the chest and felt for a pulse again. Still there was none. A siren wailed in the middle distance.

Campbell was still trying to clear the vomit from Dr Pulver's mouth when he was elbowed aside by a large uniformed woman with 'Rescue Squad' labels on her shoulders. She and a male colleague worked quickly and efficiently, doing the right sort of things with the right sort of equipment, but Dr Pulver continued to look very dead. The Dean and his surviving guests watched silently as he was borne from their midst on a stretcher. Miss Sneed was weeping, literally crying on Dr Mikoyan's shoulder. The psychiatrists observed one another. The dermatologist looked thoughtful. Campbell, for no particular reason, found himself remembering that Dr Pulver had signed himself up the previous fall to supply data for the MacHardy Index of Life Ending Satisfaction, on an eventuality basis.

PART TWO

'It's not just a turf issue, Dave, honey. You have to unner-
stand it's to do with bigger things, like the whole future of the
LEAPERS and the way it's gonna go. What those guys
decide about the leadership has to do with the whole quality
of Life Ending, not just here at MacHardy, Dave, honey, but
nationwide, because the MacHardy program is a whole
one third of the national Life Ending scene. And in Evaluation it's even more than that. It's so far out in front that the
way we go now more or less determines how Americans are
gonna Life End maybe till the end of the century.'

Campbell nodded.

'So while Phil's a great guy and we all love him, Life
Ending is basically not a Primary Care scene, and in any case
Phil just isn't up to it, because when the crunch comes he's
just not gonna do anything that upsets Teddy. And that
means that the internists get to walk all over the guys who did
all the work and got the grant. And that wouldn't be right. It
just wouldn't, would it, Dave?'

'No.'

Miss Sneed smiled up at him and moved a little, restoring
the circulation in Campbell's right arm. 'I knew you'd understand.' She sighed contentedly and settled back, making his
arm numb again. He moved a little. 'You O.K., honey?' He
nodded.

'So it's gotta be the shrinks, which is real nice. We know them and they know us. They've been in Life Ending since the LEAC set up shop. They're just so good with the problems of Life Ending and the most wonderful thing about them is, they really appreciate Evaluation. Stef's a genius the way he uses it. At this point in time ten major medical centers have already hosted him for presentations and he's been honoured with an invite to the White House Conference on Life Ending next fall. An' we've got seventy-one publications on Life Ending Evaluation either extant in the literature or in process, so I guess it'd be just false modesty if I didn't tell you that Stef, Ben and I constitute just one great team. Honest, Dave, when you've heard it so often you get so you just gotta start believin' it. Did I already show you last month's *American Thanatologic Review* editorial?'

Campbell shook his head.

'I think I've got a copy right here. Would you like to see it, honey?'

Without waiting for his reply she got up and disappeared into the next room. Clothed she had appeared simply well built. Naked she was frankly fat, with sad uneven thighs and a huge sagging dimpled bottom. She came back holding a journal with a glossy pink and white cover, looking fatter still from the front. As she drew closer he heard her thighs rubbing together. 'It's wonderful,' she said. 'Really terrific.' Campbell reached out for the journal, which was open at the first editorial. 'More coffee, honey?'

'Yes please.'

Campbell, with only the vaguest idea about what constituted brunch and what was normal behaviour on such occasions, was nonetheless surprised to discover that morning that he was the only guest, and even more surprised to find himself in bed with his hostess within the hour. He flexed his right arm and opened and closed his hand.

He did not even have the excuse of being drunk. They had had orange juice and coffee and eaten some rather heavy pancakes, then they had sat together on a sofa and talked about the Center and the dinner the previous Friday evening. Miss Sneed had begun to cry, then had sobbed against

Campbell, clutching him to her substantial and at that time decently clad bosom. Then Campbell had been surprised by an unequivocally sexual initiative, to which he had responded mainly out of politeness. Thereafter, developments had been frankly mechanical, ('Not there, honey. There. And harder. . . .) and they had adjourned to bed.

Miss Sneed got into bed again and snuggled against Campbell, looking expectantly up at him as he began to read the editorial. It was headed 'Major Impetus in Thanatologic Evaluation', and began 'No serious worker with an ongoing commitment to improved modalities in Terminal Care Situation Management could, with the upcoming prospect of Federal funding in this vital and challenging field, deny the central importance of the cost-effectiveness issue. Mikoyan and others (This issue, 1139 onwards) review their experience with the MacHardy Index of Life Ending Satisfaction (MILES) technology and there can be few thanatologists in the US or worldwide who can doubt the key contribution that it has made already to the quantification of previously loosely and subjectively evaluated parameters in the pre-terminal and terminal experience.

'A reality-based, hard-item inventory of only one hundred and ninety variables in five key areas, controlled for inter-observer bias and readily computer-codable by semi-skilled operatives, it gives clinicians and researchers a simple two-digit score, meshed to Kubler Ross staging, that facilitates individual-individual, individual-group and group-group comparisons over time and space, program evaluation, quality control and input-output inquiry as a basis for cost-effectiveness accounting. In the words of Dr J. Calbert Pulver, Director of the MacHardy Thanatology Center, the home of MILES, "Dying will never be the same again." '

'Wonderful, isn't it?'

'Hm?'

'The editorial,' said Miss Sneed. 'It's wonderful.'

'Oh, yes. It seems very enthusiastic. I'd just been reading the bit that quotes Dr Pulver.'

'Oh, I'd forgotten about that. Gee, it's tough, and just when the MILES technology was breaking out. But it's a great boost, isn't it? The rest, I mean. And the review article is on page eleven thirty-nine.' Miss Sneed nuzzled Campbell's shoulder. 'It's my eighty-seventh publication.'

For the third or fourth time Campbell realized that accepting the invitation to brunch with Miss Sneed had been an error of judgement. He leafed through the journal wondering how soon he could decently get dressed and leave.

'Ben wrote the first draft,' said Miss Sneed. 'Ben Benvenuto, our data guy. Like he's kinda good with words. His background, I guess. He was on faculty at St Brendan's a coupla years, an' he'd bin there maybe ten as a student. He's a wonderful person, Dave. We've gotta go meet him Monday. Say eleven-thirty? I've got a buncha things from eight-thirty, Transition Management Tutorials, with the new learners, you know, and a coupla video sessions on Life Ending Communication Skills. That kinda thing. But I guess I'd be through by eleven-thirty, then we could go see Ben. Hey!' She squeezed Campbell's right thigh just above the knee. 'Dave, honey, maybe we could *lunch* with him. Be kinda cute. Would you like that, honey? I could ring him as soon as I get in Monday. He's a wonderful guy, you'll love him. And if he can't make it we'll just lunch anyway, huh?'

'That's a most encouraging editorial.'

'Oh, Ben didn't write the draft of that. I meant the review. Page eleven thirty-nine. Gimme it, I'll show ya. It's really great, Dave. Yeah, Ben was a Trappist, trained an' all. Did maybe twelve years then he met Melissa. It was real romantic, she was the Old Testament Librarian at Brendan's. An' now they got a coupla wonderful kids, Bridget and Damian. Damian's three and he wants to be a priest. He's *real* cute.'

With no immediate prospect of escape, Campbell skimmed through the review article. Its prose was less dire than that of the editorial, a tribute perhaps to the literary skills acquired from twelve years of priestcraft, but it was not easy to skim, having the authentic ring of American academic English, and reading as though badly translated from German. Content also rated low. The MacHardy Index of Life Ending Satisfaction was simply another unremarkable example of the sociological vice of counting the uncountable, with large practical limitations and no very valid universal claims. Campbell had already heard enough to know that that was not how it was regarded locally. Miss Sneed, for instance, was a devotee evidently building a career on it. He decided not to share his doubts with her, at least not then, for it was unlikely she was thinking of such things. She had wriggled over him so that her right thigh covered his, and her pudgy little hands were once more exploring his groin.

On Monday morning Campbell went over to the Family Practice offices for a ten-fifteen appointment with the resident on the new Life Ending rotation. No one seemed to know about it, and he was offered coffee and a seat in the library. At quarter to eleven Dr Kravitz came looking for him. He was tall and lean, and spoke with his mouth full. They did not shake hands, because he had a large paper cup of Coca Cola in one and a half-eaten hamburger in the other. He sprawled in an armchair and continued to eat. He explained his lateness. 'Had to see mah counsellor. Only time he could fit me in. You O.K.? You find somethin' to do?'

'Yes, thanks.'

'Noo rotation an' all. Makes bein' late kinda worse. An' right now I gotta go see one of mah patients. Maybe you'd like to come along. He's in MacHardy East. Be nice if you could make it. Like, this is the Life Ending Rotation and this guy's dyin'. No problems or anythin'.'

MacHardy East was the huge white tower block dominating the campus. Hexagonal in section and flanked by two hexagonal multi-level parking decks, it would have been more suited to downtown Tokyo than to this modest and piney Southern campus. Kravitz and Campbell approached it across a huge, sunbaked, gleaming white piazza perhaps designed mainly to have been photographed for an architectural magazine. At the main door, a vast smoked-glass plate that slid automatically aside as they approached, two policemen stood guard, armed with revolvers and laden with spare ammunition.

Inside, the foyer was a softly lit hexagonal space two

hundred yards across, with a smaller one-storey hexagon in the middle, housing a bank, a gift shop, an information desk, a police post and a chapel. On top of the inner hexagon was a garden with a large sloping rockery, a waterfall and several fully grown trees. Above and around them rose the twelve hollow tiered floors of the hospital itself.

'Great place, huh?' said Kravitz. 'A hundred and twenty million bucks. Nothing else like it in the world. My guy's on the seventh floor.'

'Ischemic heart disease, chronic obstructive pulmonary disease, cerebral arteriosclerosis, oh, an' osteoarthrosis. An' I guess his kidneys are shuttin' down. He's an ole guy from one of the nursing homes here in town, MacDonnell Beechwood, I reckon. Bin my patient for a year maybe. Never did much, no relatives, an' just sat there in his wheelchair at Beechwood. Sometimes got ankle swelling which did O.K. with a diuretic. Needed a bit of sedation sometimes and Haldol used to knock him down quite nicely. Medicaid paid his nursing home bills. He came in here maybe three weeks ago, when I was outa town. The handover said he kinda stopped talkin', an' they saw him in the ER and his EKG showed infero-lateral change. Never had no pain though. They stuck him in the Intensive Care Unit an' after a coupla days he extended his infarct and had runs of VT goin' on VF. They shocked him an' got him back to sinus rhythm, I guess. It musta been hard to assess his mental status though, because he was sedated for ventilatory purposes, an' his endotracheal tube stopped him talkin'. But he did O.K. From bein' mainly blue round the edges he pinked up nicely and sorted out his blood gases, then about day ten he had a big pulmonary embolus. They got the thoracic surgeons down but they wouldn't touch him. The guy said, "He's gotta die of somethin', an' it ain't gonna be my operation." Funny. Medicare woulda paid. So we anticoagulated him an' he stabilized again, but they had a helluva job gettin' him off the respirator, an' we're still not too sure about his mental status. I looked him over when I came on the service yesterday. Oh,

59

an' his kidneys are maybe shuttin' down, they thought ECF depletion at first but he's fully hydrated and his urea's still goin' up. So I thought you might like to see him. Seein' as how he's not gonna make it unless we dialyse him. He's called. . . . He's called. . . . Oh, shit. Yeah. He's called Ron Hovey.'

Kravitz and Campbell were standing at the bedside in a single room high in the tower block. A small window at shoulder level looked out over the campus towards the center of Crimond. Walls, ceiling and floor were all white, and the bed was set diagonally, with a large colour television suspended over its foot. On the screen, in dumb show, a gang of brightly clad children scampered along a muddy lane towards a woman holding a large bag of potato chips.

An elderly white man lay on the bed, covered to his waist by a sheet. There was a slim plastic tube disappearing into his right nostril and another emerging from his neck, just under his left ear. A third tube, from an IV set suspended by a chrome-plated arm reaching down from the ceiling, entered his left arm at the elbow. From under the sheet a fourth tube led to a square plastic bag with a small amount of dark, bloodstained urine in one corner.

The old man's face was thin and yellowish and did not register any expression other than that of being comfortably asleep. His eyes were closed and his arms lay by his sides, and he had not moved when the two doctors had come in or when Kravitz had been presenting the case to Campbell.

'Hell,' said Kravitz. 'I forgot his chest problem. He got a chest infection, growin' pseudomonas, when he was on the ventilator. They zapped it with Gentamicin and it stayed zapped. The thing of it is, he ain't woke up.'

There was a knock on the door and a tall woman with acne came in. She brandished a red clipboard, perhaps by way of explaining why she had come. 'Hi, you guys, don't mind me. I'm from the LEAPERS team, just lookin' in on Mr Hovey. Like, KR stagin' and a MILES update. Won't be but a minute.' She glanced at the yellowish figure on the bed and made a line of check marks down the right-hand side of a form on her clipboard and said, 'Good ole Ronnie, Acceptance all the way. Another Five Seventeen. Thanks, guys.' As she left Campbell recognized her as the girl he had seen leaving the late Dr Pulver's office after a stormy interview.

Kravitz had picked up the old man's right hand and was taking his pulse. 'Eighty an' reg'lar.' The patient's arm fell limply to his side again. 'An' his urea's up aroun' two hundred. So whaddya reckon, Dave? Dialyse him? Like, he'll die if we don't.'

Campbell moved nearer the bedside and said, 'Mr Hovey,' several times in a loud voice. Nothing happened. Dr Kravitz leaned over him too and shouted, 'Ronnie . . . Ronnie . . .' then turned to Campbell. 'See? Like I said, he just doesn't wanna wake up.'

Campbell pinched the lobe of the old man's ear gently between his thumb and forefinger, but still he made no response. Kravitz shrugged. 'No use, Dave, he's real flat.' He bent over the old man again and ground his knuckles into the patient's ribs, still with no response.

'What was he like before all this?' Campbell asked.

'Kinda muddled, I guess. A lot of the time he reckoned he was still in the Navy.'

'I see.'

'Yup.'

'And no relatives?'

'Nope.'

'So. . . ?'

'Dave, you don't wanna dialyse him, huh? That what I'm hearin'? You wanna leave the ole guy, just because no one's gonna sue?'

'Well, I didn't exactly mean that.' Campbell reached over and opened one of the patient's eyes. There was no glimmer of response other than the slow automatic narrowing of the pupil as light fell on it. 'When did he last speak?'

'Maybe ten days ago, possibly two weeks. You reckon leave him?'

'I think so,' said Campbell. 'Maybe his troubles are over.'

Kravitz laughed. 'I heard you Brits didn't go much on defensive medicine, an', like, he's got no family that's gonna

61

sue you.' He looked at Campbell for a little while then said, 'And what are you gonna do if he codes?'

'Sorry?'

'Codes. Code Five. Like, arrests.'

'You mean if he dies?'

'Yeah, you gonna call a code? Spark him? Resuscitate him? I mean, if he dies are you gonna get the team up?'

'I shouldn't have thought so,' said Campbell. 'No.'

'Wrong, doc, you gotta.'

'What?'

'You gotta,' Kravitz was smiling as though teaching Campbell something very simple. 'He can't sign somethin' himself sayin' "No Code" an' he's got no relatives can sign it for him, so he ain't a "No Code", so if he codes, he codes.'

Kravitz laughed again. 'Don't look so worried, Dave, they might not win. For a guy like this a code's a kinda formality. You gotta try, an' it keeps the team in shape, but you don't have to win.'

'I see.'

'So I guess he'll be O.K. Like, he gets to die, eventually.'

They left the still figure of Mr Hovey in his lonely and lavishly equipped room, while before his sightless eyes a television compere introduced two young couples about to compete in a spaghetti-eating contest.

Kravitz led the way along a gleaming white corridor until they reached a bay in which several white-clad nurses sat. While the resident looked for Mr Hovey's chart, Campbell waited. At one end of the bay a wall was entirely taken up by rows of small black and white TV screens. Above them was a large sign saying 'Confidential'. At first glance all the pictures looked the same but a closer look showed them to be a series of limited variations on the theme of a patient in bed. Two dozen people lying or sitting in various degrees of distress could be seen, most with a selection of plastic tubes entering or leaving them in various places and many firmly tied down. A pretty blonde nurse sat facing the screens, her eyes flicking across them without evident interest or emotion. She was filing her nails.

As Campbell watched she focused on one in particular,

put down her nailfile, reached to a consol of controls in front of her and said, 'Yes, Mr Botticelli, what can we do for you?' The reply, relayed through some sort of intercom, was indistinct. 'We're sorry, Mr Botticelli, will you make your request again, speaking more slowly and distinctly. We are here to help you.'

Again the loudspeaker moaned in hazy distress. The nurse frowned and said, 'Mr Botticelli, you are still indistinct. One of our floor staff will endeavour to visit with you shortly.' There was no reply and the nurse picked up her nailfile again. 'Didya get that, Cindy?' she asked without turning round. 'Twelve again.' Her eyes flicked round the wall of screens once more.

Campbell watched with interest. He had not noticed any video monitoring equipment when they had been in Mr Hovey's room, but from the look of the pictures it was likely that the cameras were incorporated somewhere in the TV sets hung above the end of each bed. Campbell thought of the commercial with muddy children and the spaghetti-eating contest, and then it dawned on him that he and Kravitz must have been observed by the nurse on duty at the monitor screens. Because he had been covertly observed he felt vaguely guilty, though they had really nothing to feel guilty about. Then he realized that their conversation could have been overheard if the nurse had chosen to switch on the sound monitor in Mr Hovey's room, and spent a moment wondering how their conversation about whether or not to resuscitate him might have sounded to a detached official observer.

'Pretty good, huh?' Kravitz had found Mr Hovey's chart and was standing just behind Campbell. 'That's ole Ronnie on screen seventeen, low on the right. He looks real good from here.'

'Bedpan eight,' said the nurse in front of the screens. 'An' twenty still looks like he needs somethin'.' On the other side of the nurses' bay someone got up and headed out into the corridor.

'Hi, Tracy.' Kravitz reached past Campbell and laid a hand on the shoulder of the seated nurse. 'How are you doin'?'

63

'Hi, Don. Saw you in seventeen. Ain't he so peaceful?'

'Yea, great. Tracy, this is Dave.'

'Hi, Dave.'

'Hello.'

'Dave's from Scotland.'

The nurse turned and flashed a smile at Campbell. 'Yeah, I *loved* your accent. How long you here for?'

'A year.'

'Like it?'

'It's very interesting.'

'Mah forebears came from England.'

'Really?'

'Yeah. Glasgow. Mah grandpa's uncle was hung there for stealin' sheep.'

'Really?'

'But we love it. Like, we always watch Masterpiece Theater. It's so cute. . . . Bedpan twelve, Cindy. Looks urgent. You with Family Practice, Dave?'

'Yes.'

'Like it?'

'Just started.'

'D'you have stuff like this in England, huh?'

'No,' said Campbell.

The nurse smiled again. 'We're the first in the state. The system combines safety with the privacy of an individual room and also serves to optimize nursing efficiency.'

'I see.'

'It's wonderful. Code five in twelve.' Her voice rose. 'That guy that wanted a bedpan. Cindy! Becky! Bonny!' She flicked another switch and said, 'Code Five, room seven one two. . . . Code Five, room seven one two.' From the loud-speakers in the bay and in the corridor outside the words echoed and faded. 'Let's get outa the way,' said Kravitz. 'Codes are heavy.'

As Campbell and Kravitz stood waiting for an elevator, one with red doors stopped and disgorged a hurried little procession. First came a man in green pyjamas carrying a small red plastic case marked 'Code Five' as though it were a football and the honour of his college depended on a quick touchdown. Next came a woman, tall and blonde and similarly clad. Last was a trolley of resuscitation equipment propelled at great speed by an athletic looking young black.

'Great, huh?' said Kravitz. 'But it's mos' likely just some ole gomer with the big C everywhere an' nothin' goin' for 'im.'

Another elevator stopped and a fat clergyman puffed out and plodded off in the wake of the resuscitation team. Behind him, to Campbell's surprise, ran the tall girl with acne last seen in Mr Hovey's room not long before. Campbell and Kravitz entered a glass-walled elevator car which whispered down the inside of the glass-roofed interior of the hospital. They alighted on the second floor on a gallery surrounding the indoor forest, and descended by a broad and silent moving staircase to the ground level.

'You plannin' on lunchin' anywhere in particular?'

'No,' said Campbell, who hadn't been thinking about lunch.

'There's a place in the basement. Or maybe you'd prefer somewhere off campus.'

'Off campus, I think.'

'Fine. Let's go to Mother Nature's.'

In the line outside, waiting for a table, Campbell recalled his conversation with Dr Kidd on the way back from Split Rock. Although a certain cultural distance made these things hard to judge, the resident's general style, conversation and deportment seemed within the limits of the local norm. True, he had been late for their ten-fifteen meeting, but with reasonable cause. His appearance now gave no grounds for disquiet: he was, apart from a neat droopy moustache, clean-shaven, and he was wearing much the same as the other younger doctors Campbell had met so far. His pastel check pants were on the loud side, but hardly amounted to evidence of serious mental disorder. Campbell decided to suspend judgement.

There were no pressing doubts about the restaurant either. The waiting line included a proportion of solid citizens, and such of its unfamiliar features as were visible seemed intriguing rather than alienating. A display of small hand-written ads sought 'Aquarian of either sex to join Piscean and Taurian, both vegetarian, in caring, sharing apartment', 'New members for self-assertiveness training group – No smokers or straights please' and the like. A large poster exhorted patrons waiting on the sidewalk to Save the Whale.

'D'you have vegetarian restaurants in Scotland?' Kravitz asked after a long pause.

'I think so.'

'You don't go much on vegetarian food?'

'No. . . . I mean this place is fine.'

'I'm kinda gettin' into it. Like, I don't really enjoy hamburgers the way I used to. I guess I'm headin' for a kinda lacto-ovo-vegetarian scene, with good yin-yang balance.'

'Really?'

'Yup, like now, summer, the vegetal energy cycle's comin' up for its zenith, so there's a whole buncha yin things about. An' I kinda like what they do to me.'

The line shuffled forward as four more entered the restaurant. There was a silence between Campbell and Kravitz, and Campbell reconsidered his suspension of judgement. 'Like it's nice,' Kravitz eventually continued, 'but you gotta have yin-yang balance. So I guess I'll have the whale salad.'

Campbell looked round with concern. Kravitz was laughing. Campbell saw the joke and laughed too. A long-haired girl in a peasant skirt turned round and stared reproachfully at them through granny glasses, which seemed to increase Kravitz' enjoyment of his own joke.

Eventually they sat down and ordered.

'Uh, beans guacamole . . . and a strawberry zinger, please. Dave? What are you gonna have?'

'Greek salad and some milk, please.'

The waitress turned and disappeared into the kitchen. She was a squarish blonde girl who walked like a man and had rather a menacing bunch of brass keys dangling from the hip pocket of her denims. A red badge on the front had warned 'The Future is Female'.

'D'you have lesbians in Scotland?' Kravitz inquired when she was out of earshot.

'I suppose so. . . . Is this place sort of. . . ?'

'Sort of, I guess. But you get all sortsa folk eatin' here.'

At a table nearby three workmen in overalls were drinking beer and eating big toasted cheese sandwiches. A group of MacHardy students, with the regulation blonde hair, tanned thighs and red Gothic-printed tee-shirts giggled in a corner over milkshakes. An oriental family ate in silence. 'Interesting place,' said Campbell.

An uneasy feeling, having nothing to do with vegetarianism, lesbians or his companion's mental health, blanked out his light conversation. It was Monday and it was lunchtime. He had arranged, in the sense of having failed to disentangle himself from, a lunch with Miss Sneed and someone else. His first thoughts were guilty, but when he glanced at his watch to check that he was hopelessly late feelings of relief followed quickly. A firm if unintentional statement had been made, which might pave the way for a later and more considered dismantling of her assumptions.

'. . . in Scotland?'

'Sorry?'

'I said,' said Dr Kravitz slowly, 'do you have a whole lotta women physicians in Scotland?'

'I'm sorry,' said Campbell. 'I was thinking about something else. Yes. Well, some. More over the last ten years.'

'It's goin' that way here. Do they get to be surgeons an' all that stuff where you come from?'

'They're mainly in general practice.'

'That's like here. We got maybe a dozen in the program. I like it. It's kinda natural. In Split Rock. . . .'

The waitress reappeared with two mounds of food, and they ate without talking, like men with a lot to do. Campbell wondered how to apologize to Miss Sneed without destroying the effect.

'I guess beans are kinda yin,' Kravitz said indistinctly through a mouth of them, 'so I'm gonna have the ice-cream next. It's yang.'

Campbell made a polite inquiry.

'Some stuff I read. My buddy's into macrobiotics. Hell, he's into all kinds o' crazy things, but yin and yang's things you're supposed to balance, like hot and cold, wet and dry. Hell, I just like ice-cream. But he's really into it. I don't mind, so long as he's cookin'.'

'What does he do?'

'Neurosurgeon.'

'Really?'

'But he's into a closet alternative thing.'

'Alternative to what?'

'The MacHardy Neurosurgery Program, I guess. He's mainly into natural stuff, and gettin' your head together. Peace, brown rice and herb tea. That kinda thing. He's real laid back for a brain surgeon. I guess I'm getting into it too.'

'Really?'

'Yeah, makes you think. You know how you can bust your butt achievin' your way from first grade through a residency program? I never thought about it before, but. . . . Like, now I'm wonderin'.'

'About Family Practice?'

'Shit no. Well, I'm gonna finish my residency.'

'But having doubts?'

Dr Kravitz finished his mouthful of beans before answering. 'I guess I got stuck in a bad place, for a while.'

'Split Rock?'

Kravitz smiled and shook his head. 'No, Dave, gettin' stuck in a bad place means, uh, like it doesn't mean gettin' stuck in a bad *place*. I was kinda *thinkin'* about things, but it did happen while I was down at Split Rock. I was thinkin', shit, is this *it*? Like, is this what I've been headin' for since first grade? Lookin' after a buncha folks with nothin' goin' for 'em, you know, migrant labour, Indians and. . . .' He lowered his voice and looked around. '. . . a buncha *rednecks* who think everything's jus' *fine*, while the rest's all sad country drunks, doin' nothin' an' gettin' sick because of. . . .' Again he looked warily round. '. . . *poverty*.'

'So you started wondering?'

'I got so's I didn't wanna take their money, or anybody's money for 'em, in a slick fat Health Care Center that's really in business to look after the guys that don't need lookin' after.'

Campbell twirled some lettuce in his salad dressing, remembering his first interview with Dr Drucker and his general caution about disrespect for local values. 'So you were . . . stuck in a bad place?'

'I shoulda talked to somebody instead of foolin' around.'

'Fooling around?'

'Acting like I didn't care.'

'I see.'

'Billy came down. You know, Dr Kidd. He just appeared, and we talked for a while. Like, he was actin' like I was goin' crazy or somethin'. An' I guess I had done a coupla things ole George didn't like, things I maybe shoulda thought about first. This guy, he's about two hundred fifty pounds and real mean. Bin down there so long he's got to thinkin' he's important, but kinda sleazy, rough with the . . . the Medicaid people, hell, the poor. An' I heard a coupla things about him, real mean things. . . .'

'You guys O.K.? You wanna see the menu again?'

They ordered ice-cream and Kravitz continued to talk about Split Rock. He did not sound schizophrenic, regardless of how his father had spent the last twenty years. Campbell recalled again the conversation with Dr Kidd, and reflected on the unwisdom of trying to guess a diagnosis in a case one hadn't seen. True, there were considerable international differences in the use of the term schizophrenia: differences which had led one fierce old Edinburgh professor to remark that in America it meant that your analyst didn't like you, in Russia that you had doubts about the system. In any case, it seemed premature to label a man schizophrenic on the basis of his having turned up for work late and unshaven a couple of times and having had a personality clash with a rural physician.

When Campbell arrived for his first afternoon's attendance at the MacHardy Thanatology Center Life Ending Americans Program Evaluation and Resource Study Life Ending

Americans Clinic, there was no one else there. He found some coffee and a room marked 'David Campbell MD Director of Medical Services' and sat down at the desk. He read the wall poster ('If Life gives you Lemòns, Make Lemonade'), drank his coffee and was wondering what to do if no one else turned up when there was a cough outside and an apologetic knock at the door. The young psychiatrist from the Wednesday Conference came in, carrying a large Coca-Cola.

'Hi. Bob Nance. Assistant Director of Psychiatric Services. I guess we met already.'

'I think so,' said Campbell. 'At the dinner on Friday.'

Nance gazed intently over his Coca-Cola. 'Wasn't that just *awful*? I mean so sudden, the way he just . . . went? An' he was such a wonderful guy.' Nance shook his head in studied puzzlement at this blow of fate. 'An' LEAPERS doin' so well, I mean really takin' off. An' Cal just ain't around to see it. Maself, I still can't believe it. Like, you know people die, but the head of a major program, a man you're havin' dinner with. . . . Yea, it's tough, but I guess when you think about it, what would Cal have wanted?' Nance paused and put down his Coca-Cola. 'Cal woulda wanted us to go on.'

'I suppose so,' said Campbell. 'He seemed to be that sort of chap.'

'Good ole Cal. I guess the best thing we can do, the best thing we can all do, is go right ahead an' make this just one great program. His memorial, like. I mean, he woulda liked that. An' he always looked to us, I mean, to the Department of Psychiatry. . . . Yeah, he always looked to us an' it would be kinda sad if . . . if the program didn't go the way he woulda wanted. So we should just go on, I guess, doin' what he woulda wanted.' Nance took a mouthful of Coca-Cola. 'In fact there was a Departmental meeting this morning.'

'Really?'

'Yup. . . . So you're gonna be with us most afternoons, huh, Dave?'

Campbell nodded and Nance threw him a twinkly smile. 'That's great. An' we'd all be real glad for to help you, I mean with you bein' noo here, you're gonna need a lot of help, huh? So just don't hesitate to ask, huh?'

'Thanks. I was wondering about the clinic. I'm not awfully sure what everyone does. How could I help most?'

'Physical stuff,' said Nance crisply. 'You could do a lot just stickin' to the physical stuff. Symptoms, and routine physicals for noo Life Enders. We refer them, you see them, Stump bills them. Be nice to have that side of Life Ending covered. I think it was even in the original grant but we never got round to it. But we kinda run things, O.K.?'

'Glad to help,' said Campbell, thinking he might ring Stump. 'Soon as I get my state license.'

'How long have you been in Life Ending, Dave?'

The telephone rang and Campbell answered it. 'Dr Campbell, I have a long distance call for you,' said a female voice, possibly Candy's. 'Can you take it now or are you in conference?' Campbell said he could take it. Nance got up, smiled, waved and tiptoed out as though auditioning for a silent movie. There were some threatening clicks and another female voice came on.

'Dr Campbell?'

'Speaking.'

'Dr Campbell . . . Dave . . . Hi.'

'Hello.'

'Hi. Amy Totenberg here.'

'Hello.'

'Dave, I just wanted to call you to say thanks. . . . Mr Barbee just died, yeah, Reverend Barbee. His family were all there, an' singin', an' he just died. So I wanted to thank you for your help. You know we got him eating and drinking and his acute change of mental status got reversed. Yeah, it was wonderful. So I wanted to thank you.'

'Oh. Well, I'm glad he was all right.'

'We even stopped his restraints.'

'Good.'

'So thanks. And Dave, d'you have a minute to talk right now?'

'Yes, now's fine.'

'Dave, I hope you don't mind but I got another guy down here I want you to see. A guy who just turned up at the

71

Health Care Center with a recurrence. He's kinda difficult, an' I wondered maybe if you could help again?'

'I'll do my best. Maybe Thursday morning? Would that be soon enough?'

'Is that really O.K., Dave? Do you mind?'

'Probably mid-morning?'

'What?'

'Around ten-thirty.'

'Thanks, Dave.'

Campbell started to ask for some more clinical details, but the line had gone dead.

There were no more telephone calls. No patients came. Nothing happened. At first Campbell wondered about this, but by half past two he realized that none of these things mattered. His job was simply to be there. He was there because the Phase One LEAPERS grant said he should be there. He was there because the psychiatrists wanted him there. He was there because Dr Pulver, doubtless, would have liked him to be there. He should even have been there for a year already, but there was nothing he could do about that now. Meanwhile, he was there: the hands-on physician in Phase One, in Stump's phrase, not a psychiatrist.

Having discovered his role in life, the new Director of Medical Services went for a walk in the corridor. Candy was sitting at the front desk.

'Oh, hi, Dr Campbell. How are you?'

'Fine, thank you. How are you?'

'Good. . . . Real good. . . . Well. . . .' She turned slowly on her swivel chair and looked up at Campbell. Her eyes were big and green and more anxious than vacant. 'Would you like some coffee, Dr Campbell?'

'Just had one, thanks.'

'Huh?'

'No thanks, Candy.'

'Oh.'

'Are there many patients?'

'Coupla Mature Acceptances for Gary, an' I think Dr Nance has one comin' in later for a MILES check. An' Patti has a Denial from way back who's doin' fine, but Dr Mikoyan likes to get 'em checked. An'. . . .' She still looked troubled. Campbell recalled someone saying something about her problems.

'Dr Campbell. . . ?'

'Yes, Candy.'

'Dr Campbell, will you take a look at my beauty spot?' She pointed to her right cheek. 'I dunno, I'm kinda. . . . Oh, Dr Campbell, it's prob'ly nothin', but if you don't mind can you take a look?'

Campbell looked down at Candy's cheek. The beauty spot was about a quarter of an inch across, almost circular and very dark. 'Why are you anxious about it, Candy? Anything in particular?'

'I dunno, maybe it's gotten bigger. Like, it's kinda hard to say but I guess so, Dr Campbell. Maybe a tad bigger.'

'Anything else? Itching, pain?'

'No, Dr Campbell, it don't itch. But maybe Friday it kinda oozed.'

'Blood?'

'No more'n a drop, but blood, yeah.'

'Hm. Can I take a closer look, Candy? My office?'

Candy got up looking very pale and followed Campbell into the office and stood by the window. In daylight the lesion looked bluish black and on close inspection its edge was minutely jagged. There was a tiny red rim on the normal skin around it and a small patch of its surface was not smooth but crusted with brownish exudate. Campbell ran his fingertips over it. 'And you think it might have got bigger?'

'Only a li'l bit, Dr Campbell, an' only over the last coupla weeks.'

'And it oozed once?'

'Maybe twice. I noticed it with my cleanser. A kinda smear, like blood.'

Campbell hesitated. He would never have described himself as an enthusiast for dermatology. In the undergraduate curriculum at Edinburgh the subject had seemed dull, its teachers duller. Dermatological diagnosis had not impressed him as a rational process. It was more like wallpaper-matching: finding something in the book that looked like what the patient showed you. And the patients, it seemed, never either died or got better. A few exceptions to this rule lingered in the mind, and Candy might have one of them.

'I'm not sure what it is, Candy, but I think you should probably see a dermatologist.'

'But I don't *have* a dermatologist,' she said in a whining voice. 'I got an analyst, a gynaecologist, an orthodontist, oh, an' a chiropractor. But I never had a dermatologic problem before.'

'Well, I'm sure we can find you one. A place like Mac-Hardy's bound to have dozens. I'll have a word with Dr Nance.'

'Dr Campbell?'

'What?'

'D'you think I'll lose it?'

'What?'

'Mah beauty spot.'

Campbell looked her straight in the eye and said, 'I don't know. I think we'd better let a dermatologist take a look. Best to be sure.'

Candy straightened up and gave Campbell a wide smile. 'Thanks, Dr Campbell. Like, will you let me know when you find somebody?'

'I will.'

'Dr Campbell. . . .'

'What?'

'I'm kinda scared.'

'I'll find someone soon.'

'Thank you, Dr Campbell.'

Candy returned to her desk and Campbell went down the corridor looking for Nance. He was not in his office, but his voice could be heard from an office labelled 'Gary Ascue Director of Thanatologic Psychometric Evaluation MacHardy Thanatology Center Life Ending Americans Program Evaluation and Resource Study', the door of which was open. Campbell knocked.

'Come on in.'

'Oh, sorry to disturb you.'

'Dave, you gotta meet Gary. He's our Head of Thanatologic Psychometrics. Gary's thirty percent here and seventy percent over in the Department. . . . The Department of Psychiatry, that is. Gary, Dave's our noo Director of Medical Services. Fifty percent with Family Practice and fifty percent here at LEAC with the Department. Dave's from England.'

'Hi.'

Ascue was large and blonde, tanned like a lifeguard and showing numerous perfect teeth. 'Yeah, I'm here afternoons. Well, Monday Tuesday. Bob was sayin' you're gonna cover the physical side, huh?'

Campbell nodded.

'So it's O.K. to send you Life Enders with physical problems, huh? But I guess no psychosomatic stuff, you don't wanna see them.' Ascue smiled and Campbell asked him what he did.

'General Thanatology, evaluation and staging. Psychometrics is my specialty, but I do in-depth psychologicals, plus some counsellin'. Mainly with the Denials. My PhD's in stereotypes of death.'

Ascue was still smiling, so Campbell smiled back at him and said, 'Bob, I wonder if we could have a word. . . .'

'Why, certainly, Dave.' Nance leapt to his feet in a kind of parody of attentiveness. Campbell realized that his colleague's life was spent in a series of emphatic postures designed to portray clearly differentiated moods and functions: perhaps a professional hazard of psychiatry. Or was it that his PhD was in body language? Reluctant to discuss a clinical matter in front of the psychologist, Campbell said, 'Bob, I wonder if. . .' Nance switched instantly to a tight-lipped mode of 'Confidentiality' and ushered Campbell out into the corridor.

'Yes, Dave?'

'Bob, I was wondering if you could think of a good dermatologist, to see someone.'

Nance's eyes rolled in Deep Thought. 'We got a whole bunch of 'em.'

'What about that chap Schlepp?'

Concern gave way to Deep Anxiety. 'Uh. . . . Schlepp, huh?'

'Seemed quite a nice chap.'

'Dave, you're kinda noo on the block. I'd like to help you. See, there's things you don't know. Maybe you could leave the question with me. A coupla days, huh?'

'What's wrong with Schlepp?'

'Dave, this could turn out to be a delicate issue. It's for someone here, at LEAC?'

'Sort of.'

'Leave it with me, Dave. Coupla days, maybe the end of the week.' He smiled Reassurance. Campbell said nothing and smiled back. Nance returned to Ascue's room.

Campbell went back to his office. The only clinical problem of the afternoon was both unusual and urgent, and the management of a suspected malignant melanoma would not be improved by delays caused by a junior psychiatrist playing politics. Candy needed to be seen quickly, and Schlepp had sprung to mind. To check that he was committing no sin other than circumventing a devious psychiatrist, Campbell rang Stump.

'Thanatology. Stump.'

'Hello, David Campbell here.'

'Hi Dave. What can I do for you?'

'Randy, I've got someone who needs to be seen by a dermatologist. . . . What about that chap Schlepp?'

'Smart guy. Assistant Director of Dermatology. O.K. with the internists. Big on cancers.'

'Is he?'

'Yeah. What's the problem?'

'Might be a cancer.'

'He's supposed to be good. Like, the students think he's great.'

'Do they? Bob Nance didn't seem too keen.'

'That's political.'

'Oh.'

'So just ring him up. Schlepp, I mean. He's a good guy, you've met him, and if he's too busy he'll tell ya. He ain't shy.'

'I noticed. Thanks, Randy.'

'No trouble.'

'And Nance not liking him. . . ?'

'Political.'

'Oh. . . . Like the dinner?'

'That was political too. You're gettin' there.'

'Really?'

'But if you're askin' me if I think Schlepp's an O.K. dermatologist, well, everybody says so.'

'Thanks, Randy. How are things over there. . . ? After Dr Pulver. . . .'

'Well, you could say they were . . . political.'

'Thanks, Randy.'

'O.K., Dave. Seeya.'

'Thanks.'

Campbell reached again for the MacHardy directory, whose cover featured a full-colour glossy picture of MacHardy East, 'West Carolina's Hospital Complex for the Twenty-First Century', looked up Schlepp's number, then had doubts about just ringing up someone described as 'Dr A. K. Schlepp, MD PhD, Assistant Director Fiona K. MacHardy Institute of Dermatologic Science'. He rang the number and asked to speak to Dr Schlepp's secretary.

'Sorry, you just missed her. Schlepp here. Can I take a message or get her to ring you back?'

'Oh . . . Dr Schlepp, David Campbell here. We met last Friday.'

'Sure, sure. How you doin'? O.K., huh?'

'Yes thanks. Dr Schlepp, I've just seen a girl, a secretary at the Life Ending Clinic, who looks as if she's got a melanoma.'

'You reckon? Where? What's it like?'

Campbell described the lesion. Schlepp said, 'Jeeze, I better see her. Say around five, whenever she quits work. Know where my office is?'

Schlepp explained. Campbell wrote down the directions and thanked him. As soon as he had put the phone down it rang again. It was Candy.

'Dr Campbell, can you take a call?'

'Thanks, Candy.'

'Hello, Dave, honey. . . . Did somethin' happen?'

'Hello?'

77

'Dave, honey. Sharron here. You didn't make it to lunch. You O.K.?'

'Yes, thank you. No, I mean. . . . I'm sorry. . . . Look, can I ring you back. I'm in the middle of a clinic.'

'Sure, honey. You got my number?'

Campbell wrote it down, wondering how long he could decently leave it before ringing her, then went out and found Candy. She was sitting dabbing her right cheek with a paper handkerchief. He told her about his telephone call to Dr Schlepp, and how to get to his office. 'He's a very nice man,' he added. 'I was sitting next to him at a dinner last week.'

Candy looked up at him dolefully, still dabbing her cheek. 'You mean, when Dr Pulver passed away?'

Two days later Campbell was late for the Life Ending Americans Clinic Wednesday Teaching Conference. At twenty past eleven he stood in the corridor thinking about the unpredictable nature of psychiatric response to minor social lapses and wondering if it was worth going in at all. In the end he did, and found a gathering much larger than that of the previous week. Most of the new people were unfamiliar, but among them Campbell recognized Dr Bottger, the Chief of Psychiatry. The tall girl with acne was presenting a case. She was talking from untidy notes, stumbling and hesitating, and paused just as Campbell came in. In the silence he found his way clumsily round the room to the last vacant seat. Dr Mikoyan looked up but did not say anything. The girl presenting the case looked sadly round, scrabbled among her notes and resumed her story.

'So then she found another lump, and got kinda angry, and quit takin' her, uh, her chemotherapy, an' saw a third internist. . . . Well, maybe he was an internist, Miz Bird's kinda vague, maybe he was one of those personal counsellors on Holcombe Street. . . . Anyway, this guy told her it was nothin' to worry about an' her hair would grow in again because it only fell out on account of the change. I guess you call that Collusive Denial, so she's back at a K R One, third time aroun', with a physical problem an' I guess a Regressive

Transition problem because all the time she's seein' the radiotherapist just to be on the safe side. . . . I told you this was a mess. Then. . . . No, that was before that. . . . I'm sorry. . . .'

'Dave, honey,' said a determined whisper very close to Campbell. He turned to his left and found he was sitting next to Miss Sneed. She looked better with clothes on, but seemed tense and angry. 'You bin busy, huh?' she whispered. Campbell had not called her to explain why he had not turned up for lunch and had not even spent time thinking of an excuse. He smiled at Miss Sneed and nodded and then devoted obvious attention to the case presentation. Dr Mikoyan was looking at them through clouds of cigar smoke.

'Then she ran outa Medicare, so she had a one outa five financial situation, an' had to find another apartment. So she had a social problem there. . . . Like, she had before, but it had gotten worse. So by now she's in real trouble. A messed-up KR One with a MILES aroun' seven or somethin', at least until this guy Washington she calls her third husband showed up again, maybe the end of June. No, mid-April. So maybe a nine, but still stuck in Denial. Then she quit comin' to the Life Ending Clinic, she said because of the fees.'

The girl paused. Dr Mikoyan sighed. 'Patti?'

Miss Love, the Coordinator of Clinical Thanatology, smiled at Mikoyan and at the girl with acne. 'Willa did her best,' she said, 'an' arranged several appointments, an' we redooced her to the Economically Disadvantaged Rate with maximally spaced payments, but this Washington was a bad influence and Miz Bird was lost to the clinic.'

Mikoyan took the cigar out of his mouth. 'These non-progressin' Denials. . . . These folks who go roun' an' roun' in a kinda Denial-Anger thing, they're one o' the greatest problems left in Life Ending.'

'I think she's dead now,' said Miss Love.

'I'm not sayin' they don't die. . . . I'm sayin' they present a problem that Thanatology ain't cracked yet.' He turned to the girl who had presented the case. 'They quit the Clinic because they can't face up to things, you know that, huh? Didja try usin' that knowledge to help her?'

The girl was now quite pink. 'Dr Mikoyan,' she said, 'the last time she came up we spent the whole time on that sorta stuff. We got into the Denial and we worked on her symptoms with Advanced Therapeutic Vocabulary Training. We went through the lot: you got the pain comin' on, it's a tickle; you got the pain, it's a twinge. We went through all that. You got fear, this is an adventure. You got a lump, it's fullness. I know all that stuff, Dr Mikoyan, I majored in Thanatologic Communication. Dr Mikoyan, I'm a Zelda MacHardy Life Ending Fellow.'

'No use fightin' with me,' said Mikoyan. 'It's not me you let down. It's the patient.'

'Maybe Willa got kinda involved here, Dr Mikoyan,' said Miss Love. 'Bessie Bird was her first breast disease Life Ender.' Turning to the girl, who was now not far from tears, she said, 'We gotta stay professional, Willa, otherwise we'd be cryin' all the time.' Instead of being comforted Willa sniffed and then sobbed.

'Be a pity if she's dead,' said Mikoyan, ignoring the tears and the handkerchief. He blew a smoke ring. 'Phase Two coulda helped her a lot. If she'd made it to August, the economic thing woulda been taken care of, she coulda paid us and all her physicians, an' kept on her apartment, and she coulda gotten through all that Denial stuff into a nicer place. But if she's dead, like Patti says, well, I guess she missed out on Anger, Depression, Bargaining and Acceptance. Tough, huh?' The chairman of the meeting leaned back, looked in the direction of Dr Bottger and blew smoke towards the ceiling. 'Phase Two's gonna open a whole lotta new doors in Life Ending. From August we got access an' we got follow-through. We get to look at the big questions an' we get to stop fussin' about the little questions. Patti, what we got now?'

There was a pause as Mikoyan and Miss Love conferred about the agenda. Miss Sneed turned to Campbell and whispered, 'I still think you gotta meet with the data team. . . . Especially Ben.'

'Perhaps I could ring him up,' Campbell said, 'then go round and see him.'

Miss Sneed looked at him oddly and said, 'I think I know where you're coming from.'

A black lady social worker with frizzy hair began to recount the woes of an alcoholic cotton worker with a liver tumour, and a deep peace settled over Campbell. Without planning and almost without effort he had solved the principal problem of his new life in Crimond. On his left Miss Sneed listened intently and took copious notes, splattered with things like 'KR3M17', 'KR4?5 M12', with dates and odd little squiggles appended. Perhaps, as people were said sometimes to do in the circumstances, she would now throw herself into her work, producing another hundred or so publications, and live happily ever after as a thoroughly fulfilled thanatologist.

'When I said Irving was the treasurer of the AMA,' said Kravitz, handing Campbell a glass of turbid green liquid, 'I shoulda explained. We got the secretary coming along too, and a coupla other people from the committee. Woulda had the president, but he's up in Pulpit Hill precepting in a Transcendental Massage Workshop. He's really into massage. . . . Rolfing mainly, but like he says, every massage therapist's gotta be to some extent eclectic if he's gonna do any good.'

Irving had gone back to the kitchen, leaving Kravitz and Campbell in a large room with no furniture, in the strictest sense. 'Sit down, Dave.' Kravitz indicated a large purple cushion. 'Maybe you'd like to take your shoes off. Most people will. But do whatever you feel comfortable with.'

Kravitz, in white jeans and a green tee-shirt with 'AMA for Health' on the front, was barefoot, as was Irving, who wore a long dark caftan with short gold-laced sleeves. Campbell, earlier in the evening, had wondered what to wear for an evening described as 'a kinda get-together' and now, not for the first time in West Carolina, he felt over-dressed. Kravitz looked at him sympathetically. 'Couple more of these,' he said indicating Campbell's green drink, 'Maybe you'll feel like takin' off your necktie.'

The cushion, perhaps filled with beans, rustled but was comfortable. The drink tasted strongly of mint and gave the impression it might also contain a fair amount of alcohol. Campbell made a polite remark about it.

'Irving's kinda experimenting with herb cocktails,' said Kravitz. 'That's a Mint Mule you got there. Plenty more if you like it.'

Campbell had arrived punctually, a habit which in West Carolina seemed to make him early for things. However, promising Middle Eastern cooking smells filled the air. He sat back and wondered who else had been invited and concluded that the AMA referred to must be something other than the American Medical Association. The room in which they sat, the front parlour of a white wooden house on Dogwood Avenue, was done mainly in reds, purples and maroons, with wall-hangings, ornaments and a selection of oriental rugs that looked as though they had been collected, thoughtfully but with a strict regard to economy, over a period of time. A joss stick burned and there were two large wall-posters with elaborate circular designs. Between them a small framed certificate proclaimed that Irving K. Bronstein had been honourably discharged from the US Army.

'I guess by now you got acclimated some,' said Kravitz, talking with the careful enunciation he still employed when speaking to Campbell.

'More so,' said Campbell. 'Still getting some surprises, mainly with driving.'

'How about the women? Different than English women, huh? Kinda upfront?'

'Yes,' said Campbell, hoping the word meant what he thought it meant.

'So at least you're gettin' to find out.'

Voices on the porch outside and a tinkle of bells announced the arrival of more guests. Kravitz got up to let them in. Irving emerged from the kitchen again, carrying a mixing bowl and thoughtfully stirring its contents with a wooden spoon. He was a short dark man, with shiny black hair in ringlets round his neck, a gold earring and the general air of a lesser disciple in a biblical epic film. He lifted his spoon and watched as the creamy mixture ran back into the bowl. Kravitz came back with three more people, and there were smiles and introductions.

'Martha, I wancha to meet Dave from England. He's with the Program. Maggie. . . . Maggie's big in AMA. Dave. And Carl. Carl is the secretary.'

Martha and Maggie were both approximately blonde and in their thirties. Carl was thin and serious-looking, distinctly secretarial in wire-rimmed glasses, and older than everyone else present. More of the cloudy green liquid was produced and the girls both took glasses of it. Carl asked for an orange juice. Campbell took a top-up, deciding that the active ingredient was probably gin. Irving stayed for a moment to chat, still stirring carefully, then went back to his kitchen. Everyone else sat down.

Maggie, the thinner of the two girls, was beside Campbell. She was dressed in a long, unadorned white garment and sat with her legs curled invisibly under it. She sipped from her glass and smiled.

'Isn't that just awful about Skunk Bend?'

Campbell looked blank.

'You don't care?' she asked.

Campbell continued to look blank.

'You don't know?'

'No. . . . I'm. . . .'

'You a physician?'

'Yeah, but. . . .'

'An' you don't know about Skunk Bend?'

'No.'

She looked at him as though she had suddenly begun to dislike him. 'Like it's only shaping up to be our very own TMI.'

'TMI?'

'Three Mile Island.'

'Oh, power stations.'

'*Nuclear* power stations,' she said firmly.

'I see,' said Campbell. 'There's been an accident?'

'Not yet. It ain't built yet. We're gonna protest it.' She lifted her chin in a gesture of defiance suggesting imminent nuclear martyrdom, for which her simple white outfit would have been quite appropriate. 'Are you with us,' she asked with a challenging stare, 'for the Skunk Bend Day of Peaceful Action?'

'When's that?'

'The twentieth. A Sunday. You should come. Everybody should come. Like, everybody here's probably gonna come.'

Campbell expressed polite interest and Maggie smiled again. 'There's gonna be authentic crafts, folk stuff, an' clogging. An' a health fair. That's the AMA event. An' Lemmy Gravel's gonna be there. An' it ends with a firelight swim-in against nuclear power. That could be just beautiful. You gonna come?'

'It sounds interesting.'

'You work with Irving? Neurosurgery?'

'No. I'm in the same program as Don. What do you do?'

'You mean my job?'

'Yes.'

'At MacHardy. Medieval English.'

'Really?'

'But mainly I teach freshmen advanced use of English. Like, you know, sentences, verbs, that kinda stuff.'

'I see.'

'Don said you were from England.'

'Well, yes. Scotland actually.'

'Isn't that the same? You got socialized medicine in Scotland same as England.'

'It's the same system.'

'So you came here?'

'Only for a year.'

'For the money. . . ? As a physician?'

'Not really.'

'Gary, my husband, was a physician.'

'Was he?'

'A psychiatrist.'

'Oh.'

'Went off with a patient.'

84

'Really?'

'I shoulda expected it. I mean, when he left his first wife I was a patient.' Campbell could think of nothing to say but tried to look interested.

'This other kid was an anorexic,' said Maggie dolefully. 'Same as me. Well, I was. So he's a sick guy. I mean, stuck in a bad place.'

There was another tinkle of bells and more people came in: first a pair of men in matching flowered shirts, then two women, both in their twenties, holding hands. Campbell finished his second Mint Mule, wondering if the party was now complete. A few minutes later Kravitz filled his glass from a jug, asking, 'You like these, Dave?'

Maggie was still scrutinizing him, looking at his watch and his tie. 'Are you into, like, money?'

'Sorry, Maggie.'

'I said are you into money?'

'I don't think so.'

'A lot of physicians are. Gary was.'

'I don't think I am.'

'I guess Irving isn't.'

'I don't think Don is either.'

'He's a neat guy. Irving, I mean. The Alliance is lucky to have him.'

'The Alliance?'

'Yeah, the Alternative Medicine Alliance.'

'Oh, the AMA?'

'Yea, the *other* AMA, we sometimes call ourselves.'

'Are you in it?'

'I'm on the committee.'

'What does it do?'

'Promotes health. Positively, you know, with regard to individual life styles. And it offers alternative modalities in health care. Mainly natural things. Irving's the treasurer, Carl over there's the secretary and I do workshops in feminist consciousness-raising. It's a how-to series aimed at victims of chauvinism.'

'I see.'

'But the Alliance does all kinds of things. Everything from

85

dream interpretation groups to herbal first aid. Things you might have negative feelings about.'

'I really don't. . . .'

'Lotsa physicians do. Gary did.'

Campbell had another mouthful of Mule and wondered if he was drinking too fast. More people arrived, including some conventional one-of-each couples, and an opportunity arose for Campbell to stand up and mingle a bit. For a while he talked to a man with a beard who had just come back from an Indian reservation, then he talked, or rather listened, to a short, strident girl who described herself as a mother and maintained that American medicine was a conspiracy against women because they had shaved her pubic hair. The evening seemed to be settling down as a fairly conventional party, and Campbell began to drink more slowly.

At about nine o'clock Irving raised his arms as though blessing a substantial multitude and announced that the food was ready. People formed into a slow, sociable line. Campbell found himself beside Martha, who said she was a cook, and they talked generally then went together round the kitchen table, helping themselves from a selection of vegetarian foods. There was a choice of wines, mainly of Californian origin. The red turned out to be quite good. They made their way back to the other room and sat down.

Campbell asked Martha about the food. She explained, using words like 'sorghum' and 'tabouli' which did not mean much to him. He asked her what kind of cooking she did and she eventually admitted that she was a restaurateur, and the owner of Mother Nature's. Campbell, who had liked the place and enjoyed his meal there, told her so then asked a bit more about it.

She was a big, pleasant girl with blue eyes and a thoughtful smile. She spoke about her business. 'It sounds obvious, but everything's got to be good. So you check stuff coming in, and things like shellfish you've just got to be sure about. And even then, if something's not right you chuck it out. Two nights ago we threw out a whole lot of shrimp salad because, well, it just wasn't right.'

Campbell asked about the staff. 'They're good people,' she

said, 'and they want people to come and eat there, and they eat the same food, so they want it to be good. And no funny business.'

'Funny business?'

'Anything. Well, drugs and dishonesty. So the place is clean, I know it's clean and the police department knows it's clean, so they don't bother us.'

'Really?'

'I run a tight ship.'

That was not a phrase Campbell would have expected from the owner of a health food restaurant. He said so. She smiled. 'My father was an admiral.'

Opposite them the two girls who had come in holding hands were sitting very close together, laughing, with their heads practically touching, and eating from the same plate. Martha noticed Campbell noticing and smiled.

'D'you know them?' he asked.

'Quite well,' she said. 'Molly, on the right, is a wait.'

'Oh?'

'At Mother Nature's. We don't have waiters and waitresses. Everyone's a wait.'

'Are those two. . . ?'

Martha was smiling. 'They're in love, I guess.'

Campbell, having softened on vegetarianism, prepared for another jolt to his unexamined assumptions.

'You mean there aren't any lesbians where you come from?' she asked.

'I suppose there are.' Campbell was surprised to hear that question twice in only a few days.

'I think it's beautiful,' she said. 'They're so together, more than anyone else in the room. But you're shocked? Why should you be? Women are nicer than men.'

Campbell thought about that and agreed.

'They're softer and nicer and they know what they're doing.' She had lowered her voice, but only a little. 'You'd be surprised if you knew how many women liked women.'

Campbell dipped some possible sorghum into a puddle of creamy sauce. 'I suppose it's more understandable than men and men.'

87

'I'm not so sure about that either,' said Martha, 'but it seems to suit some guys.'

In the social reshuffle brought about by the trip back to the kitchen for another course Campbell found himself standing next to Irving and complimented him on the food.

'Glad you like it,' he said. 'It's just food. Like, no additives. Uh, just natural things . . . that grow. Maself I find that more, you know, *in touch* with things than, say, a Dunkin' Donut or a Big Mac. . . . It's more . . . *natural*.'

Campbell found that a bit difficult to follow. Irving did not express himself clearly, and did not even appear to be trying very hard to do so. His dark brown eyes were out of focus, perhaps even squinting. It was all somewhat unexpected for a neurosurgeon with an Army background. Irving smiled back at Campbell, giggled to himself and took a slice of sticky brown pecan pie.

Campbell helped himself to a glass of white wine to go with his fruit salad and made his way back to the other room. Kravitz was sitting in a corner with the two men wearing matching shirts and beckoned him over to join them and made some more introductions, but conversation did not become general as the matching pair seemed interested only in talking to each other. Kravitz asked Campbell how he was enjoying the party.

'Very much, thank you. Interesting people.'

'Who've you bin talkin' to?'

'Maggie. And Martha.'

'Martha's wonderful. You know she's dietary adviser to the AMA?'

'She didn't mention that.'

'You should join it, Dave. They do some real good things.'

'Perhaps I shall.'

'We got a day of peaceful action comin' up.'

'Someone mentioned that.'

'At least it's supposed to be peaceful.'

'Oh?'

'You hear rumours. Some power company's gonna build a nuclear installation real near. An' some folks think they jus' won't notice *peaceful* action.'

'Really?'

'But that's nothin' to do with us. The AMA's just doin' a health event.'

'Nuclear-free green salads?'

'That kinda thing. You should come.'

'Maybe I will.'

For some reason, perhaps to do with Campbell turning over in his mind the proposed visit to see a patient there with recurrent cancer, he and Kravitz began to talk about Split Rock.

'There's some kinda neat things goin' on down there,' Kravitz said. 'Maybe the last time we talked about it I was kinda negative. Like, some guys wouldn't touch Indians, even with Federal funding. An' they do a neat OB package at around four hundred bucks. An' their record system's at least half good.'

'How many partners are there?'

'There's ole George, the fat guy, an' a guy Worz, a bit younger, came out the Air Force a coupla years ago. An' Amy. Dr Totenberg.'

'What's she like?' Two or three gins and the wine permitted a fairly direct approach.

Kravitz paused. 'Amy's O.K. Like, she knew where I was comin' from with ole George an' even kinda indicated I should cool it. An' she's the sharpest physician down there, even sharp enough to let ole George think he is. An' the folks think she's just great. Like, workin' down there for them when her daddy's Mr Big in Ole Mac's medical college. They like that.'

'I met him,' said Campbell. 'Dr Totenberg, the Dean.'

'The horse's ass?'

'Sorry?'

'That's what Billy, you know, our Director, calls him.'

'He mentioned that.'

'The *Dean* did?'

'No, Dr Kidd.'

'They say Teddy thinks the Family Practice Program is MacHardy's only mistake. Ever.'

'He seemed quite a nice old chap.'

'Amy's nicer. She really cares. Like, she really does.'

'Does she?' Campbell had a sudden but controllable urge to pursue his inquiry by asking Kravitz, in a phrase of British naval origin he would not have understood, who was hanging out of her. Instead, he said, 'Life must be fairly quiet down in Split Rock.'

'Oh, I don't know,' said Kravitz. 'Saturdays, everybody goes downtown to watch the haircuts.' Campbell laughed. 'An' people get shot.'

'Do they?'

'Sure do. Mainly blacks and Indians. Domestic, like. Hot night, folks are drinkin', somebody switches channels. Maybe five bullet wounds a weekend go up to the ER at Pittsville. Just from Split Rock, mainly from the tribe. . . . You know they're supposed to be British?'

'Somebody mentioned that.'

'Kinda neat, British Indians. "I say, old chap, how about a puff at the jolly old pipe of peace?" '

'How about the migrant workers?'

'They can't afford health care, an' a lot o' them's illegals, so they don't want no trouble. Hell, some of 'em's *slaves*, 'cept they don't get looked after. Ole George, he can't stand 'em. I guess Amy sees one or two.'

'Really?'

'Like I said, she's a nice person. You know she started out in pediatric neuro-oncology?'

'Oh?'

'Then her marriage split up an' she quit MacHardy. But she's got this guy she really likes now.' Campbell took a thoughtful gulp of white wine. 'Yeah,' said Kravitz. 'A marine. Well, a major in the marines. Heavy. Like, you know what they say. . . . If God had meant us to join the Marines he'd have given us green baggy skin. But this guy's apparently really into all that stuff. His problem, I guess. Hers too, maybe.'

'Some marines are really O.K.,' said one of the matching shirts, smiling at Kravitz. 'You know, beat the shit out of you, *gently*.'

By eleven o'clock the atmosphere of the party had changed considerably. To the sound of oriental music from an endless and eventually hypnotic tape, people lay around in groups, talking little but sometimes whispering or giggling. The last of the cooking smells from Irving's kitchen mingled with the sharper fragrance of the joss stick and a hazy benignity enveloped the guests, some of whom were smoking. Several times Campbell refused a cigarette, he hoped without causing offence. He continued, with due regard to the additional problems posed by driving on the wrong side of the road, to drink the white Californian wine.

Around midnight the guests started to go home. Campbell thanked Kravitz and Irving who, after a successful party, was radiant but inarticulate. He made his way back to his apartment without any mishaps other than one attempt to change gear with the door handle. That night his sleep was disturbed by a series of foreboding dreams, in one of which he was taken by a detachment of Marines to appear before the West Carolina State Licensing Committee. In his dream they met in a starkly furnished rural church surrounded by a cemetery which included a high proportion of very recent graves. The members of the committee wore white robes and pointed hoods and asked him if he was or ever had been a member of the British National Health Service.

Next day Campbell despatched Kravitz to read up on the management of pain in terminal illness from the vast resources of the Felix MacHardy Medical Library and Information Center and went down by himself to Split Rock. Dr Totenberg seemed pleased to see him. They had coffee and she told him a little more about the last days of the old black preacher. More and more of his relatives and descendants had turned up, until at the end he had been visited by no less than forty-four, including a Black Power activist on special parole from a Federal penitentiary. She recounted these scenes with a kind of touching enthusiasm then, with equal enthusiasm, talked about his pre-terminal fluid and electrolyte intake and his deteriorating chest X-ray. She even showed Campbell the laboratory report confirming his clinical diagnosis of candida in the old man's mouth.

If Campbell had been asked to describe Dr Totenberg at that point, he would have said that she was a good doctor: not, like some of his colleagues, for all the wrong reasons; but genuinely enthusiastic about the details of practical management; and, if anything, pleasantly naive. She also had long dark hair, big eyes, nice hands and an air about her that Campbell had seen before, usually in people who subsequently turned out to be nice to be with in bed.

They sat in Amy's office. The customary framed certificates were on display in more than average numbers and Campbell cast an eye over them. Both her premedical and medical degrees were from MacHardy. At the time of the latter her name had been Amy Scopes Totenberg Mudd. Four years later, on a certificate relating to Family Practice, it had reverted to the first three only, as in the premedical degree. A glance at her bookshelf was also informative. Standard multiauthor textbooks rubbed shoulders with obscure volumes about pediatric neurology and, more worryingly, *Jonathan Livingstone Seagull* and a selection of vaguely self-help books with titles like *Be What You Are*, *By Yourself*, *For Yourself* and the like.

They talked generally and happily, as if it were a purely social occasion, until conversation ran out and Campbell remembered why he was down there. 'You mentioned some chap,' he said. 'With a recurrence.'

'Oh, Boaz?' Amy brightened again. 'Boaz Tulliver, a migrant farm worker. He's stabilized right now, but he's got a whole lot of problems. Things I've never seen before.' She looked sad again, pretty and sad, with her coffee mug between her fingertips. 'We'll go see him,' she said. She sipped her coffee and looked at Campbell over the top of her mug. 'He's got nobody and he can't talk. A thirty-three-year-old black unmarried male. Farm worker, lives in camps. We think he's from Georgia but he hasn't been there for years. Does fruit-picking, tobacco, anything on farms. His primary was resected two years ago.'

'Where?' Campbell asked. 'Where was that?'

'In Altamount, at Memorial. It's a big state school and medical center.'

'Oh. Yes. And where was his primary?'

'I'm sorry. Tongue.'

'And they took it out?'

'Yes.'

'His primary?'

'Yes. And his tongue. I'm sorry, I'm not explaining this very well. It's all kind of horrible. This poor black man gets a lump in his tongue, posterior third. An' he goes to Memorial and comes out with no tongue. They say, fine, come back in six months, but he's scared so he doesn't go and just goes back to work for a couple of years. And then a few weeks back he starts to get pain, but he still doesn't want to go see anybody because he can't talk and he can hardly write and he's scared what's going to happen. Then some union guy says c'mon, Boaz, get in the car, and brings him here. . . . He was working just a couple of miles away.'

'And he's got a recurrence?'

'Local. Root of tongue, plus mets. You know, big nodes in his neck.'

'Constant pain?'

'Probably. I mean, I guess so. It's hard to tell. He nods and shakes his head when you ask him questions, but writin's kind of hard for him. He never got much school.'

'Can he swallow?'

'Some. But he coughs and splutters, and that seems to hurt. We got an I V I up so his hydration's O.K. now, but he's kinda thin, maybe a hundred and ten pounds, so I guess he had trouble eating for maybe a few months. Your guys have seen him. The LEAPERS team.'

Campbell thought about the story, then about the last bit, and said, 'They're not exactly my people.'

'The guy in the wheelchair came with Sneed.'

That seemed an odd way for Dr Totenberg to refer to her former housemate but Campbell, who thought of himself as relearning the colloquial use of English, did not know what to make of it. 'What did they think?' he asked.

'Oh, you know their sort of stuff.' Dr Totenberg smiled sadly. ' "K R Three going on Four with a MILES maybe aroun' fifteen". I mean, that's what they usually say.' She put

93

down her coffee. 'That's why I wanted you to see him, David.'

'Fine.'

'I'm glad you came down, I really am.'

Campbell wondered if she were being naive about him too, and began to worry about his credentials. 'I don't know much, in fact hardly anything, about head and neck cancers. What about the people who saw him first?'

'I thought of that,' said Dr Totenberg. 'And when I talked with him about it he cried. So, no.'

'And he's got spread to neck now. Both sides?'

'Yes.'

'Sounds grim.'

'I don't think anybody's gonna try and cure him.'

'Good,' said Campbell, thinking of the more futile and gruesome mutilations said to be practised by optimists in the field.

'I should have said, he's got some pain in his arm now.'

'Brachial plexus spread?'

'I think so.'

'So nobody would do anything.'

'Well,' said Dr Totenberg, 'some guys might want to try to clear his neck. Maybe even take his arm. But really, David, he's had enough.'

'Sounds like it.'

'He's over in the Facility.'

'Boaz, I got someone to see you.'

The patient reached out towards Campbell and they shook hands. He was a short thin black man lying on his bed wearing only pyjama trousers. There was an IV line in his left arm.

'How are you, Boaz?' Dr Totenberg asked. The man shrugged and reached into a locker at his bedside, found a notepad and, steadying it against his knee, wrote in large shaky letters 'IM HURTIN' '.

'Where are you hurtin', Boaz?'

The man pointed to his neck and throat, and ran his left hand over the outer aspect of his right arm.

'Your neck and your arm?'

He nodded.

'You hurtin' all the time?'

The man wrote 'MOSLY'.

'Which is worse, Boaz, your neck or your arm?'

He pointed to his right arm.

'On the outside?'

He nodded.

'But it doesn't stop you writing, huh?' The man nodded again. 'David, you want to ask him some questions?'

'Mr . . . Mr Tulliver, can you swallow all right?'

The man made a face.

'Can we see?' There was a jug of water on the locker, with a plastic beaker. Campbell offered him some and he drank it slowly, wincing as he did so, but getting it down without choking, tipping his head back to swallow. 'Did that hurt?'

The man nodded.

'I want to look at your arms.'

Campbell wanted to find out the extent to which the nerves in the man's right arm had been affected by the tumour spreading from his neck into his shoulder. Normally he would have tested for touch sensation, but with a patient who could only nod his head or shake it or write things slowly it would not be easy. Instead he simply tested for muscle power.

'Grip my hands.' The man did so, rather diffidently. 'Grip them hard.' The man smiled and squeezed Campbell's hands in his own. Campbell pretended to wince and the man laughed. The hands which gripped his were both quite strong but the right was less so. 'Do this,' Campbell said, making a movement like playing the piano. 'Move your fingers like that.' The man did so, clumsily. 'You having a lot of trouble writing?' The man nodded.

'Is that getting worse?' The man nodded sadly. 'Because your fingers are kind of clumsy?' He nodded again.

'Just your right hand?' Campbell asked. The man agreed. 'Are you right-handed?' The man nodded again and sniffed.

'I want to examine your neck.' The man reached out and switched on his bedlight. The little room was gloomy, and the light helped. Campbell thanked him and leaned forward to look. There was a small irregular mass just under the skin above the right collarbone. Campbell felt it gently. The mass was fixed, both to skin and the deeper tissues below. 'That sore, when I touch you there?' The man shook his head. Campbell ran his fingertips under the man's jaw. He grimaced. 'I'm sorry. Nearly finished. Can I look in your mouth?'

Mr Tulliver opened his mouth. His tongue had been completely removed. The floor of his mouth was rough and unhealthy looking and had probably been invaded by tumour. Mr Tulliver turned round towards the bed light so that Campbell could see better. At the back of his mouth there were ragged, firm-looking masses of tumour on the hard and soft palates and almost entirely replacing the tonsils. His breath was thick and unpleasant.

'Thanks,' said Campbell. The man looked up at him and swallowed, flinching again. He looked anxious and very sad. Campbell put a hand on his shoulder and said, 'I think Dr Totenberg and I should have a talk, about how to help your pain.'

Campbell and Dr Totenberg went out into the corridor. 'It's awful,' she said. 'Soon he's not even gonna be able to write.'

'Looks like it. I don't know how he can still swallow. It's mostly tumour in there. What's he on for pain?'

'Tylenol.'

'What's that?'

'A really simple analgesic. Not enough, I guess. What do you think?'

'Well, the big stuff, I suppose. Morphine.'

'I guess so. Injection? IM?'

'Not if he can swallow.'

'It's O.K. by mouth?'

'Makes some people sick, but it's worth a try.'

'In water?'

'At home they get it in stuff like gin.'

'This guy was an alcoholic.'

'Was he?'

96

'But we got him off it.'

'Not much point now.'

'So let him drink again?'

'If he wants to. . . . Why not, if it makes him feel better?'

'So morphine and booze?'

'What did he drink?'

'What they all drink. Terrible red stuff called Cardinal.'

'Well, I'd let him drink it. And morphine. . . . He can't talk, he can hardly write and he's having pain from something we can't cure.'

'So just let him. . . ?'

'Well, it's treating the pain, and he's going to die, so why not comfortably?'

Dr Totenberg looked troubled. 'What if. . . ? I mean, what if he just dies after some morphine?'

'He's going to die so that's not a reason for not treating the pain. But he'll probably die of pneumonia, because he's going to have trouble coping with his secretions.'

'I wouldn't treat that. Pneumonia, I mean, if he got it.' She sounded quite resolute about that. 'If he gets pneumonia, that's it.'

'He's going to aspirate sooner or later. He'll lose his cough reflex in all that tumour. I'm surprised he hasn't already, but until he does and gets his pneumonia at least we can make him comfortable.'

'I suppose so,' said Dr Totenberg. 'I mean, we should. And guys like him get heroin where you come from?'

'If they're lucky.'

'Well, he'll get morphine from me. Say ten milligrams?'

'Minimum, and regularly. Every four hours.'

'O.K. An' he's got a welfare check, so we can get him some Cardinal from that. How long do you think. . . ?'

Campbell, who was aware that he was sounding more expert than he felt, said, 'Well, hard to say. Definitely not months. Maybe weeks. But probably longer than a few days.'

'But for now we make him comfortable.'

'Why not?'

'Thank you, David.'

They walked in hot sunlight back to the Health Care

Center. Campbell went through the case in his head. The man was certainly going to die, miserably unless they controlled his pain. No one, not even the most manic surgical optimist, would wish to intervene in any other way. He had local recurrence and incontrovertible evidence of spread deep into his neck and shoulder. He needed something for the pain, even if it shortened his life a little by depressing his cough reflex. And if he wanted to drink he could.

'The nurses kinda like him,' said Dr Totenberg. 'It's nice, because he's got no one else. If I tell them to get him some liquor, they will.'

'Good.'

'And how do we know if he's getting enough morphine?'

'Ask him. Ask him about the pain. His head's clear, even though he has trouble telling you anything. And if he even just looks less miserable we're winning. I'd like to know how he does.'

'I'll call you.'

'Thanks.'

Sooner than Campbell would have wished they were standing by his car. It was just after eleven, which left time to drive back to Crimond, have lunch and be at the Life Ending Americans Clinic by two. 'Interesting case,' he said. 'Thank you for asking me to see him.' Where he came from that was a polite convention at medical consultations, usually expressed in that hallowed formula. Dr Totenberg looked a bit puzzled. Perhaps it wasn't in West Carolina.

'Will you be O.K. getting back?'

'I think so.'

'There's a quick way. Did Billy take you by Hyperion, or by Athens?'

'Athens?'

'Athens, West Carolina.'

'Oh. I'm not sure. . . . There's a map somewhere.' Campbell found his map and spread it out on the roof of the Thanatology Center Oldsmobile. 'I must have come that way,' he said, pointing. 'I think I would have noticed Athens.'

Dr Totenberg stood quite close and showed him another

route to Crimond which avoided a series of small towns and saved fifteen minutes. She smelt nice. They straightened up and she said, 'Where do I find you to tell you about Boaz?'

'I'm at the Life Ending Americans Clinic most afternoons.'

'In a couple of weeks I have to come up to Crimond, to a meeting about the Life Ending Program. Cal fixed it.'

'Cal? Haven't you heard? Dr Pulver died. . . . At dinner last Friday.'

Dr Totenberg put a hand on Campbell's arm. 'Cal's dead?'

'Yes, on Friday. It was pretty gruesome. He just dropped at the table.'

'His heart?'

'I suppose so. We sort of tried to start him up but it didn't work. He was probably dead by the time he got to the ER.'

'On Friday? At dinner?'

'Yes.'

'Was Daddy there?'

'The Dean? Yes, it was a sort of dinner meeting, and he was chairing it.'

Dr Totenberg still had her hand on Campbell's arm. Her face was paler than usual and her expression troubled rather than surprised. 'Cal's dead?' she asked again. 'That's just awful.' Her grip on Campbell's arm tightened.

'I'm sorry,' said Campbell. 'Perhaps I should have told you earlier, but I really thought you would have heard. Did you know him well?'

'Years. He was a friend of the family, and then when Split Rock Health Care came in on the Program I had to see him quite often at meetings as well.'

'He seemed a nice man,' said Campbell, not feeling too insincere. 'I mean, he was very enthusiastic.'

'That's terrible, David.'

'I would have told you earlier if I'd thought you didn't know.'

'It's all right. I guess I should have heard somehow, but I didn't. . . . Do you know what's happening about the LEAPERS thing. . . ? I suppose it's too early to know.'

'It seems to be going on, but I don't think it's clear yet who's going to be in charge.'

'I wonder what's happening about that Steering Committee meeting. Have you heard?'

'I haven't, but I could probably find out.'

'Please, David. . . . But that's awful. He always looked so healthy. . . . What happened? What was it like?' She was standing very close to Campbell, still holding his arm.

'He sort of slumped and gurgled a bit. Vomited, I suppose. And someone went to get the Rescue Squad, and we tried to resuscitate him. . . .'

'But he was a goner?'

'I think so.'

Dr Totenberg let go of Campbell's arm, and sighed. 'Poor Cal. . . . Is it O.K. if I ring you, David? About Boaz, I mean. If something else comes up.'

'Fine,' said Campbell.

'Thank you for coming down to see him, David.'

'No trouble.'

'See you.'

'See you.'

When Campbell went to the Life Ending Americans Clinic at two there was no sign of Candy, the Office Manager. Her place at the desk had been taken by a buxom black girl. He asked what had happened.

'Apparently she needed some kinda procedure on her face. Her beauty spot, you know. Somebody said it was a melon-somethin'. . . .'

'A melanoma?'

'Yeah, that's what they said. But maybe they got this melanoma in time.'

PART THREE

'How lovely is Thy dwelling place, O Lord of Hosts, O Lord of Hosts. . . .'

On wings of near-perfect amplification the soprano line soared from the choir stalls up into the remotest air-conditioned recesses of the MacHardy Chapel. In the nave below a gathering of two or three hundred people sat listening and waiting, not all of them with the air of people who came to church often. Through the anthem they variously craned to examine the stained-glass windows, shifted in unaccustomed discomfort, looked around for friends and acquaintances or read the service card, issued at the door by a matching pair of blonde, red-robed co-eds, which outlined the proceedings and carried on its obverse a brief life of the late Japheth Calbert Pulver, thanatologist and teacher.

Campbell went through this with interest. The four or five paragraphs were modest and factual and presumably written by someone other than the deceased. On reflection, it was hardly surprising to learn that the late Dr Pulver had been the son of a preacher, or that he had shown early promise in college and accumulated over the years a resounding litany of academic credentials. These things were only to be expected. Potentially more intriguing was the change of career, the transition outlined by Stump from evangelism to anthropology. Stump's account remained the more detailed and

101

convincing, the card confining itself to '. . . after service overseas in the mission field. . . .' and resuming its tale of relentless progress up the academic ladder. Only in the final paragraph did grandiloquence creep in. Successive sentences hinted at a place in the higher councils of the nation and mentioned a mighty work of scholarship, a sifting and ordering of the whole universe of thanatologic theory and practice, with a hundred and two contributing editors, seventeen associate editors and now, alas, no editor-in-chief.

How many of that galaxy of contributing editors were present at this memorial gathering, and how many of the twenty-seven disciplines participating in the MacHardy Thanatology Program were here represented? Campbell, seated between a fragrant little librarian from the Thanatology Center and Dr Billy Kidd, head of the Department of Family Practice in the Division of Primary Care, looked round and was impressed. In the transept, diagonally opposite, was a pew occupied by, among others, a clinical psychologist, a statistician, an educationalist, a sociologist, several psychiatrists (looking less familiar than most with their surroundings) and a clutch of social workers. Behind them, in rather heavier ensemble, sat the Dean, Dr Totenberg, with Dr Bottger and Dr Drucker. Behind them were rows more of solid-looking men in lightweight suits. Campbell thought about those present and imagined the deceased grinning and baring his teeth and saying something along the lines of there being nothing like a multidisciplinary memorial service for bringing people together from all over the campus.

'. . . My thirsty soul longs vehemently, yea faints Thy courts to see. My very heart and flesh cry out, O living God, for Thee. . . .'

The MacHardy Chapel singers, drilled from the front by a man who, without his red robe, would have looked like a mad scientist on the run in a movie, gave a controlled rendering of religious passion by enunciating their vowels a little better and biting off the consonants. In the front pew of the transept Miss Sneed, dressed in a subdued pink cotton suit, leaned across her neighbour to talk to a thin dark man with a

beard who might well be the hitherto elusive Benvenuto. To
the right of them in the same pew, seated almost under the
pulpit and nearest the choir stalls, was an odd little group,
atypical of the gathering in that its members seemed quite
upset. A thin, faded fiftyish woman sat with three young
men perhaps in their twenties, all thickset and vaguely
simian about the jaw. A family resemblance asserted itself.
Presumably this was the newly widowed Mrs Pulver with her
sons.

The anthem's last verse faded and the conductor drew his
robe around him and stole furtively for the anonymity of the
choir stalls. Another red-robed figure emerged briefly into
the aisle then mounted the pulpit steps with an eagerness and
spring of step that seemed in the circumstances unusual.
Campbell glanced at his service card: after the anthem came
'Words of Comfort – The Rev. Estelle Novak, Associate
Chaplain, MacHardy University'. He looked again at the
figure in the pulpit. The Rev. Novak was in her late twenties
or early thirties, apple-cheeked and good-looking if not
exactly pretty, with cropped curly hair and a general appearance of preternatural good health.

'Friends . . .' She leaned forward and addressed the microphone as if it were an intimate or even a lover, so that the
word sprang breathily from speakers behind every Gothic
pillar. 'Friends, we are all joggers on the great highway of
life. . . . Some of us have just set out. . . . Some of us have
got the rhythm an' are runnin' real easy. . . . Some of us are
beginnin' to hurt. . . . An' some of us, I guess, have already,
as we joggers say, "hit the wall" – an' by that let me tell you
right away I don't mean we stopped runnin', but just that we
got to a hard place, the way we all do sometime, when the
important thing to do is not give up, so you keep right on
runnin' till it gets easier, as it almost always does. . . . An' of
course for some of us, the pain just isn't goin' to go away until
we finally stop from runnin' altogether.

'Just as there are so many ways of starting out jogging
down the great highway, there are so many ways of stop-
pin'. . . . I don't mind tellin' you, friends, that I don't know
whether Calbert Pulver – Cal, to so many of us – actually

103

jogged or not. An', friends, whether he did or didn't is in so many ways neither here nor there. But that should not prevent those of us who have gathered here together today from honourin' his memory an' givin' thanks for the race now over from seein' it, his life, that is, for what it truly was . . . a race well run.'

It would have been difficult to tell from the expression on his widow's face whether the late Dr Pulver had been a running man or not. She looked dumbly miserable, untouched if not alienated as the words of comfort unfolded. One of his sons, perhaps not a jogger, glared up at the pulpit with a cold and distant hate. Unaware of this, since she was directing most of her attention to the higher academics present, the preacher carried on, referring occasionally, and in general terms only, to the topics of death and the deceased, and relying for the bulk of her discourse upon a series of apparently unconnected biblical references to athletic pursuits. Campbell won a little bet with himself as she finished by exhorting those present to run with patience the race set before them, looking unto Jesus the author and finisher (a word she particularly relished). There was a moment of heavy-breathed prayer, then the preacher descended, in a manner reminiscent of a circus trapeze artist, to ground level.

After another hymn, the Dean made his way to a lectern in the shadow of the pulpit. His address was brief, specific and by all appearances sincere. A newcomer to MacHardy, unexposed to campus whispers, would have thought highly both of the eulogist and the deceased. The widow began to weep, and was comforted by her sons.

'. . . No foes shall stay his might, though he with giants fight;
He will make good his right, to be a pilgrim.'

Bunyan's fairy-tale words and steady, marching tune were familiar enough to be sung loudly and well. Campbell, who always found the last hymn of any church occasion vaguely uplifting, if only by association with the promise of early release, sang out with Dr Kidd and the little librarian and the assembled hosts of all disciplines, and thought that the shade of Dr Pulver would have enjoyed it.

104

The hymn over, the congregation was dismissed with a blessing unexpectedly free from any athletic reference, and spread itself down the aisles and towards the door. As that happened there was a small disturbance in the space below the pulpit. Two young men held a woman. It was hard to tell, at the distance and through the crowd, whether they were supporting or restraining her. Dark-suited and stern, they moved her sideways through the crowd, which opened fastidiously at their approach. Somewhat belatedly Campbell recognized the family group that had been seated near Miss Sneed. The abiding impression of these moments was one of a minor scuffle at a public occasion, in which security guards dealt with a harmless nuisance. No one seemed to recognize them.

On the steps outside Miss Sneed was waiting with the dark, bearded man as Campbell and Dr Kidd emerged.

'Hi, Dave. . . . How are you doin'. . . ? I don't know if you ever got to meet Ben. . . . Ben Benvenuto, who's just *wonderful* with data. An' Dave. . . . Dave's from Scotland and is *deeply* committed to the thanatology program.'

Campbell and Benvenuto shook hands. As they did so Campbell felt uneasy, partly about the depth of his commitment to the program, but mainly because of his non-appearance on a previous occasion. Matters were further complicated by the presence of Dr Kidd, who as Director of the Family Practice Program had a claim to fifty percent of his time. Unfortunately, for a variety of reasons to do with endless and pointless meetings, conferences, seminars and case-presentations at the Thanatology Center, Campbell's contact with Family Practice had dwindled to occasional visits there to check his mailbox. He decided that at the next available opportunity he would go across and meet Dr Kidd and try to work out something that would restore the balance.

'. . . since after all data and what you do with it is the real outcome of the whole Life Ending gestalt, huh, Dave?'

'Quite,' said Campbell. 'Dr Benvenuto, I'd been hoping to get across to the data place. . . . But I'm afraid it's. . . .'

Benvenuto smiled. 'There's not a whole lot to see. But we

could talk. . . . You going back over to the Center now?'

The two left Sneed so abruptly that Campbell was led to wonder if Benvenuto was as generally unkeen about her and her efforts as he was himself. They walked away from the chapel, down a long line of parked cars.

'Very sad about Dr Pulver.'

'He was a very special guy,' said Benvenuto. 'Did a lot for MacHardy. An' not just in thanatology. Committees all over the place. All kinda things, but he was real big in thanatology.'

Campbell recalled more about Benvenuto, in particular his lapsed religious vocation: something he shared with the lost leader. 'Have you been in thanatology long, Dr Benvenuto?'

'Ben. Maybe six years. . . . It's a living.'

'Oh?'

'I guess I'm in data processing, but you can't just be a pure data processor. An' the way I started, the way I came into this, like, I couldn't exactly pick and choose. So Thanatology.'

'Oh.'

'Ever hear of Willie Sutton?'

'In thanatology?'

Benvenuto laughed. 'No, Willie Sutton robbed banks. Kinda famous for it. One time they caught him and some dumb reporter asked him why he did it. Willie Sutton was a neat, straightforward guy an' told him straight out. "Because that's where the money is." So right now I'm in thanatology.'

'Your guess is as good as mine, Dave. All I know right now is who's gonna show up for the poker game.'

'The Steering Committee?'

'Right, the Steering Committee, an' you're there because Phil thinks it'd be a good idea. The shrinks are gonna bring two or three maybe, so Primary Care lines up its toy soldiers too.'

'Oh.'

'You and Amy.'

'I see. And the internists?'

'Interesting question. Schlepp carries their flag, alone for now. But you're never alone at MacHardy if Teddy Totenberg's backin' you.'

'So what do we have to do?'

'Just be there. Nothin's gonna be decided today.'

'Thanks, Randy. I thought it'd be best to check first.'

'That's fine . . . How about lunch after the poker game?'

'Hm, might be difficult . . . I think I've already arranged . . .'

'Jeeze, you guys from Edenburg. Is everybody like that where you come from?'

Campbell laughed. 'See you at the meeting, Randy.'

'See you, Dave. Thanks for callin'.'

'Thanks, Randy. See you Thursday.'

On Thursday morning Campbell got to the Thanatology Center Conference room a little early. There was no one else around, but at five past eleven Dr Schlepp came in and sat down beside Campbell.

'Hi, Dave . . . I guess this *is* the place. Nobody else showed up?'

'Not yet.'

'You doin' O.K., Dave . . . ? Get your license an' all?'

'Yes, thanks. No problem.'

'How long have you been on this committee, Dave?'

'I don't think I'm actually on it. Dr Drucker just asked me to come to this meeting. I think I'm just in attendance. You know, not actually a member.'

'First time for me, too.' Dr Schlepp put down a file marked 'LEAPERS Steering Committee'. 'I guess I'm on it. Teddy kinda insisted. So did Phil.'

'Has Dr Drucker taken over from Dr Pulver?' Campbell asked, exercising a newcomer's privilege.

Schlepp smiled. 'Phil doesn't go around takin' things over. Teddy asked him to take over as interim chairman, an' try an' get things together again. Phil thought it'd only be for a coupla meetings, but he'd see.'

107

'He seems a nice man.'

'Phil's been around a long time,' Schlepp said. 'Knows where the bones are buried, everybody likes him and a lot of guys owe him a favour . . . So you guys from Primary Care gonna be buyin' into Life Ending?'

'I wouldn't know,' said Campbell. 'What about the dermatologists?'

'We see a lot of cancers in this state . . . More people'n you think die of skin malignancies. Some of them kinda messy.'

Campbell thought of Candy. 'I sent a girl across. You kindly said you'd see her . . . A girl who might have had a melanoma.'

'She had . . . Gee, I shoulda told you. Deep, anaplastic as hell. Real nasty. She got an excision and graft, which is difficult on the face, an' real tough on a pretty kid like her.'

'Will she be all right?'

'Well, no . . . Every now and then people get seeding in their graft, an' she's got it. So . . . Gee, it's tough, an' she's a nice young kid. Dumb but sweet.'

'So . . . ?'

'Yeah, she will. She's got a bit of spread already. Like I said, it's real aggressive. And nobody'd go digging in her neck, so . . .'

'How awful . . . Does she know?'

'We had a talk,' said Schlepp. 'She knows the score. She's a tough little kid, in her dumb way. She's gonna take a vacation, go see her folks in the mountains an' keep in touch with us, so we know what's goin' on. We'll see, but it might not take too long.'

Campbell thought about that. It was all rather horrible. A further horrible thought struck him. 'I don't suppose . . .' he said. 'I mean you wouldn't refer her to the Life Ending Clinic?'

'Sure wouldn't,' said Schlepp. 'At least not while those guys are still runnin' it.' Campbell admired his frankness.

There were voices in the corridor and more people came into the Conference Room. Stump, carrying an armful of files, was followed by Dr Drucker. After them came Mikoyan and Nance, both wearing ties. Last came Dr Amy

Totenberg. She was prettier than Campbell had remembered her, or perhaps just a bit more tanned. She smiled when she saw him, greeted him as if they were old friends and came and sat down beside him.

Over the two weeks or so since his trip down to Split Rock they had kept in touch by means of a series of phone calls, each beginning with a clinical problem of some sort. Once she had rung him at his apartment about something not very urgent and they had chatted for a while then Campbell had suggested lunch together after this meeting. She had agreed with some enthusiasm. Now she was sitting beside him, smelling nice and talking so close that he could feel her breath in his ear. With any luck it would be a short meeting.

They were called to order at quarter past eleven. Dr Drucker, whom Campbell now recognized as almost drably sane in comparison with most MacHardy physicians, thanked everyone for coming and said low-key, obvious things about recent events. He referred with perhaps sincere respect to the efforts of the late Director of the Thanatology Center, and stressed the interim nature of his present duties.

He talked quietly and referred frequently to his notes. All present except Dr Mikoyan listened carefully. Proceeding in the manner of someone who suspects he is viewed as worthy but dull, Dr Drucker outlined Phase Two of the Program and the various ways it would alleviate the financial consequences of terminal illness while at the same time preserving the patient's freedom to choose his doctor and the doctor's freedom to do what he thought best for the patient.

As Dr Mikoyan lit a cigar, Dr Drucker started a fresh page of notes and reminded those present of their responsibilities to the public, the institution and the Federal agency that had provided the funds for what he called 'this humane and courageous initiative on behalf of a group more than ordinarily vulnerable to the less fortunate consequences of our present way of doing things'. Campbell, who had come to like Dr Drucker, wondered if that might not be a rather dangerous way of putting it, but no one else in the room seemed to mind.

After a pause and a glance at his notes, the interim chairman

109

began to enlarge on his themes, particularly the special responsibilities falling on those taking part in one of only three projects, each of which had a million-dollar budget. A special attitude, a spirit of tolerance and cooperation was required. Campbell stopped listening and turned his mind to the more interesting question of what Dr Totenberg, sitting on his left and scribbling occasional notes on what Dr Drucker was saying, would look like without her clothes on.

A few minutes later (slender but not thin and probably rather nice, he thought) Stump was talking. 'I guess it depends on whether this is a trend or just the beginning of a trend. . . . In the first full week of Phase Two we got seventy referrals. In the next three days we got sixty. If it goes on getting busier like that we'll be hitting our half-year projected budget by the end of the month. Like, it's through the roof. So even if it doesn't get worse there's a helluva problem.'

'You can't turn business away,' Dr Mikoyan blew smoke and chuckled. 'This is a humanitarian Project.'

'Let's back up for a second,' said Dr Drucker. 'Randy, where are all these referrals comin' from?'

'Well, that's the problem,' Stump said. 'More'n half of 'em's comin' from the MacDonnell chain. Half the rest's from around the Medical Center an' the difference is from up and down the state. An' we had a bunch of inquiries from outa state. Not eligible. They get a note about the guidelines, sayin' sorry.'

'These nursin' home referrals,' said Dr Drucker. 'Perhaps we better get a handle on them . . . Randy?'

'Well, the MacDonnell chain has four nursing homes in town. MacDonnell Avalon, MacDonnell Beechwood, MacDonnell Cypress and MacDonnell Dogwood. Let's call 'em A, B, C and D. A an' B's Medical Director is Orville Doe, an' most of the patients in 'em are either with him or with Alzheimer Physician Associates. C and D's only sent us about four patients between 'em.'

'So it's Orville,' said Schlepp. 'He smelt the money.'

'But as I recall, the guidelines say you have to have two independent physicians certifying a high probability of death within the ensuing six months.' Dr Drucker was being reasonable again. 'So that any additional professional fees related to a patient's Life Ending are under some sort of control.'

Dr Mikoyan leaned back and chuckled. 'Ole Joe Alzheimer's old, but he ain't slow. . . An' he's an ole buddy of Orville's.'

Dr Drucker gave every appearance of not having heard that. 'Randy, it seems there's a whole lot of terminal illness in Avalon and Beechwood. You got any idea what those referrals are comin' in as?'

Stump shrugged. 'I'm only a dumb administrator, but I guess I saw the word "arteriosclerosis" quite often on forms comin' in last week.'

'It's a fatal illness,' said Mikoyan. 'Kills a whole lotta Americans.'

'I see,' said Dr Drucker. 'And as I recall the guidelines, there's some sort of contingency clause for patients who outlive the initial six-month benefit period.'

'Peer review groups of physicians,' Stump said. 'We got two planned, one for malignant, one for non-malignant diagnoses.'

'Well,' Dr Drucker sighed. 'Maybe the non-malignant peer review group's gonna be kinda busy in six months . . . Who's on that?'

Mikoyan blew a smoke ring. 'That might be the one I chair, Phil. I took a look at the regulations a few days ago. Sump'n' about a high probability of death in the ensuing three-month period. You know, for an extension of Life Ending status, cover an' all. Cases discussed anonymously of course, with no way of tellin' which physician's involved. Kinda like the Medicare review procedures for skilled nursing facilities in the homes. I guess we can handle that.'

'Well,' said Dr Drucker, 'that's why we have pilot projects. Work the bugs out of the system.' He did not sound happy.

'Mr Chairman,' Mikoyan said, 'I'd like to say how pleased I am that our Clinic here's attracting referrals. I know there's lotsa physicians resent Big Government interfering with the doctor-patient relationship, an' we're all aware of the issues it

111

raises about control and the threat of socialized medicine, but for maself I'm real happy with the openmindedness Orville's shown towards us so far. Joe, too, an' he's a real old-fashioned town doc. If we can get guys like him in, this Program's sure gonna be a success. An' as a researcher in the field I think you all know I have a special interest in the nursing home Life Ending situation, an' you're all aware of the special arrangement we got with the MacDonnell chain to have a MILES computer terminal in all the nursing homes in town. They're fine people, that corporation, an' we should be glad to help them and their patients any way we can.' Nance, sitting beside Mikoyan, was smiling inanely and nodding in time with his superior's assertions.

Campbell listened. If this was a power struggle it was a decently veiled one. No one was talking crudely about who would succeed Dr Pulver at the head of the million-dollar project. Perhaps, as Stump had suggested, the occasion was a polite and relatively formal preliminary to something altogether more intense, a campaign to be conducted by telephone and in corridors, in committee rooms and off campus, between rival individuals and interest groups, with all the traditional ferocity of routine medical politics.

Dr Drucker, the interim chairman and the representative of a speciality with which Campbell himself identified, seemed to have few advantages and perhaps even little inclination for the job apart from a vague sense of duty about preventing worse things happening. To Campbell he seemed too nice, too fair: in Miss Sneed's words 'not up to it,' though her disapproval must surely be seen as signifying some useful qualities. And Dr Schlepp had spoken highly of him, if only in general terms.

Schlepp himself, said to be 'O.K. with the internists' and a protégé of the Dean, might be more the man to watch. He had been at the dinner at which matters had been precipitated, for reasons more obvious now than at the time, and was, so far as could be judged from one referral, a prompt, energetic and humane physician. Was he interested? Campbell could see how it would be possible to become bored with the routine, wallpaper-matching aspects of Schlepp's speciality, and Schlepp's own phrase, 'not while those guys are in charge,' seemed at least to envisage the possibility of changes at LEAC. As with Sneed and Dr Drucker, Nance's reaction to Schlepp's name could only be a point in the latter's favour. Campbell tried to think what Dr Schlepp might have to say about the wilder flights of psychiatry as seen at LEAC, and concluded that the psychiatrists were right to be anxious.

Meantime the psychiatrists were in charge: sitting tenants with a lot invested in the status quo, however fatuous. They would not give up so much without a fight. Mikoyan, egregiously lazy and absurd even by the standards of his speciality, had been stirred by recent events to the extent of making long and relatively coherent remarks, and wearing a proper tie. And his allies included the vaguely powerful Bottger and presumably Nance and Miss Sneed and all the other nebulously qualified non-physician appendages such as the psychologists, social workers and sundry counsellors. The only problem was that when it came to looking after dying people they didn't seem to be any good.

It was all rather complex. Campbell listened off and on, and watched Amy taking notes and idly lusted after her in, among other places, his heart, forgetting for the moment the various questions associated with the future of LEAPERS at MacHardy. He could easily catch up with them over a beer or two with Stump at a later date.

Not long afterwards the meeting ended quite suddenly. Amy touched Campbell's hand and said, 'Soon we can go and have lunch,' and went over to talk to Dr Drucker. Campbell waited in the corridor. Nance and Mikoyan passed him, whispering gleefully. Amy came out and they walked in the sun across the campus talking about where to go for lunch. She suggested the Oxford Room. He made a face and suggested Mother Nature's, which surprised her. She looked thoughtful then agreed. They spent an hour there and a further hour sitting by the lily pond in the Rose G. MacHardy Memorial Gardens. As they prepared to say goodbye, in the

113

parking lot outside the Life Ending Americans Clinic at two
o'clock, she asked him quite casually if he would like to come
down and have dinner with her the following Saturday evening. It seemed a good idea.

Inside the Clinic, Candy's black replacement seemed hard
pressed. A tall thin man with a silvery crew cut was beating
on her desk with a silver topped cane and shouting, 'Don't
you talk back like that to me, miss. I got a tumour growin' in
me and this yere is a Life Ending Clinic.' A scrawny woman
almost as tall was pulling at his elbow. 'Pay no heed,
miss . . . Engelbert, you jus' don' know what you're *doin'*.
They fixed that tumour for you *years* ago!' The black girl was
no longer listening to them, but trying to get some information from a man in a wheelchair behind them who was
evidently deaf. Behind him, the line stretched three quarters
of the way along the corridor. There were blacks and whites,
mostly middle-aged or older, and perhaps a third of them
were in wheelchairs. Campbell hesitated briefly and a man
seized his arm. 'Son,' he said, 'son, you gotta help me. . . .
Ah'm dyin'.' The man was white, in the sense that his face
was mainly reddish purple. A huge belly drooped over his
waistband. The hand that held Campbell was large and
hairy. 'Ah need help.'

'What's wrong?'

'Like I *tole* you, son, I'm dyin' . . . T'let you unnerstan',
the docs over at the VA hospital tole me I'd be dead in a
coupla years, an' that was *five years ago*. An' I heard this noo
clinic's gonna help the dyin', an' they tole me I'd be dead in
two years . . . five years ago mind . . . if I didn't stop
drinkin' . . . You gotta help me, son . . . I *cain't stop drinkin'*.'

Campbell, who had a vague idea that the VA hospital
specialized in health problems related to tobacco and alcohol
abuse, was unsure as to whether its physicians were encouraged to refer people to the Life Ending Americans Clinic,
but promised to find out and suggested that meantime the
man should wait in the queue.

'In the what?'

'Sorry. The line.'

The man let go Campbell's arm but before he could move someone else had grabbed it. A little old lady in a pink print dress asked him, 'Sir, does this clinic pay for cancer surgery?' Campbell said he wasn't sure and it might depend on the details of the individual case, and that she would probably be best to wait in the line and register at the desk. She said she had waited three hours already and that was a long time for someone with cancer. He said he was sorry the Clinic was so busy. She smiled and said that with the prices she'd heard for cancer surgery it would still be worth it, and thanked him.

Half way through the afternoon Campbell found Nance and tried to discuss with him the problems raised for the Clinic by the large numbers of new patients. Nance seemed uninterested but did remark, 'Most of these people don't have any feelings worth working on, except maybe about getting somebody else to pay their bills.'

After coffee Campbell rang Stump and suggested that they might meet for a chat. Stump agreed. 'Come round to Mr Woody's, around six. A couple of us are taking Willa out for a drink. She's leavin'.'

'Where's Mr Woody's?'

'On Billup, near K-Mart. See you there around six.'

In the latter part of the afternoon there was only one more patient, a retired insurance executive with a lung tumour that didn't seem to have bothered him very much for about two years. He complained of pain in his knees, and Campbell examined him and found that he had osteoarthrosis quite unrelated to his tumour. When he explained this to the old man he seemed pleased at the news, but surprised that Campbell had not ordered an X-ray to ensure there were no secondary deposits there. Campbell explained about osteoarthrosis and why it was different from tumour. The man thanked him, reflecting aloud that he should have known that psychiatrists wouldn't know much about knee pains.

'Hi, Dave. . . . Dave, come on an' meet Willa. Willa's leavin'. She's got a great job on the West Coast.'

'Hello. Congratulations.'

'Hi, Dave. I guess we've sorta bumped into each other. . . .'

Willa was the tall girl with acne whom Campbell had first seen coming out of Dr Pulver's office and who had more recently presented a case at the Teaching Conference. She was drinking something that looked like a Bloody Mary, perhaps not her first that day.

Few others were present. The psychologist who looked like a lifeguard and whose name Campbell could not remember was there, as was a girl who worked as a research assistant in the LEAPERS Data Storage Systems and Information Center. Campbell sat down on a bench opposite Willa and beside Stump, who signalled for a waiter.

'Whereabouts is your new job, Willa?'

'Montana,' said Willa sullenly, stirring her drink with a small pink plastic tomahawk.

'Still in thanatology?'

'Not exactly. . . . Well maybe. It's in the psychology section of the State Department of Correction.' Campbell looked blank. 'Jails.'

'Have you worked in the West before?'

'Yeah.'

'So you'll know a bit about it.'

'Montana isn't San Francisco.'

A waiter appeared and Campbell ordered a beer. Stump, presiding over this strange and joyless occasion, attempted to make conversation more general. The psychologist and the girl from Data Storage continued to talk quietly to each other.

Mr Woody's, Stump informed Campbell, sought to recapture the atmosphere of the 1880s, and had been opened three weeks before. The interior was subdivided into sections and decorated and furnished in the manner of a saloon, a stagecoach office and a jail of the period. Willa's little farewell party was being held round a plain pine table in the jail section, perhaps in arch reference to her future employment. A young black waiter in a coarse black and white horizontally striped suit was serving them. The place was not busy and they had a fair-sized cell to themselves.

116

Conversation remained sporadic. The girl from Data Storage told Willa that Ben had said he'd try to come along later, for a few minutes at least. The psychologist thought he had once played football with someone who had just had a vacation in Montana and enjoyed it. They ordered more drinks.

'Hi, you guys! Hi, everybody. . . .' A girl's voice very loud made everyone turn round, as perhaps it had been intended to. Miss Sneed, in a fiercely pink outfit, ran down the steps from the entrance to the jail section waving both hands like the star of a TV spectacular. She arrived at the table and did a breathless-but-happy, great-to-see-everybody routine which included all present except Campbell. She sat down beside Stump.

'Thanks, Randy, a beer'd be great. I got a lot to drink to. The reason I'm late. . . . Sorry, everybody . . . is that I just spent an hour and a half with Jake and Stef talking about the way things are gonna go evaluation-wise, research-wise and communication-wise. I'm taking over the Thanatologic Communication Module task from today, from yesterday in fact.'

No other conversation prospered. Willa, who had been looking thoughtful before Miss Sneed had arrived, now looked dumbly despondent. Campbell recalled that she had had something to do with Thanatologic Communication.

'We looked at my career development opportunities too,' said Miss Sneed. 'Randy, I tell you, I was hardly ready for what they were sayin', but I guess they're the guys who know. Right now I don't even have to pick a track. With the way things are, I just sit in Evaluation, with Communication, Research and Data Handling as major interests, and still keep in touch with the Interpersonal Skills Program, of course, an' they're happy to let me do all that. You know what they said, Randy? They said I was good at interfaces. That's what they said, an' I just never heard it put so good before. Like I kinda know I'm comfortable with multi-track self-organization, but it would never have gotten to be so clear to me why that is unless Stef, who's so wonderfully *perceptive*, had put it together and showed me why. Isn't that wonderful?' A beer arrived for her and she smiled round the table, again not getting quite so far as Campbell. 'Willa,' she said. 'I'm sure you're gonna have just one great time in Montana. . . . Let us know . . .' Spotty, red-nosed and by now a little red-eyed too, Willa looked down into the last drops of her Bloody Mary.

'Drink, anyone?' Stump asked, looking round for the prison-garbed black. 'Willa? Cherylene . . . ? Uh, Dave? That a beer?'

'No thanks, Randy,' said Willa. 'I gotta whole lotta things to do tonight.'

'You sure?'

'Oh, well . . . Thanks.'

'Cherylene? A Mr Woody's Ambrosia?'

'Uh, yeah.' Cherylene giggled, displaying perfect teeth marred only by a brace. 'It makes me feel so good.'

The black youth went off with the order and as he did so a seventh person joined the party, a slender, fair-haired girl who stood for a moment beside Willa with a hand on her shoulder, wishing her luck in her new job.

'Thanks, Candy,' said Willa. 'It's real good of you to bother . . . Especially, you know, with everything you've been goin' through.'

'I wanted to say goodbye,' said Candy in her little-girl-in-a-movie voice, 'and wish you luck.'

'That's real sweet of you, Candy. I appreciate it.'

Candy sat down beside Willa and said hello to Stump and Campbell. It was impossible not to look at her right cheek, in the middle of which there was now a rectangular patch of discoloured skin about two inches long, pale and mottled with a fine bluish black rash: the 'seeding into her graft' described by Schlepp. Campbell tried not to inspect it too closely, but Candy lifted her hand towards it. She was pale and perhaps already thinner than before.

'How are you, Candy?'

'Maybe Dr Schlepp told you, Dr Campbell. They had to cut out mah beauty spot.'

'So I heard, Candy. How do you feel?'

'O.K., I guess. It's kinda itchy an' I keep wantin' to scratch it . . . You know it's a cancer.'

Miss Sneed was still talking about her career but no one

was listening. Willa sniffed and lifted her empty glass, put it down and started to sob. Once again Candy put a hand on her shoulder then she too started to sniff. In a moment they were both weeping, jerking forward over the pine table towards each other. The others sat still and embarrassed.

At the other end of the table the psychologist shuffled his feet and then stood up, waved goodbye to Stump and Campbell and tiptoed out. The girl from Data Storage followed him without waving goodbye, and so, a few steps behind, did Miss Sneed.

'C'mon, honey, you try this.'

Candy looked up through her tears. The youth in convict dress was holding out a glass of fizzing opaque golden liquid, topped with cream and thin slices of fruit. 'You gonna drink this?' Candy blinked and took the Mr Woody's Ambrosia ordered for Cherylene, who had now left. The two girls looked vaguely alike, so that Campbell wondered whether the waiter was improvising heroically or merely confused. Either way he was doing simple human good. 'An' a Bloody Mary fo' you, ma'am, same as before. Make you feel better too. An' your beers . . . All on the tab, sir?'

'Yeah, thanks,' said Stump, lifting his beer.

Fifteen minutes or so the remainder of the party broke up, Willa and Candy leaving together, still talking sadly. Stump paid. Campbell waited for him, reading the 'Wanted' notices beside the cash desk. When Stump rejoined him he offered to contribute to the cost of the drinks.

'Nope,' said Stump. 'That came outa the Center's entertainment budget. Call it conscience money.'

'Oh?'

'For the way they fired her.'

'I didn't realize . . . Was it her work?'

'Her work was fine, but Sneed didn't like her, wanted her job and kinda canned her, through Cal. She got Cal convinced that Willa couldn't handle people.'

Campbell thought of how Miss Sneed and the late Dr Pulver 'handled people', and wondered what Willa might have done that did not measure up to their standards. 'So she was sacked?'

'Well, she had a talk with Cal, an' he told her she'd be smart to start lookin' for somethin' else. . . . Jeeze, Montana.'

'I see.'

They moved towards the door. Stump paused. 'Feel like a drink, Dave? After a drink like that, I feel like a drink.'

'Fine.'

'Let's try the saloon.'

The saloon was almost as quiet as the jail. They took a corner table in a little alcove and were served beer by a blonde girl wearing a long flounced skirt and track shoes.

'Cheeyahs.'

'Cheers, Randy.'

'How did you get on with Amy?'

'Hm?'

'At lunch.' Stump winked. 'Saw you sneakin' off with her. Ongoing discussions on rural Life Ending, huh?'

'That sort of thing.'

'And that green marine guy she's gonna marry, he can hardly object to her maintaining her professional contacts.'

'I suppose not.' There was rather more to it than that but Campbell did not want to go into details. 'Randy, I was wondering about one or two things about the Center, and LEAPERS, and the Clinic . . .'

'Like, what the hell's goin' on?'

'More or less. You know, Phase Two and all those patients this afternoon. Is that what people expected?'

'Some of us did, but nobody thanked us for sayin' there might be a problem. Back in February we talked about a quota, so many new referrals a week, and that's it for now, folks. Not Cal's style, though. The Pulver way of doin' things is to go for broke, get yourself a good-lookin' crisis an' then go on TV an' preach some. And now we got a crisis and Cal ain't around any more.'

'So?'

'One or two people are beginning to get nervous.'

'Phil? Dr Drucker?'

'Right. Not the sort of guy who gets down the hole at the bank. Likewise Totenberg. Likewise Schlepp.'

'And the shrinks?'

Stump drank half a glass of beer, perhaps to stop himself saying something uncharitable. 'To those guys balancing the books is anal-obsessional. Not their problem. You've seen Stef. "We should be glad to help these wonderful corporations and physicians who are so afraid of Big Government", and all that shit.'

'But they're not in charge,' said Campbell, wondering if perhaps they were now.

'A Federally financed terminal care talk show is their idea of heaven. They've just about got it and they'll take a whole lot of shifting. They suited Cal fine. "Look, we got lotsa MDs on the team", he could say, without the hassle of havin' real hard-nosed whitecoats that cost a lot and want to run things. Neat, huh? Keeps Teddy an' the rest off his back, an' he gets to run his own show.'

Once or twice Campbell had noted Stump and others talking about Dr Pulver as though he were still alive. 'But now he's not around any more . . .'

'Interesting, huh? But even before he died he was havin' trouble. A million dollars made a whole lot of guys take a fresh look at the problems of Life Ending. That dinner was probably the beginning of the end for Cal anyway.'

'Oh . . . Schlepp?'

'Well, not really as simple as that, but, yeah, it was meant to be a nice way of getting people to think about maybe gettin' some more people on board, maybe with a view . . . All that stuff.'

There was a longish silence. The mirrors in the saloon offered half a dozen views of the waitress polishing glasses behind the bar.

'I rather like Dr Schlepp,' Campbell ventured.

'So do I,' said Stump. 'Only problem is, the shrinks loathe him.'

'They might not want to stay around.'

Stump laughed and shook his head. 'I guess these things look simpler from a little way off, like the distance from here to Scotland. But from close up like where I am it's kinda complicated . . . Turf issues . . . The shrinks have always

121

been big in MacHardy an' they were the first to get into thanatology, well, the first MDs. Myself, I'd fire 'em all tomorrow, but it's not my decision. Have you heard of Jake Bottger?'

'The short man at that dinner?'

'You got him. See, Jake's a big guy, an' Teddy an' the rest can't just push him around, an' everybody knows that. An' Jake sees a lot of important issues in a million dollars.'

'So what's going to happen?'

'Nothin', I guess, for a while at least. Phil does his caretaker administration thing an' everybody gets together an' tries to take out the shrinks.'

'And the money side?'

'That's a nightmare.' Stump reached for his glass again. 'The way things are shapin' up we could wipe out a year's budget in a coupla months.'

Campbell remembered Dr Drucker's remark about working the bugs out of the system, and quoted it approximately.

'So far,' said Stump, 'only the bugs have showed up. We're still lookin' for the system. It's definitions again. You can't run a program for Life Ending Americans unless you can define one. The best way we've thought of is for two independent physicians to agree about it an' we gotta pay them both for even thinkin' about it, an' then the one whose patient it is gets a Special Needs Supplementation for that patient until it's all over. So it's definition by incentive again, with no pay for holdin' back an' only the well-known clinical objectivity of the American physician to protect the Federal dollar. They shoulda learned from Medicare, but they didn't, an' we're goin' broke.'

'How much do they get?'

'For a guy from a socialized medicine background you're cottonin' on fast. Fifty dollars at the time of registering an' a hundred dollars a week thereafter plus all the usual fees plus as many other specialist referrals as you want. I mean as the patient needs. So all your friends get a cut. An' it's all guaranteed income, there bein' no such things as bad debts in this business. And of course fifty dollars for the other guy who agreed your patient needed it in the first place, an' you'll do the same for him anytime. For patients in nursin' homes, the institution gets a cut too. Special needs, so special facilities. You know, the FLEAs, like that one down in Split Rock.'

'Do those MacDonnell places have FLEAs?'

'The way things are goin' they'll have nothin' else.'

'And those patients this afternoon? The clinic was mobbed.'.

'They shouldn't have been there. They should get referred by their own physicians. But unfortunately Cal has a gift for mobilizing the media. The *Bear Fork Examiner* did a feature on us. "MacHardy brings hope to millions." You know the kind of stuff. Boy, have we got a problem.'

At lunchtime next day Campbell still felt unwell. A beer with Stump had turned into two or three, then they had gone to a seafood restaurant with a good wine list. Stump took eating and drinking seriously and also knew a great deal about the workings of the MacHardy Medical Center, and they had sat late over a series of bourbons. They had talked of many things and Campbell could not remember in detail how he had got home, but through the ensuing phases of oblivion and headachy wakefulness several points remained with him.

It seemed that the Life Ending Program at MacHardy was heading, under loose psychiatric direction, for disaster. For a variety of reasons powerful men thought changes now necessary. Schlepp was the favourite to be the instrument of such change, but only once things had got a little worse. Meanwhile, the psychiatrists held sway.

In the Life Ending Americans Clinic at two o'clock Campbell found a note lying on his desk. It was pink and had a printed heading 'From the Desk of Candy Konopka'. 'Candy Konopka' had been scored out and 'Ethelanne Johnson' substituted in a round childish hand. The message read 'Dr Cambel Please Call 9-847-8163 (Dr Todburg)'. Campbell rang the number.

'Hello?'

'Hello, Amy?'

'Oh, David . . . Thank you for calling back. I just wanted to say how much you helped me yesterday.'

123

'No trouble. I mean I didn't do very much.'

'You were really helpful . . . More helpful than I can say.'

'No trouble . . . A pleasure.'

'And by the lily pond . . . That was just beautiful. . . . I can't believe all that, but it happened. Wasn't it just amazing?'

'Um, yes.'

'For me it was like, well, being really in touch with myself after months and months of not being, like of even being someone else. And you've no idea how much that means to me.'

'Quite.'

'I've been thinking a lot about myself recently, and I really reckoned I had myself figured out. But talking with you made me realize just how much I was kidding myself, and I guess I could easily have gone on kidding myself, just gone on and on, until it was too late. Gee, isn't that awful, that that *happens* to people . . . It does all the time, I guess. Oh, David, thanks for not letting it happen to me.'

'Glad to be of help.'

'You were really wonderful.'

'Have you seen . . . ?'

'No . . . And I feel kinda mean about that. Like, me knowing and him not. I was going to try and call him but he hates me to call while he has access.'

'Access?'

'You know, access to Larry and Walt and little Barbara. I told you about them, his family. And he always has access on Thursdays, so I rang him at the camp this morning. He doesn't like that either, but it's not so bad as ringing him when he has access. Anyway, we couldn't really talk, because he had gunnies in his office.'

'Oh.'

'He's just commencing a five-day field exercise.'

Campbell made a little calculation which proved reassuring about Saturday evening, then realized he might not have been invited unless she had made that calculation too. 'So you couldn't really talk.'

'No. So I'll have to leave it until next week. But I really

know now, like I said, I'm really in touch with myself again. And I'm so grateful . . . How are things up at LEAPERS?'

'Fine, I think. Phase Two is bringing in a lot of referrals.'

'Oh good . . . David, I meant to tell you, Boaz is doing real well. You know, the black guy you saw for me.'

'Oh yes. Good.'

'Well, he's having a lot less pain, and he usually has a drink in the evening and the nurses got him a little radio and he lies drinking and listening to country and western music.'

'Sounds fine.'

'Everybody's real happy with the way things are goin' for him. We got him a picture board so's he can point to things he wants, and it doesn't matter so much him not bein' able to write. He's great. You can take a look at him when you come down.'

'Be glad to.'

'Well, if you get here maybe around five-thirty we can see him, then come on over here and have a drink and eat. Do you like Italian food?'

'Sounds fine. Shall I bring a bottle of something red?'

'Good idea, if you don't mind, David. Most of the wine down here's that stuff the Indians drink.'

'I'll try and find something.'

'And you know the way down?'

'I'm getting the idea.'

'See you Saturday.'

'Around half past five . . . Oh. Where?'

'The FLEA?'

'Fine.'

'David, I can't thank you enough.'

'No trouble. See you Saturday.'

Campbell put the phone down and wrote 'FLEA 1730 hrs Sat' on the pink piece of paper. It was all rather strange.

Over lunch they had chatted generally and later, seated on a stone bench by the lily pond near a fountain commemorating a lesser MacHardy who had succumbed in infancy, Amy had told him her life story.

After a childhood fraught with privilege and college years dominated by the mighty shadow of the Dean, she had tried to deal with her feelings about her father by marrying a psychiatrist. These feelings dealt with, ('I was grateful, David, I really was, but you can't have transference every morning with the orange juice') she found herself on her own again and making decisions.

She had left her home town and started a new life in Connecticut, ('Honestly, David, I just wasn't *allowed* to adolesce till I was twenty-five') and had begun her career afresh in the speciality of Family Medicine, for a variety of compelling reasons. ('I wanted to help people, really help them. And I guess I knew it'd annoy the hell out of Daddy.')

Campbell had sat watching a bullfrog under a stone and listening as the story evolved. Split Rock, where she had now practised for two years, was conveniently distant from Crimond ('I need space, but not too much of it') but had limitations, particularly those affecting her social life.

As a result of those limitations she had become involved with one Dan, an officer in the US Marine Corps. Dan was a Vietnam veteran, a major in the Field Training Section at Camp Oswald, near Split Rock. Amy described him as a dedicated but only moderately successful officer, and 'basically a deeply caring person who's had a lot of tough things to handle'. She explained that he had had family difficulties and was now divorced, and added, in a faintly apologetic afterthought, that she was engaged to him.

Campbell had listened to all this and wondered if Amy, having been married to a psychiatrist, was now going rather too far in the opposite direction. The more details emerged, the less likely the relationship seemed. The deeply caring person evidently spent his days teaching otherwise unemployable young Americans to hide in the woods and kill people. His recent marriage turned out to have been at least his second. He drank a lot. It was difficult to imagine Amy as a Marine Corps wife suddenly responsible for a half-grown and, from the sound of things, thoroughly disturbed family. Campbell had refrained from saying so and was gratified shortly afterwards to hear her saying it for herself.

Still unfamiliar with the solemn casualness of American marital behaviour, he had listened in awe as Amy, in the

126

space of half an hour or so, had talked herself out of her impending marriage. Side by side they had sat in the sun, looking out over the water, Amy speaking to a mellow sardonic bullfrog accompaniment, and Campbell listening and reflecting successfully upon the vanity of human wishes and the various fleshly possibilities now arising in relation to his proposed trip down to Split Rock on Saturday.

Sitting idly now in his office, he went over their strange conversation again. The awesome speed of the collapse of her intentions presumably meant that for weeks she had been aware of the sort of mess she had got into. Down there among the tobacco farms it might have been possible, even necessary, to suppress that recognition, perhaps indefinitely. Half a day in town had clarified the matter considerably.

Campbell, who had long suspected that rural life was prejudicial to mental health, felt somehow pleased to have acted in the matter as a sympathetic representative of urban culture. It was just a pity she had invited him down to Split Rock before he had thought of suggesting she come up to a town with restaurants and more than one make of wine.

There was a knock at the door. Campbell folded the pink message slip, put it into his pocket and said, 'Come in'. The psychologist whose name he could not remember put his head round the edge of the door. 'You got a minute, Dave?'

'Fine. Come in.'

The psychologist sat down on the couch and looked solemnly at Campbell. 'Wasn't that just awful about Willa?'

'She certainly seemed quite upset.'

'No, I mean later.'

'Oh, after Mr Woody's?'

'Yeah. . . . She did somethin' she maybe shoulda thought better of.'

'Oh?'

'In fact she, uh, ended her life.'

'Really?'

'She took her own life by means of a combined overdose of antidepressant medication and, uh, alcohol. Vodka, maybe a quart. Unfortunately she lay overnight in her apartment and

127

was unfortunately dead on arrival at the ER. Her apartment complex manageress found her. You know she hadn't even begun to pack?'

'She seemed quite upset at Mr Woody's.'

The psychologist gazed across the room and said with a vibrant sincerity reminiscent of Nance, 'I was there'.

'But she seemed less unhappy when we left. She went off with Candy. I thought they were friends.'

'When somethin' like this happens I guess we all try to make excuses. Anyhow, Dr Mikoyan was deeply upset when I told him.'

'Oh?'

'He said it was a tragedy and a great loss to the program.'

Campbell thought about that and said, 'But I thought she was leaving anyway.'

'Oh. I guess maybe Dr Mikoyan didn't know that. I mean, he can't know everything, can he?'

Kravitz muttered something under his breath and started to drive round the block again. 'Sorry, Dave. Harvey told me roughly where it was an' I thought I knew anyway. Maybe I was thinking of MacDonnell Beechwood. But I know it's this side of the tracks and not as far west as the Loop.'

They were in a part of town that Campbell had not seen before. Small, shabby frame houses, evidently inhabited by blacks, fronted a series of derelict industrial sites. On the other side of the road was an old railway track overgrown with weeds. They were looking for MacDonnell Cypress.

'I never had any patients there myself, so I never . . . Hell, let's ask this guy.' Kravitz pulled over, skidding to a dusty halt beside a car with no wheels and no windows. A black man sat on its hood. 'Hi there,' he said to Kravitz.

'How you doin'?'

'Jus' fine.'

'We're lookin' for Cypress, MacDonnell Cypress.'

The black man's eyes narrowed. He was toothless and his jaw writhed in an endless chewing movement even when he was talking. 'Son, you got the wrong street.'

'Huh?'

'He don't live here any more.'

'No, MacDonnell Cypress is a nursing home.'

'Maybe he's dead.'

'Yeah, O.K. Thanks . . .' Kravitz let out the clutch and the car jerked forward again. 'Some kinda schizoholic, or maybe an alcophrenic. With these guys it's hard to tell. We could go west a block.'

The road and the railway separated and derelict land fell away between them. Kravitz braked hard. 'Got it. It's down here.' They turned off on to a bumpy unmade road and clouds of dust billowed behind them. 'Cypress is not their top-rated place, but I guess it's O.K. as these places go. You got a lot of nursing homes in Scotland?'

'Very few.'

'You seen some here?'

'One, at Split Rock.'

'Theirs is quite good. I mean, they got a popcorn stall, you know, run by the inmates. It makes the place smell nice. These MacDonnell places don't usually smell nice.'

MacDonnell Cypress, which they must have passed several times in the previous ten minutes, lay down a slope and was particularly concealed from the main road. It was a cheap brick building with a parking lot of stony, shrub-fringed waste. A sign read 'MacDonnell Cypress: Crimond's Quality Downtown Convalescent Center'.

'Harvey got the biopsy report yesterday and told me about it at Family Practice rounds this morning. Billy said it'd be a good idea for us to go take a look.'

'Do they know?'

'Do who know?'

'The MacDonnell people.'

'They don't need to. We just go. If the guy's O.K. for LEAPERS I guess we tell 'em. They'll be interested in that. A circular came round from the MacDonnell chain local office announcing individual Life Ending Care Plans in conjunction with MacHardy and the LEAPERS bunch. I guess you know all that stuff. Harvey thought this guy'd be nice for you to see, an' I believe Billy's quite keen, you know, from the remuneration side. Like, we gotta make money like everybody else. Oh, an' his Medicare just ran out.'

'And he's got a sarcoma?'

'Well, they said an anaplastic leiomyosarcoma. But good enough for Life Ending. I mean, malignant as hell.'

They went into the nursing home. In a small entrance hall a dozen or so people, mainly old and black, sat in wheelchairs. They were arranged in an irregular semicircle centred on the door as though the most interesting foreseeable event in their lives might be someone coming through it. Campbell stopped and looked round. Kravitz stopped with him. Nearest was an old man, slumped forward so that all that could be seen of his head was a smooth chestnut-brown expanse flecked with little curly white tufts. He was prevented from falling further forward by a blotchy grey canvas vest secured by stout cords to the frame of his wheelchair. He was tied in, as was everyone else in the semicircle. Some looked up expectantly, some stared vacantly. One or two were asleep. There was an overpowering smell of stale urine. Above a little reception desk with no one behind it hung a large framed notice headed in stylish capitals 'The MacDonnell Philosophy of Care'. The rest was too small to read.

Kravitz pressed a bell push at the reception desk. No one came, which seemed to surprise Kravitz less than it did Campbell. Kravitz said, 'Sometimes they got a list up of where folks are,' and started to look round the entrance hall. A few from the semicircle watched them.

'He's called Sullivan. Stroked out last year. Funny little guy, insurance clerk, white. High blood pressure, an' real difficult to control. He used to come round Family Practice a lot, wearin' these wild yellow and blue check pants. Eccentric, I guess, rather than crazy. Stroked out, was in MacHardy East maybe a month, then came here for rehabilitation.'

'Rehabilitation?'

'Yeah. Medicare pays.'

'What's the rehabilitation like here?'

'They got a physical therapist.'

'Is this chap likely to get home?'

Kravitz laughed. 'No way. He's too crazy now. Grabs ass. Harvey says the MacDonnell people keep complaining, so he sent the psychologist round, to see why he grabs ass. He's on behaviour modification for that now, but if he's on his way out it might not be too much of a problem. . . . Yeah. This is the guy. Sullivan, R. They call him Rob. Now all we gotta do is find his room.'

A youngish man in a wheelchair had manouvered himself over towards Kravitz and Campbell as they stood by the list of residents. 'You lookin' for Mr Sullivan?'

'Yeah.'

'He's in D.17,' said the man in the wheelchair.

'Where's that?'

'You go roun' to the left, past Management, Accounts and Social Activities Coordination, through the Interaction Area an' it's just by the Skilled Nursing Office.'

Further into MacDonnell Cypress the smell got worse. In the Interaction Area, an irregular space lit only by a few grimy skylights, the odours of stale food and unwashed bodies were added to those of excreta. Three old women were slumped in wheelchairs in front of a blaring television set. In the corridor labelled 'Skilled Nursing' an old man stood rigid and staring, leaning on an aluminium walking frame. There was a puddle round his feet. They had not yet seen anyone who might be a member of staff. It seemed a strange place to send someone for rehabilitation after a stroke.

There was no one in the room marked 'Skilled Nursing Office'. Kravitz checked through a file of clinical records and found a folder labelled 'Sullivan'.

'We got 'im. Let's see. Yeah, this is the guy. "Difficult and aggressive. Dinner withheld for one hour in accordance with Behavior Modification Care Plan". That was Tuesday last week. Wednesday he was trouble, Thursday he grabbed ass again. Then they found this thing on his shoulder, so biopsy under local. Deeply fixed to bone and kinda rubbery, an' it turned out to be this horrendoma. Harvey told me about it this morning an' we talked about it at rounds. Some folks thought do a forequarter, take his shoulder and arm. Seems there was a series with a fifteen percent survival. Harvey said it might stop him grabbing ass, I guess he was joking. But Billy said the hell with it, get the Life Ending rotation guys to see him. Makes a lotta sense. Like, his Medicare's run out.'

D.17 was a small dark room looking out onto a railway embankment. In one bed lay an old black man watching portable television, in the other an emaciated white in late middle age. The left side of his face dropped slackly and his left arm hung limp. He waved at Campbell and Kravitz with his right hand. In the little room the smell of urine and stale bedding was nauseating.

'How are you guys doin'?'

'Mr Sullivan, we're the Life. . . . We're from Family Practice. Dr Harvey Klein asked us to come along an' take a look at you. You got somethin' on your shoulder, huh?'

'Sure have.'

'Which shoulder?'

The man nodded down to his right.

'Can we take a look?'

'You sure can.'

Kravitz unbuttoned the man's pyjamas and bared his right shoulder. There was an irregular pink mass overlying the outer third of the scapula. A Bandaid covered part of it.

'You havin' pain?'

'Only when they cut out that piece a coupla days back.'

'You can move your shoulder O.K.?'

'Sure can.' Suddenly he reached out and lifted the pen from Kravitz' top pocket. 'Ah sure got all my wits about me.'

The man laughed and Kravitz smiled sheepishly and held out his hand for the return of his pen. Campbell remembered that left-sided strokes sometimes went a bit strange, but as far as he could recall the strangeness was virtually untreatable, and almost certainly not susceptible to the dubious techniques of behaviour modification. Perhaps Medicare paid psychologists too.

'You wanna take a look, Dave.' Campbell inspected the lesion from a safe distance and palpated it briefly.

'Gonna be O.K., doc?' Mr Sullivan asked.

'Might need some treatment,' Campbell said. 'Depending on the final report on the piece they took out.'

'I ain't havin' no operation.'

'That probably won't be necessary.'

'You guys from Family Practice?' A nurse, a tall woman with a fiery crown of copper-coloured hair, stood in the doorway of D.17. Mr Sullivan leered enthusiastically at her. Campbell and Kravitz turned round.

Kravitz said, 'Dr Klein asked us to come and see Mr Sullivan.'

'You the behaviour guys?' Kravitz shook his head. 'His shoulder, huh? He gonna have surgery?'

'I guess not,' Kravitz said. 'In fact, Dr Campbell here was asked to advise about his . . . care. Dr Campbell's from Scotland.'

'Hi, Dr Campbell.'

It seemed to Campbell that an opportunity had arisen to get out of the rank and stifling room. The nurse was not to be moved. 'Your first visit to MacDonnell Cypress, Dr Campbell?'

'Yes,' said Campbell, trying not to breathe unnecessarily.

'Beth Knopf, head nurse. I'm responsible for all nursing care here at Cypress.'

Campbell nodded. Her manner was complacent though it was difficult to see why. The room was grubby and smelt awful, the beds were unclean and untidy and both patients looked unshaven and neglected. There was a squadron of flies buzzing at the window.

'Hi there, Mr Sullivan.'

'Hi, nurse.'

'Hi there, Mr Helms.'

The old black man watching television grunted and continued to watch television. The head nurse flashed a plastic smile at Campbell. 'Here at Cypress,' she said, 'we make no distinction on grounds of race or creed. It's part of the MacDonnell Philosophy of Care.'

The room was stiflingly hot as well as smelly. Campbell began to feel sick and moved towards the door, murmuring, 'Perhaps we can discuss things outside.' When he and Kravitz and the head nurse were out in the corridor again he said, 'I suppose there are some problems with patients who are incontinent. . . .'

133

The head nurse flashed another gleaming plastic smile and said, 'Here at Cypress we have an Incontinence Program.'

Kravitz, perhaps sensing trouble, said, 'We came to assess Mr Sullivan for the LEAPERS Life Ending Americans Program.'

The nurse beamed and said, 'Mr Holyoak would be real happy if you could step along to his office. . . . He has very positive feelings about the Life Ending Program. . . . Mr Holyoak is our manager, here at Cypress.'

Mr Holyoak was a short fat man in a bulging pale blue shirt with one button missing and a grey line round the collar. He waddled round his desk to greet Kravitz and Campbell.

'Garth Holyoak. . . . Hi. . . . Hi. . . . I jus' wanna say you guys are doin' a magnificent job and we here at Cypress wanna help you all we can. Your Dr Mikoyan is a wonderful physician an' one of mah most cherished friends here in Crimond. I cain't speak too highly of him, an' any physician who works with him is an automatic friend of the MacDonnell Corporation. . . . You wanna cuppa coffee.'

Mindful of hygiene, Campbell declined. So did Kravitz. As they sat down a telephone rang and Mr Holyoak answered it, saying, 'I'll call you back,' and put it down.

'I love this work. . . .' He shrugged and shook his head. '. . . but sometimes. . . .' He smiled bravely. 'What I wanted to say is that here at Cypress we are one hundred percent behind you in your efforts. We want your program to feel welcome here. . . . Stef. . . . Yeah, he's Stef to me . . . knows that, an' I want you to know it too. As a MacDonnell manager I'm here to *help people help people*. That's my philosophy and I don't care who knows it. An' my office door stays open. . . . I wanted to see you guys to tell you that with head office approval we are planning to increase our Facility for Life Ending Americans bed complement by two hunner percent over the next three weeks, simply to help Stef and his people help our people here at Cypress. Now I don't wanna take any more of your time, but I want you to know that our Corporation will always be firmly on your side.'

As they rose to go Campbell noticed on the corner of the manager's desk a little stack of business cards which read

'Garth's Funeral Home: for Dignity on a Budget when it Matters Most'. Outside there was no sign of the head nurse or any other member of staff. Campbell held his breath all the way across the lobby and half way across the parking lot.

At twenty-eight minutes past five on Saturday Campbell arrived outside the nursing home at Split Rock. He parked in a slot marked 'Physicians Only' and waited. Another car drew up and Amy got out. She was wearing a tee-shirt and short, tight tennis shorts. She seemed pleased to see him. Campbell got out of the car, his shirt sticking sweatily to his back.

'Hi, David.'

'Hello.'

'Good trip down?'

'Yes, thanks.'

'You look kinda warm.'

'I am a bit. . . . You don't.'

'I've just been playing tennis but my car's got air.'

'Air?'

'Air conditioning. Down here you gotta have it.'

'This one doesn't. It's one of the Thanatology Center's. The car I mean.' Campbell tried to work out how stupid all that sounded.

'You gonna get one of your own?'

'Yes, soon.'

'Don't let 'em sell you one without air. . . . David, why don't you leave your car here and come on over in mine?'

Campbell retrieved his lukewarm Beaujolais from the Oldsmobile and got into her car. A bleeper lay on the passenger seat. 'You on call?'

'Yes, but it's quiet. Right now all the guys who cause trouble are out fishing. Later they get to drinking some more, wrecking their four by fours and shooting people.'

'Shooting people?'

'Down here guns are part of the culture. Everybody carries 'em. Well, certainly all the men.' She revved the engine and her car lurched forward spurting gravel. 'My home's just two blocks down.'

That night no one in Split Rock shot anyone, at least not in circumstances that led to the summoning of the physician on call for Split Rock Health Care Inc. In Amy's white frame house they dined early. Conscientiously on call, she drank only token amounts of the Beaujolais. Campbell drank the rest. For that reason, among others, he did not drive back from Split Rock that night. Amy's duty remained quiet. They sat and talked. At about nine o'clock she was called over to the nursing home. When she came back they went upstairs.

Her bedroom was small and old-fashioned, with lacy net curtains and a dressing table of oak, on which stood a portrait photograph of a fanatically tidy-looking marine officer, clean-shaven and bemedalled.

They stripped unromantically and lay on the bed. The marine on the dressing table glared at Campbell as if he were a recruit who had just dropped his rifle. The effect was disconcerting, indeed not dissimilar. Amy worked on him with a cheerful dexterity that would have made her a first-rate sex therapist, but to no avail.

Eventually she said, 'I'm sorry, David,' and got up and turned the marine's face to the wall. After that things went splendidly. Half an hour later Amy reached out to turn off the light, and smiled. 'I may not have got my head together yet,' she said, 'but I'm a wonderful fuck.' Not simply out of politeness, Campbell agreed.

Campbell had just entered his apartment when the phone rang. His first thought was that it would be Amy, but it was not. A man's voice, distant and unfamiliar, said, 'Is that David Campbell?'

'Yes.'

'You just got back?'

'Yes.'

'You just got back, huh?'

'Who's speaking, please?'

'Don,' said the voice. Or perhaps it said 'Dan'.

'Dan?'

'No, Don. Don Kravitz.'

'Oh, hello. I've just got in.'

'I rang you last night . . . And this morning.'

'Oh?'

'You O.K. for two o'clock?'

'Hm?'

'Two o'clock. You don't remember, huh?'

'Sorry.'

'The Day of Peaceful Action.'

'Oh, yes. Sorry, Don. Yes, of course. Skunk Bend. Looking forward to it.'

'Fine. I'll pick you up at two.'

'You know the way?'

'To Skunk Bend?'

'I meant here.'

'I think so. You're where Gus used to be, huh? Apartment B.7?'

'Yes.'

'You explained all that when we made the arrangement.'

'Of course.'

'Fine. See you at two.'

'Thanks, Don.'

Campbell put down the phone, glad that it had been Don, not anyone called Dan.

The arrangements about going to the Skunk Bend Day of Peaceful Action had been made towards the end of the party at Dr Bronstein's and Campbell, who now recalled them in outline only, was happy to have been reminded. There was just time to have a shower and change into something that might be suitable for a Day of Peaceful Action.

'They said west maybe twenty on seventy-five then look for a big red barn, then it's dirt roads. So maybe a couple more miles and we should pick up the barn. I'm pretty sure she said it was red.'

Apart from a certain vagueness in his navigation, Kravitz was an agreeable travelling companion. His car was old but luxurious, and had 'air'. The stereo system was playing a restful piece for sitar or mantra or something, the sort of music that evoked one of Edinburgh's better Indian restaurants.

A long upward slope ended in a view of mountains, blue in the distance. Above the intervening plateau and perhaps a couple of miles away a helicopter circled, black against the sky. 'We need a red barn,' Kravitz said. None appeared. The restaurant music stopped and the tape jumped out. A voice said '. . . or alternatively in the event of rain in the Hoskins Auditorium. That's the UWC Women's Baroque Recorder Group Summer Concert. All welcome, no admission charge . . . And here in Pulpit Hill it's ninety-five with a humidity of eighty-nine and the weather forecasters tell us it's a zero percent chance of rain this afternoon through tomorrow. A great day for a picnic and for those baroque recording folks . . . An' now to while away the time before the upcoming WUWC newsbreak we gotta li'l thing by Ludwig van Beethoven. It's a quartet, his Rasum . . . His Rasum-something . . . Anyhow, it's Opus Fifty-Nine, an' it's a new recording by a foreign group . . . from, uh, Amadeus. Take it away, boys . . .'

'That's it,' said Kravitz. 'The barn, an' it's red. We hang a left maybe a coupla hundred yards west of it. Yeah, we did it . . . Well, looks like we're gonna do it.'

The car slowed and Kravitz paused while a huge eastbound truck rumbled past, then he turned down an unmarked dirt road and accelerated again. Dust billowed behind as the car hit thirty then forty and lurched and slithered into a long bend shaded by trees. Suddenly Kravitz cursed and they skidded to a halt only ten feet or so short of a large grey and black car parked so as to block half the road.

'Goin' somewhere in a hurry, sir?' said a voice.

Kravitz switched off his engine. A state trooper in an old-fashioned scout hat leaned down and scrutinized him at length then peered across the car at Campbell. 'These li'l country roads, sir, they need extra care.'

'I'll remember.' Kravitz looked straight ahead.

'May I see your license, sir?'

'Sure can.' Kravitz fished it from his pocket.

'An', sir, may we check your trunk?'

'Go right ahead, it's open.'

The trooper moved back round the car. 'Maybe a gaol break,' Kravitz said, turning to Campbell. 'Gee, shit.'

On the right of the road, standing back a little under the trees, were two more state troopers. Both were festooned like assault infantry in arms and ammunition. One was holding a shotgun levelled firmly at Kravitz and Campbell.

The trooper who had checked the trunk returned to Kravitz' side. 'That's fine, sir . . . Heading for the Day of Peaceful Action?'

'Sure are.'

'Have a good day, sir.'

'Thanks.'

Kravitz drove carefully round the partial roadblock. The Beethoven quartet, played rather better than it had been announced, evolved serenely over the engine noise.

'Kinda soothing, that stuff.'

Campbell agreed.

'Yeah, cool. Like, if it had been Schoenberg or somethin', we coulda had our heads blown off.'

He drove on with the sedate watchfulness of one who has just had a brush with the law. The helicopter was much closer now, still circling against the blue.

'How many people might turn up at a thing like this?' Campbell inquired.

'The Day of Peaceful Action?'

'Yes.'

'The committee hoped thousands. But hundreds maybe, I guess. Hell, who knows? But a bunch of the folks from the AMA reckoned it'd be nice to make, like, a kind of Health Fair of it. Bud, our president, like the president of the AMA, Bud's gonna do a drop-in workshop on Transcendental Rolfing. An' Maggie and a coupla the women are putting together something on Biorhythms and Feminist Anger.'

'Who's on the committee for the Day of Peaceful Action?'

'Some AMA guys and some ecology groups. Ecology is big in Holcombe county, with the Skunk Bend development, I guess. And then there are one or two wild guys. . . .'

'You mentioned them.'

'Fringe-of-fringe people, not so fussy as the AMA. Against more, maybe. Like, we're against big bad medicine and nuclear power. But they're just . . . angry. Oh, an' Mother Nature's is doin' the official food.'

'Good.'

Clouds of dust from previous cars marked the line of the road ahead. Kravitz slowed for a narrow wooden bridge. A track led off to the right to a river-bed dried by summer. In it Campbell glimpsed a small military vehicle, perhaps a wireless truck. Beside it two soldiers worked at a table under a camouflaged canvas awning. At home in the UK such things would have signified a reservist exercise. Here, and after the roadblock, it might not be so simple. Kravitz had noticed nothing and Campbell did not tell him. The moment passed.

Only a few hundred yards further on Kravitz slowed again then pulled into the side of the road behind a line of parked cars. They got out and walked in the sun for perhaps quarter of a mile. Ahead the sounds of amplified music mingled with the clatter from the helicopter above. To the right a small forest of orange construction cranes shimmered in the haze.

'That must be the nuclear installation we're protesting. The AMA guys said we keep real clear of it. But the commune right next to it has got land, an' they want us. . . . It's all legal. Irving went into it. . . . Gee that's heavy.'

Parked in the line of cars, with big nervous spaces in front and behind, were two more military vehicles, larger and more formidable than the wireless truck. They were tracked, open-topped, lightly armoured personnel carriers, their engines running. Each was full of armed soldiers. Rifles pointed skywards. Young eyes looked humourlessly out from under helmets.

'National Guard,' said Kravitz. 'But heavy, huh? An' I guess the chopper belongs to them too. I mean, they don't paint TV helicopters like for *Apocalypse Now*. . . . Shit, it's a Day of *Peaceful* Action.'

'I hope so.'

'You up for it?'

'Sure.'

'People get kinda funny about nuclear stuff.'

'You mean the ecology people? Or the angry lot?'

'I meant the law.'

The entrance to the commune came into view. Two untidy rows of policemen, mostly tall and fat and laden with nightsticks, guns, ammunition and nasty little black canisters that might well contain tear-gas, formed a funnel leading to a rickety wooden archway topped by a pokerwork shingle which read 'Peace Love Freedom'. The two biggest and nastiest looking policemen of all, bulging irregularly from their accoutrements and sweating in the sun, stood at the innermost ends of the lines, flanking the gate like heraldic beasts. Framed between them, like a glimpse of another world, was a stretch of open land dotted with brightly dressed people in picnicky groups. Beyond them, down a gentle slope, was an old-fashioned white wooden farmhouse.

In the space before the gate lingered a curious trio. Two were young: one tall and bronzed with a trim blonde moustache and a classic early-American profile; the other small, slender and Hispanic, with eye make-up and garments of garish unisex motley. In an attitude of defiance and martyrdom, and quite ignored by the police, they held between them a stylish banner proclaiming, 'UWC Gays Against Nuclear Power'. The third man was middle-aged: a rustic, perhaps even a simpleton, with high cheekbones, sunbleared eyes and the standard redneck plaid shirt, who looked around him as though such scenes were rare in Holcombe County. As Campbell and Kravitz passed he peered at them and said, 'It's a scain-dal. . . . Ain't ever seen nuthin' laike it. . . .' Campbell, unsure as to which faction he meant, nodded politely.

Soon the various unsettling preliminaries to the Day of Peaceful Action took on the unreality of a bad dream. Within the gates, Peace, Love and Freedom prevailed as advertised, in fine old-fashioned style. Most of the two or three hundred adults around seemed to be in their middle to late thirties: the men bearded, the women in denim or baggy peasant attires of folky print. It was, Campbell gradually realized, an occasion for long-serving sixties people.

They strolled around the farm, past family groups lying in

141

the sun and round a series of odd little sideshows and strange alfresco businesses. A billowing untidy girl with ringlets presided over a table of 'Authentic Outer Banks Natural Seashell Jewellery'. A legless young black, blind and possibly psychotic, drugged or shell-shocked, sat by himself in a wheelchair, playing a bamboo flute. From a stall labelled 'Country Herb Tea No Capital or Exploited Labour Involved' two fat girls dispensed half-gourd cups of a steaming liquid at 15¢, or 50¢ for a family pitcher.

The farmhouse and its outbuildings formed the focus of events. In front of it, overlooking a grassy slope down to the river, a makeshift stage consisting of a flatbed truck with a sound amplifying system stood empty and for the moment silent, and in the courtyard a crew from Mother Nature's ran a service of food and drink from trestle tables with a very business-like cash register clanging away at the end of the line. Campbell and Kravitz had a coffee and a wholefood snack then further explored the various attractions of the Day of Peaceful Action, ending up at the riverside with representatives of the Alternative Medicine Alliance. Dr Bronstein was there in some administrative capacity. He smiled at Campbell. 'Peaceful, huh?'

The helicopter had gone away. A loose coalition of idealists, eccentric but not harmful, had assembled for a day together in a probably futile gesture against something they didn't like. Out in the sun on an old farm by a river they were variously engaged in amusing each other, selling things that did not seem worth much and preaching fads and faiths of similarly dubious value. Buyers and listeners were both in short supply but that did not seem to matter. All concerned, perhaps even the policemen at the gate, appeared to be enjoying themselves. Yes, Campbell agreed, it was peaceful.

'You gonna stay a while? We got entertainment . . . We even got Lemmy Gravel.'

'Oh?'

'He sings.'

'Oh.'

'Great ole guy . . . Really great.' Kravitz was embarrassed by Campbell's lack of sophistication. 'Maybe the last of the

142

chain-gang blues bunch. Did twenty-somethin' years in pokey.'

'Oh?'

'Alabama,' said Kravitz respectfully.

'He's kinda old,' Bronstein said. 'That's another reason everybody should catch him now.' He smiled and went away.

'Ever had a foot massage . . . ?' Kravitz asked. 'They're just great. As a member of the Alliance I can get cut rates for both of us . . . A coupla girls I know said they'd be here . . .'

For only a dollar Campbell was relieved of his shoes and socks and lay back on the grass while a middle-aged lady with fierce grey hair held back by a woven sweatband that made her look like an Indian brave pulled his toes one by one until they cracked then, with a thing like a wooden rolling pin carved into knobbly ridges, worked back and forward over his soles until they felt as if they had been sandpapered. She explained as she worked that the foot contained a representation of the whole body, which would benefit accordingly, then added that she did whole body massage too, but only by special appointment. Campbell imagined what it would feel like and demurred. Nearby Kravitz received similar treatment from a lively blonde girl, perhaps twenty years younger than Campbell's attendant, who giggled a lot in a way which suggested that she and Kravitz had done at least as much together before.

The afternoon passed agreeably enough. Campbell watched a solemn little team of clog-dancers, clumsy and unskilled but respectfully applauded for their sincerity. Then he listened to a fiddler who had at least taken the trouble to master his instrument as a preliminary to public performance. A girl from one of the Alliance stalls engaged him in earnest conversation, and he suffered for the sins of his profession as seen and described by Ivan Illich, though his assailant failed to recognize the sage's name when Campbell mentioned it. She was perhaps sincere, which seemed to count for a lot in this company, and she was undoubtedly pretty, so Campbell heard her out, and when he found that she had majored in Law got her to talk about that, which made her sound more intelligent. Kravitz, meanwhile, had drifted off with his masseuse.

The sun dipped towards the mountains and around six o'clock someone tested the sound system on the stage, then an old black man was hoisted up. He shuffled towards the forward edge and was stopped just in time by a young assistant and placed carefully in front of the microphone. To a guitar accompaniment played by a scholarly young white in denims he sang in hoarse complaint about the sun, the roads of Alabama, the cruelties of prison and the wider injustices of life. His audience, white, well-fed and free, loved him, and applauded louder and longer until he was finally led shuffling away as dusk fell. Campbell, who had provisionally diagnosed Parkinson's Disease, wondered whether successful treatment would improve the act or not.

'So you think Mount St Helen's was a *natural* disaster, huh? You think that mountain just suddenly decided to blow itself up? Well, I guess you can think that if you want, and that's exactly what they want you to think. But we got sources, and our sources say that there were geologists, *and* seismologists, staking out the whole area *six months* before anything started to happen. Our sources say their experiment went wrong, *but it was a deliberate experiment*! How else could they have been there for six months? *That's* how much these people care. An' we're just *not* gonna let them do it *here*. Right?'

The small dark girl stopped talking and a man with a beard said, 'No way.'

'They just don't care what they do. They only care if somebody gets to know about it. D'ya see those pigs at the gate? And the deliberate and repetitive overflying of *this* farm by *their* helicopter? And those guys in the *tanks*? Skunk Bend is no power station, it's another of their *experiments*!'

'Right,' said the beard.

'The power station shit is just *cover*.' The girl leaned across the table towards the man whom Kravitz had said was the Rolfing expert.

'We've blown their cover!' she shrieked. '*They know we know*!'

The Rolfing man was less sure. 'We think it's a power

144

station,' he said mildly. 'And we don't like nucular power stations. So we're protesting it.'

'We're protesting ecodisaster,' said the girl.

'We're against it.'

The Rolfing man was calm. 'We looked at the Three Mile Island stuff. If the same thing happened here, we'd be evacuated.'

'We looked at Mount St Helen's,' said the girl. 'If the same thing happened, we'd be under *six feet* of nucular ashes! *Doesn't anyone care?*'

They were in the farmhouse kitchen, a big untidy wood-lined room. The organizers and their guests sat around, aglow from the day's sun, dining from the riches of the Mother Nature's wholefood menu. A few bottles of wine had appeared and people were relaxing. Kravitz, who had fixed late invitations for himself and Campbell, was at another table with his blonde masseuse. Campbell, less fortunate or less organized, was trapped between rival factions of the committee.

'I guess you're scared about property values.' The small dark girl had returned to the attack.

'That's only part of it. A very small part.'

'Some of us are grappling with forces that could *destroy* the *world*!' She paused. 'And most of us are more concerned about that than we are about property values. Our sources say those guys have been here too. Geologists *and* seismologists.'

'That's normal, I guess, for any . . .'

'No . . . No. It's *cover*. They're gonna try it all over again, *away* from the fault line.'

'Yup.'

Someone tapped Campbell's shoulder. He turned round to face a pleasant-looking blonde woman in a blue shirt. She was familiar but he had forgotten her name.

'Martha,' she said helpfully.

'Sorry . . . Of course. Great food.'

'You getting to like it?'

'I really am. Still have the occasional furtive sausage. But this was really nice.'

145

She pulled up a chair, and Campbell said something else about the food and asked how the day had gone.

'You saw it,' she said. 'Pretty good, I suppose. The waits did well . . . This place isn't anything like a restaurant, so we made the stuff up early and brought it out here in bulk . . . Everybody worked hard. How's MacHardy treating you?'

'Interesting.'

She smiled. 'You into this protest? Or just taking a look?'

'Taking a look, I suppose.'

'There was plenty to look at.'

It occurred to Campbell that she must have had a busy day, and while she might simply be taking a rest it was kind of her to have come and rescued him from the surrounding conversation. ('Mount St Helen's was just a beginning,' the girl hissed. 'Wait till they start testing the crust *undersea*.') They talked about Crimond and MacHardy and when the wine came round again she had a glass and then lit a cigarette, which rather surprised Campbell in one who was so rational about what she ate.

She finished her cigarette and stubbed it out, and shortly afterwards the waits descended and began to clear the tables. The company rose and stretched and conversation turned to the last event of the day, something called a firelight skinny dip. Slowly the farmhouse kitchen emptied.

A quarter moon had risen, and in the distance the mountains were faint but somehow larger. A few hundred yards down the slope half a dozen small fires twinkled at the river's edge. It was cooler outside but still comfortable. They walked slowly, savouring the evening and talking about skinny dipping. With some trepidation Campbell realized what was involved.

Down the slope a crowd had gathered to the right of the line of fires, and from it a hubbub of voices carried upward on the still air. As they drew nearer Campbell heard not laughter but shrieks and angry shouting.

A hundred or so people, most of them naked, crowded in a tight inward-looking huddle. In the flickering firelight their movements were dim and jerky, as if in an amateur movie or

146

some primeval rite. As far as could be seen, no one was swimming.

A naked man ran up the hill, shouting. 'Any of you guys MDs? You AMA guys . . . ? You gotta come on down real quick.'

Bronstein ran towards the man. Kravitz and Campbell followed, and as they stumbled down the slope in semidarkness the naked man, panting for breath, gasped, 'Those guys are real sick . . . Maybe dead, some of 'em . . . It's awful . . . You gotta help . . .'

The naked firelit crowd opened. At its centre lay two children and a woman. Everyone was shouting and gesticulating except the three figures lying still on the pebble river-bank. Bronstein took charge. 'Stand back, please . . . Except you guys. You carry 'em over here by the fires so we can see . . . Stand back please. . . .'

Kravitz, Campbell and a few naked helpers lifted the woman and the two children over to the nearest fire. Campbell, who had taken the woman by the armpits, began to suspect the worst. If she was breathing at all, she was not breathing much. Still carrying her, he tried to feel for the pulse in her neck and could find none.

Examined by firelight, she was simply not breathing. Her pupils were fixed and dilated. She was dead, and so was one of her children. The other had a pulse of around two hundred and was breathing in short tiny gasps. The crowd murmured, and some shouted angrily.

The two corpses and the sick child were fully clothed and dry. A quick look revealed no superficial marks of violence. There was no obvious explanation.

'Where d'you find 'em?' Kravitz asked the nearest onlookers. 'How did this happen?'

'Over there by that fence,' said a voice. 'Somebody tripped over 'em in the dark. . . . Next to that place. . . .'

'Go back and see if there's any more.' Bronstein looked and sounded authoritative, if only because he still had his clothes on. People paid attention. 'Go on,' he said. 'Make a reg'lar search. . . . Spread out and keep looking.' Kravitz and Campbell knelt over the sick child, who was breathing a little better now and muttering rapid, delirious words they could not make out.

'They're killing us!' a voice screamed. It was the small dark girl from dinner. 'Those pigs are killing us! It's Jonestown all over again . . . They're killing us because we *know*!' The crowd around bayed and shrieked.

Campbell took the child's pulse again. It was racing, faster than two hundred, almost too fast to count. As he held her wrist he noticed something else. 'She's hot,' he said to Kravitz. Kravitz laid a palm on her forehead. 'Jeeze, she's hot as hell.'

Screams broke from the darkness up the hill and soon another little group stumbled into the circle of firelight, half carrying, half dragging a young man whose head lolled back limply. Behind them came another group, and another. In a few minutes eight figures lay side by side on the pebble shore.

Campbell and Kravitz checked the newcomers. Three were dead and two, like the still living child, were hot with racing pulses and hectic, gasping respiration. Bronstein, Kravitz and Campbell conferred.

'Poisoning,' said Bronstein.

'Not nucular,' said Kravitz. 'Nothin' in radiation sickness like this . . .'

'Hot . . . Dry . . . Tachycardic and tachypneic . . .'

'A plant poisoning? Something like atropine?'

'Jeeze . . .'

The small dark girl was shrieking, 'They're killing our people . . . They're killing our people . . .' In the circle of naked onlookers children screamed and wept, and angry shouting echoed back and forward across the river.

'An atropinic plant poisoning,' said Bronstein. 'Something some crazy guys might eat . . . Oh, jeeze.'

'Oh Christ! The crazy bastards . . .' Martha knelt over a dead man, beating her fists together. 'They drank that crazy herb tea and some crazy bastard put some pretty berries in to make it look nice . . . Oh Christ!'

'Keep lookin' for 'em . . .' Bronstein shouted over the noise. 'We don't know who's here or how many. Just keep lookin'. . .'

148

'They're killing us . . .' the dark girl screamed.

'Don, go ring from the farm . . . The rescue squad . . . And ambulances. Say six to start . . . We just don't know . . .'

'There's no phone at that fucking farm.' Martha was shouting.

'Hell, no.'

'How about the police at the gate? They'll have radio, and cars or vans or something. You know, at the gate. If they're still there.'

'Gee, shit,' said Kravitz, clenching his fists in fury and running off up the hill.

'Oh Christ,' said Bronstein quietly. 'Stupid, stupid crazy bastards . . . Deaths, deaths, deaths.'

More little groups stumbled down into the firelight carrying people. Campbell thought of the two fat girls at their stall, with country herb tea at 15¢ a half-gourd cup and 50¢ a family pitcher. They were not around.

PART FOUR

'Welcome to the MacHardy Thanatology Center . . . A nationwide leader in the sociologic, psychologic, psychiatric and medical evaluation and care of the dying . . . The Center looks back proudly over five decades of leadership in basic research, multi-disciplinary professional training and delivery of service and is probably the most respected center of its kind in the world. But we do not fall into the error of resting on our laurels . . . No . . . We have a great future too, as recent events have demonstrated. The award of a Federal Life Ending Americans Program Evaluation and Resource Study grant of no less than one million dollars has given us here at the Center a new and important recognition of our place at the forefront, nationwide and worldwide, in our field.

'Welcome to the Center . . .' There was a pause and a smile. Dr Pulver's regrettably ape-like teeth shone and glistened. 'As Director I want you to know that your weeks here in the Multi-Professional Thanatologic Training Program may be the most formative of your life. Many practitioners with backgrounds ranging from pastoral care to advanced and specialized studies in oncology. . . . That's the branch of medical science dealing with malignant tumour . . . have sat where you are sitting now and in due course have subsequently gone on to positions of great distinction in their own fields, carrying with them that sensitivity, academic discipline and straightforward applied humanity which is the hallmark of Thanatologic training here at MacHardy.'

'Some of you . . .' Dr Pulver's voice dropped a little. 'Some of you from further afield or from continents other than ours may be wondering about the name MacHardy . . . You can ·take it from me that Ephraim MacHardy was a great man, a great American, a man of wealth and ideals both, who is chiefly remembered today because he was from the beginning a supporter of the then newly emerging discipline of Thanatology . . .

'It would be a mistake, although a pardonable one, to think of the Thanatology Center as an outgrowth of the University. In reality, the reverse is . . .'

A disfiguring Technicolor stripe appeared, dividing and distorting Dr Pulver's face and for a moment the sound too was lost.

'But here at the Center . . .' the stripe disappeared, revealing a good-natured simian grin '. . . we take a tolerant view.

'So welcome to the Center, and welcome to our facilities. Whatever your discipline of origin, you will find here something to help you develop your research interests. And we do encourage you to "think research" from the very beginning. Funds are available both from generous trusts established by Ephraim MacHardy and his family and from Federal sources which recognize the value of a MacHardy Thanatologic training. And we certainly have the facilities. By arrangement with the MacHardy University Medical Center Rodent Unit, over a thousand terminal rats of various high-quality laboratory strains pass into our care each week, so that over the years many of the most basic biologic mechanisms of the various stages of mammalian death, from psychologic adaptation to molecular biodegradation, have been elucidated here by teams of investigators in this Center. And some of these investigators . . .' the voice dropped in come-to-Jesus sincerity, '. . . initially started out in the basic introductory course you are now commencing.

'The MacHardy Rodent Thanatology Program is a small but important part of our activities. However, if one thing is characteristic of our work here at this Center it is the pride we take in our breadth of vision. A few examples will demonstrate . . .'

Campbell was sitting in the conference room of the Thanatology Center with new intake for TC 206. Miss Love, the Director of Clinical Thanatologic Services, was in charge and had introduced the videotape, mentioning only as an afterthought that Dr Pulver had 'unfortunately at this point in time passed on'.

For the benefit of the assembled trainee nurses, psychologists, social workers, dietitians, speech pathologists, physical therapists, podiatrists and lesser breeds of health professional, Dr Pulver posthumously outlined the activities of the Center. Most were by now familiar to Campbell. Only a few, like the Intercultural Bereavement Program in conjunction with an obscure university in Paraguay and the Longitudinal Study of Multiracial Death Sentencees evidently waiting around in various States of the Union, were either unknown to him or perhaps now defunct. Campbell listened with interest to the customary Pulver mixture of bombast and exhortation, thinking that it was quite pleasant to be hearing from the old boy again.

Dr Pulver had raised his voice and was using his hands a bit more, perhaps working up to some sort of peroration, when Ethelanne, Candy's black replacement, popped her head round the door of the conference room and beckoned Campbell with a grin, rolling eyes and a hand signal probably denoting a telephone call. He smiled deferentially to Miss Love and left.

'Hello.'
  'Hello?'
  'Hello . . . David?'
  'Yes?'
  'Amy here.'
  'Oh, hello. How are you?'
  'Just fine. I'm at the office. I just had a no-show, so I thought I'd call you.'

'A what?'

'What?'

'You had a what?'

'A no-show. A guy booked in who didn't turn up.'

'Oh.'

'He'll be O.K. He was a cast check. We charge twenty dollars so I guess he checked it himself.'

'I see.'

'So I called you . . . How are you?'

'Fine. I was listening to Dr Pulver.'

'You what?'

'On a videotape thing. It was odd. I'm beginning to think I liked him.'

'He was a great guy. Daddy was real sorry when he . . . when he . . .'

'Died?'

'Well, no. Yes, then as well. I really meant when it looked like he had to go . . . from the LEAPERS thing. But when he died as well. Anyway, how are you?'

'Just fine . . .'

There was a pause then Amy said, 'I enjoyed the weekend.'

There was another pause while Campbell set aside in his mind the events of Sunday evening and realized what she meant. 'So did I . . . it was nice.'

On the other end of the line Amy giggled and said, 'That sounds very British . . . "It was nice".'

Campbell laughed. 'Sorry. It was nicer than just nice.'

'David, I have to come up to Crimond this evening. Some family stuff . . . But maybe we could meet.'

'That would be nice.'

She giggled again. 'I'll call you from home . . . Crimond home, I mean. Maybe around nine?'

'Fine.'

They chatted a little longer and began to talk about patients. Campbell remembered the man in the nursing home. 'How's that black chap? With the tongue? I mean the carcinoma of tongue.'

'Boaz?'

153

'Yes, him.'

'He died.'

'Oh?'

'Real peaceful.'

'Recently?'

'Saturday evening. I got called, remember?'

'Oh.'

'Yeah, it was real peaceful. Like the nurses said, "He's gawn to Jesus . . ." David, I got patients. See you tonight . . . Bye.'

'Bye.'

Campbell went back to the conference room. Miz Love was fielding a question from a black youth with mirror glasses and a huge fuzzy coiffeur. 'No, Humbert, the Thanatology Program isn't morbid. We're very positive about death . . . In fact we hardly ever mention it at all, as such, per se.'

There were no more questions and Miz Love went over some administrative points with her students. Campbell thought about death and about Amy, then about Amy and death: how she had first reacted to the news of Dr Pulver's passing; her seemingly casual acceptance of the toll of domestic violence in Split Rock; the matter-of-fact way she had come straight from certifying the death of the tongueless black to their exhilarating encounter in the old-fashioned bedroom. But it was not, he thought, 'morbid' or in any way sinister, more a reflection of her impulsive, immediate character and the healthy American tradition of naive realism. And the trouble with death in America was simply that there was an awful lot of it about.

'I shoulda mentioned, Dave, Dr Mikoyan particularly asked me to say how pleased he is with the way things are going in the Clinic since you joined. He's not had a chance to speak to you himself but he really made a point of it. "You tell Dave, Bob," he said. "You'll be seein' Dave on the Phase Two LEAPERS rounds".' Nance touched Campbell's arm, a gesture which he seemed to use to convey especially profound sincerity, and smiled sweetly. A fat man in dungarees sharing the elevator glanced warily at them, and when he got out at the sixth floor grunted disapproval, as though certain that worse things would happen now the two were left alone together.

'Dr Mikoyan says hospital rounds will give us what he calls follow-through. Like, this guy Claypole we're seein'. He was a real pillar of strength, you know, a key contributor, in the Prostate Cancer Peer Support Group when he was up to it, and in his turn he's come to expect we're still gonna be there when he needs us, say . . . further on in his disease process. Folks get the wrong idea about psychiatry . . . I'm sure you've come across 'em, Dave . . . Folks think that when you get sick, like physically sick, your psychiatrist just ain't innerested in you any more. I'm sure *you* don't think that at all, Dave, but lotsa folks seem to. Kinda negative image problem we got, I guess, an' it's just so silly because people don't just leave their conflicts, their life-prioritization problems, their identity work and their life-crises in the hospital lobby when they check in. No, sir. They need us, maybe more'n ever, an' the way Phase Two is structured we can, you know, *be with them*.

'Take Goober Claypole. He was gettin' into some real innerestin' places with the Prostrate Group, touchin' on issues that, well, didn't surprise us, but were real impressive comin' from him. Subtle, gender-identity stuff in sync with a whole buncha things to do with gender-specific childhood experience. You know the kinda stuff, Dave, I'm sure you know it well, but when a blue-collar redneck with a grade-school education and a life in timber comes right out in a group an' says, "Well, why *shouldn't* I have breasts?" I tell ya, it makes a whole lot of the other guys sit up straight.

'Then he missed a coupla meetings. Said he wasn't up to it. Backing off, we thought. Gone too far, you know? He *said* he was havin' trouble walkin', an' *we* thought, uh-oh. You know the way we do. I tell you, I could have bitten mah tongue out when I heard he had spinal secondaries and was *paraplegic*. . . . But we sure are glad you picked it up, Dave. Kinda underlines what Dr Mikoyan was sayin' about the importance of havin' a spread of expertise within the Clinic. Like he says, it's great to have you on board.'

At first glance Mr Claypole seemed an unlikely candidate for psychiatric support, even taking into account what Nance had just been saying about 'follow-through'. He lay in a single room with the customary ceiling-mounted television set, in this instance showing a silent, maniacally gesticulating preacher in flapping purple vestments. An old man sat on a chair by the window, his hands folded over an ebony walking cane. The only sound in the room was a dreadful convulsive spluttering occasioned by a third man, perhaps a respiratory technician, who was manipulating a polythene catheter in the patient's endotracheal tube and sucking out his lungs.

The old man by the window smiled at Nance and Campbell as they came in. The technician, intent on his work, ignored them, probing and sucking and being rewarded from time to time by glutinous, snoring gurgles and more bouts of apocalyptic coughing.

The room was hot and humid, presumably as part of intensive respiratory care. Mr Claypole was naked but for white modesty pants. His wrists had been tied to the frame of the bed by white felt bands but his ankles were free. Campbell wondered if there had been some mistake but then remembered that Mr Claypole was now paraplegic.

An IV line entered his right arm at the elbow. A catheter draining cloudy urine emerged from his modesty pants. Two wide polythene tubes pierced his left forearm and led to a device by his bedside the size and shape of a domestic washing machine. A mechanical ventilator stood idly by, no doubt to be reconnected as soon as the respiratory person had finished his healing work.

The old gentleman by the window looked serenely on. He was fat, pink and well-dressed in the Southern manner of pale linen suit, dark string tie and elaborate gleaming shoes. After the first flicker of acknowledgement his face was blank and on a closer look his eyes had the red, dead sheen of a hardened drinker's. Some patriarch of the Claypole tribe, Campbell thought, come to see young Goober off.

The respiratory man showed no sign of finishing and until

he did there was no question of psychiatric or any other intervention. Campbell and Nance stood for a moment, with Nance smiling ingratiatingly at the old man, presumably just out of habit. The TV preacher flapped above and Mr Claypole coughed and heaved sporadically. Nance moved over towards the window.

'Dr Alzheimer, sir.'

The old man shook his jowls as though suddenly wakened. 'Son?'

'Dr Alzheimer, sir, I'd like for you to meet Dr Campbell. He's noo, sir, from Scotland. Dr Campbell is on Dr Mikoyan's team.'

'Dr Mikoyan's team, huh?'

Nance smiled. 'Dr Mikoyan, of the Thanatology Center, as you know, sir . . . Dr Mikoyan asked me to give you his special regards, Dr Alzheimer.'

'Dr Mikoyan, huh?'

'Yessir, Dr Stef Mikoyan.'

'Stef, huh?' The old man shook his head. 'Why didn't ya say Stef, son? Ole Stef, huh . . . ? How's he doin'?'

'Well, his Program's doin' real well, sir . . . Into Phase Two, as I'm sure you know, Dr Alzheimer. In fact Mr Claypole here's benefiting from the noo LEAPERS reimbursement plan.'

'Oh . . . Reimbursement? The LEAPERS plan, huh? Sure . . . Sure . . . An' how's ole Stef?'

'He's real happy the plan's helpful to you an' your patients, Dr Alzheimer, sir.'

The old man thought about that then said, 'That's real nice of him . . . Ole . . . Ole Stef . . . An' where you fum, son, huh? England?'

Campbell smiled.

'Son . . . Ah ain't bin there, but I know you got problems over there, huh?'

Campbell agreed there were problems in England and then asked the old man a polite and not too difficult question about his patient. 'Have you been looking after Mr Claypole long?'

'Son, I've known young Catchpole maybe sixty years. I

guess I may've even bin the first to slap his bottom . . . Cain't exactly recall. . . . There were a whole lotta them Catchpoles. Did I say Claypoles? Anyhow, there wuz a whole lotta them. . . . Son, if the Lord spares me I'll be eighty sooner'n I like to think . . . so I guess I've gotten to know a bit about . . . about . . . uh, medicine. An' over there in England you gotta whole lotta problems . . .'

The old man clasped his hands over his stick again and looked vacantly to his front. The respiratory technician finished the tracheal toilet, reconnected various tubes and prepared to go. On the way out he patted his mechanical ventilator affectionately, waved to the three physicians and said, 'Have a good day.' It occurred to Campbell that at no time had he addressed Mr Claypole.

Nance coughed in a prefatory way and went to the bed-side. Campbell followed and felt Nance's elbow nudging his own. His attention was being drawn to the patient's chest, where, festooned with EKG leads, was the beginnings of a modest bust, of a sort fairly common in men taking oestrogens for prostate cancer. To make the point absolutely clear Nance mouthed the word 'boobs' to Campbell then turned with a winsome smile to the patient.

'Well, Goober, a whole lot's happened to you since we last saw you at the Group, huh?'

Mr Claypole had a large green plastic tube in his mouth and throat which prevented him talking and even limited his range of facial expressions. As far as could be guessed from his eyes his strongest emotion was one of sheer terror. He struggled against his bonds, perhaps trying to point out to the psychiatrist why he could not talk.

'Everything's goin' just fine, Goober . . . I just dropped by to tell you that, an' I'm real pleased to see Dr Alzheimer's dropped by too. An' I believe you've met Dr Campbell . . . He's from England.'

Mr Claypole stared up in uncomprehending anguish, sweat breaking from his brow.

'An' the boys in the Group said to say hello, Goober. You sure helped 'em along with all that stuff you said last time you came up. A lot of them spoke up an' said how much they'd appreciated it . . . An' I think Dr Campbell here wants a word with you too.'

Campbell had not thought so, but moved nearer Mr Claypole and took his hand and said, 'I'm sorry to hear you've been having all this trouble.' Mr Claypole rolled his eyes then nodded his head. His hand was warm and pouring sweat. It clutched desperately at Campbell's.

The door opened and a tall fair-haired man came in. He wore operating room whites and a badge which read, 'Ed Rickard MD Division of Neurosurgery'.

'Hi there, Dr Alzheimer . . . You doin' O.K., sir? Bob? An' I don't believe I've met . . .'

Nance introduced Campbell and again waved the Mikoyan flag, in a way which made Campbell feel it was time he had another chat with Stump about developments in the leadership of the LEAPERS Program.

'Glad to meet you, Dave . . . Bob, you know we're involved, I guess. You seen the SAR? No? Well, we're involved. We got on to something in the work up. A routine CAT scan showed a solitary anterior lesion. Should do well with a resection.'

'In his spine?' Nance sounded puzzled.

The neurosurgeon guffawed. 'Hell, no . . . That's just a malignant collapse. Nothin' we'd do about that 'cept get the radio-oncologists in an' fry it. No, he's got a *cerebral* secondary, but solitary and real frontal. Non-dominant, a bit of brain this guy'll never miss.'

Dr Alzheimer had lost interest again and was gazing at the respirator. Nance seemed if anything pleased by the neurosurgical interest now being shown in the case. Campbell was somewhat surprised but hoped, for the sake of politeness, that it did not show.

'Is it set up?' Nance asked.

'Not yet,' said Rickard. 'But I was hoping to find the SAR here to talk about all this . . .' He waved in the direction of the ventilator and the dialysis machine '. . . sounded like he's comin' up for extubation an' his kidneys might be better'n we thought, so he could go for months. . . . So, who needs a brain tumour?' He laughed and Dr Alzheimer looked round to see where the noise was coming from. 'Right, Dr Alzheimer, sir?' Dr Alzheimer nodded.

'Ed,' said Nance. His brow was furrowed by a sensitive portrayal of Concern. 'Ed . . . Just run that by me again, huh? You found a solitary met in his brain, right?'

'Right.'

'In his right frontal lobe, right?'

'Right.'

'An' you're gonna take it out, right?'

'Right.'

Nance paused. 'Ed . . . That's a *lobotomy*.'

'Right.'

'Ed, this man is in therapy, an' he's doin' real good. His MILES scores have been twenties right through. He's in the middle of a wonderful Mature Acceptance an' he's helpin' a whole buncha folks. . . . An' you're planning a *lobotomy*?'

'Bob, as far as we're concerned he's got a brain tumour so he gets it out.'

'But a lobotomy . . . Ed . . .'

'It's the least that'll do him any good . . . He'll be O.K. I mean, he could go weeks if we don't, maybe years if we do.'

'Ed, I know where you're comin' from. Don't think I don't unnerstan, but it's a real complex issue . . . An', gee, a lobotomy . . .'

'C'mon, Bob, we gotta decide. A live patient or a dead guy who had therapy. An' Dr Alzheimer . . . Dr Alzheimer, sir? Dr Alzheimer says go ahead.'

'Uh?'

'See?' Dr Rickard smiled generously. Nance shrugged and smiled his decent-guy smile then turned to Campbell. 'See, Dave, Life Ending is full of real delicate issues.'

Campbell thought about that, and about another delicate issue which appeared to have escaped the attention of his colleagues. Although Mr Claypole could not speak there was no reason to suppose he could not hear and understand everything that was being said in the room. He looked not simply troubled but unwell.

The door opened again and a fat man with a moustache

came in. To no one in particular he said, 'Rodriguez. Nephrology . . . Y'all doin' O.K.?' then set to work on the larger of the two bedside machines. Rickard, momentarily distracted, returned to saying something fierce about what would happen to the S A R if he did not get his ass up here real soon.

He was interrupted again, this time by a high-pitched buzz. At work on his machine, Dr Rodriguez pressed various buttons but the noise went on. He then checked the lines running from his machine to the patient. The noise, an insistent, rasping hum no doubt devised not to be ignored, continued. Dr Rodriguez then checked the patient.

'Hey, you guys . . . This guy's real sick . . . In fact . . . Hey. Well whaddabout that. I guess he's coded.'

'Coded?' said Nance.

'Coded?' said Rickard. 'Where's that jackass of an S A R?'

'Well,' said Nance, 'let's just call a code. Is that O.K. with you guys? Huh? Everybody comfortable with that? I guess we just use this red phone . . . Hello . . . Hello? Pardon me . . . Yes . . . I think we have . . . Well, he looks real . . . Yes, I guess it's a code situation. Huh? Oh. Somewhere on nine, I guess. Hey, Dave? Oh, pardon me. You're right . . . The number's right here on the phone. Thank you . . . It's nine one nine . . . Yes. Thank you, ma'am . . .'

The noise was coming not from the renal dialysis machine but from the cardiac monitor, and across its display screen tracked a frantically dancing green line. Mr Claypole was in ventricular fibrillation, and if the E K G was bad, the patient was worse. He was breathing, but only because he was on a mechanical ventilator. Everything else about him looked dead. He was waxy pale and lustrous with agonal sweat. His limbs lay slack and he stared lifelessly at a point somewhere above the T V preacher.

The door burst open and a large fit-looking man in green pyjamas sprang into the room rather like Superman emerging from his telephone booth. He was smiling and confident, and with one hand lifted the limp torso from the bed and with the other slid under it a plain white board marked 'Code 5' which had been slotted discreetly beside the cardiac monitor.

161

Then he sprang into a kneeling position on the edge of the bed and stooped over the patient's chest.

'Hi there, Dr Alzheimer. You doin' O.K.?'

It seemed an odd time for social chit-chat but no one could have suggested the man's efficiency was suffering. He compressed Mr Claypole's chest as though to do so were a simple gymnasium exercise and smiled round the room as he did so. Behind him lesser members of the code squad changed the IV infusion and unshipped a formidable collection of vials and syringes from red plastic boxes. By the door a tough-looking blonde drew a pair of metal paddles from a shiny red trolley while another turned knobs and checked dials.

'O.K., Fritz.'

'Check.'

The lead man got up and stood back and the first blonde leaned forward and placed her paddles, one on the front, one on the left side of Mr Claypole's chest.

'Two hundred.'

'Two hundred.'

Mr Claypole heaved like a landed fish, arching from his bed then falling back. He looked as dead as ever. There was a silence as three members of the team perused the monitor screen. The stench of recent defecation filled the room.

'Dissociation, huh?'

'So pace. Go subclavian.'

'Check.'

The lead man resumed his simple gymnastics. The blonde unsheathed a pacing catheter and crouched over a vein in Mr Claypole's neck. A third stabbed at his groin for arterial blood and a fourth, whistling 'Dixie', added the contents of a large brown vial to the infusion. They talked very little and worked quickly in a display of teamwork more impressive in its technique than in its results. Mr Claypole remained dead.

The code squad and its equipment blockaded the only door. Along with the neurosurgeon, the nephrologist, the psychiatrist and Dr Alzheimer, Campbell was trapped in the room almost as surely as was Mr Claypole. He watched the proceedings with interest but without enthusiasm.

On the monitor a slow regular rhythm of slurred complexes progressed across the screen in the EKG equivalent of a funeral march. On the TV screen opposite the preacher fell to prayer, his flamboyant figure for the moment hunched and humble as the credits rolled before him. The end was nigh.

Pacing did no good. The slow slurred complexes speeded up a little but diminished in amplitude, and only the last rite of all remained. The blonde who had pierced Mr Claypole's neck drew up the contents of a vial and, with a four-inch needle, stabbed his chest and emptied the syringe straight into his heart. On the monitor there was a last jumbled flutter. The team straightened up and stood watching as the green trace flattened for all time.

'Asystole, twelve oh two,' said the blonde with the syringe. The rest shrugged and began to clear up. A fat and wheezing chaplain tiptoed in, surveyed the wreckage, nodded, smiled gravely in the direction of Dr Alzheimer, and left. In the corridor someone whistled and footsteps approached then the door swung open again. A small oriental stood blinking at the dozen or so people gathered where he might have expected one or two. Rickard sprang to life and elbowed his way over to the newcomer. Nance nudged Campbell. 'I guess that's the SAR . . . Dave, maybe we should go now. I don't know about you, but . . .' He sounded as if he might be about to faint so Campbell steered him through the crowd and towards the door. As they passed Rickard was starting on the SAR.

In the corridor Nance brightened. 'I think I'll try to remember ole Goober the way he was in the Group,' he said. 'Like, all that stuff just now . . . Well, I guess the important thing is we covered all the bases. And we were with him to the end. I guess he appreciated that.'

'Did he have a family?' Campbell asked.

'Goober?' Nance laughed. 'A family? Hell, like Dr Alzheimer said, "There were a whole lotta thaim Claypoles." Maybe five brothers an' I think three sisters, maybe four. Most of 'em aroun' town here.'

'Did he have a wife?'

'Lovely lady, Miz Claypole . . . An' a whole nice buncha kids, mainly in their twenties now, I guess.'

'Did they know?'

Nance shrugged. 'How would I know? I s'pose maybe some of 'em knew he was in here, certainly his wife. An' maybe Dr Alzheimer told them it was serious.'

That seemed unlikely. Campbell asked Nance a general question about the old physician.

'Typical old-fashioned town doc, Dave. You know the kind. New Caddy every year, packs a gun an' real big in the masons.'

This dementing and possibly drunken old man was presumably Dr Mikoyan's esteemed colleague: not, Campbell thought, the sort of chap one liked to think of driving a large fast car, or carrying a handgun, though he was probably quite safe doing funny handshakes with one of his trouser legs rolled up, or whatever it was that masons were supposed to do.

'Yes,' Nance mused. 'Ole Joe Alzheimer's a real influential guy here in town . . . Let's walk down the stairs, Dave. Be nice to get some fresh air after all that.'

They went through swing doors on to a stairway encased in glass and clinging to the outside of the building. Below them the MacHardy Chapel, a gleaming white stone toy, sat at the centre of the campus. Minute among the trees and lawns and stately mock-Gothic buildings, students strolled and sprawled. Beyond the campus the roofs of Crimond were dotted among dark green treetops and beyond that a wooded landscape receded to a blue misty horizon. Campbell remembered Nance's phrase about Mr Claypole having had a 'life in timber'.

At the foot of the stairs they met Dr Alzheimer again, puffing and limping. He was lost and looking for a way out of the hospital. They helped him. At first he did not appear to recognize them then, as they were passing the police post on the ground floor concourse, he levelled his cane accusingly at Campbell. 'You the physician from England, huh?' Campbell said he was. The old man stopped and looked at him. 'Never bin there mahself, but I hear you gotta whole lotta problems.'

Outside, Nance did a touching little Goodbye routine and

went home for lunch. Campbell had been vaguely expecting to lunch with Don Kravitz, but he was not around. As resident on the Life Ending rotation he should have been with Campbell all morning, but perhaps his counsellor, or even his masseuse, had had prior claims. Campbell lunched alone in the basement of MacHardy East, watching obese, carnivorous hospital employees and wishing he had gone to Mother Nature's instead.

At around two he drove across to the Department of Family Practice. An old black man in a straw hat was cutting the grass outside one of the frame houses. Campbell stopped and chatted with him. He had been the gardener and odd-job man since the start, he said, and seemed quietly proud of his efforts. Each of the three houses had its own little garden, with a lawn and flower beds, neat on the wide, tree-lined street. Campbell decided to try to spend more time over here, and less at LEAC and MacHardy East, if future developments in the LEAPERS Program gave him any opportunity to do so.

In the front office, Miz Jo, the Director's secretary, was sitting at her desk. She looked upset. 'Dr Campbell, I've been tryin' to get a hold of you . . . Have you heard about Dr Kravitz?'

Campbell said he hadn't.

'It was just awful . . .' She sniffed and reached for a handkerchief.' Dr Campbell, Dr Kravitz is dead . . . Some crazy guy shot him this morning. In the ER, you know, the emergency room, up at Buchananville. Oh, Dr Campbell, he was such a nice man . . .' By now she was in helpless floods of tears. 'I'm sorry, Dr Campbell, bein' like this, but he was jus' such a nice man, an' nobody ever died on the Program before . . . It's just so awful . . . I cain't help cryin' like this . . . I'm sorry . . . An' the saddest part is Dr Kidd *tole* him he shouldn't be moonlightin' up there, an' he said he wouldn't no more, but they said they were real stuck, jus' this once, an' could he come up, an' he went . . . An' Dr Kidd's real upset, an it's just so . . .'

Campbell sat down. Don Kravitz, who had been reading things about pain control in the dying for a tutorial with him

165

in the cool, comfortable, untidy little Family Practice library at two-thirty, was dead. As dead as Mr Claypole. As dead as Dr Pulver and the girl who couldn't face going to Montana. 'That's awful,' he said. Miz Jo sighed and wept afresh, dabbing her eyes with a sodden tissue.

'Some crazy mean guy,' she sobbed, 'shot our Dr Kravitz in the head . . . An' he's dead . . . He's dead.' She pronounced it 'day-eed'.

Campbell spent part of the afternoon on his own in the library then went off early and drove out into the country. By four the heat of the day was over. He parked his car and walked on the outskirts of a little town called Pittsville. Old black people drowsed on their porches and though dozing dogs woke as he passed they barked only half-heartedly. Houses gave way to fields and he found himself wandering along a country road where mockingbirds sang and blue jays dipped and darted from tree to tree. It was all very peaceful, apart from those silent reminders of another side of Southern country life, the bullet-holes patterning every road sign and telephone pole.

The road crossed another then curved down into a wood. Campbell followed it past an overgrown orchard then through the wood, arriving eventually at a lake. There was a boathouse and a floating pier, alongside which lay a dozen green rowing boats.

On the porch of the boathouse a deaf, red-faced man laboriously deciphered what Campbell was trying to say, then asked him where he came from and told him he'd been there himself in the war, and the whisky was real good. For two dollars Campbell got a pair of oars, a life-jacket and a little green boat for the rest of the day. He struck out from the pier, explored a long reach of tree-lined water, observed and was observed by a family of turtles, glimpsed a possible osprey and just lay for a while in the boat, drifting under a slow-turning sky, thinking about a number of things.

An hour later he was back at the landing stage, with blistered palms and a variety of not unpleasant aches around the shoulders. He sat for a while with the deaf boat-hirer and a man who had been fishing then, as he left, asked about the lake and the times it was open. The deaf man told him and said, 'Next time bring yore fishin' pole, an' some whisky maybe.'

By ten Amy had not rung, and Campbell wondered if she had forgotten, or even changed her mind about her proposed visit. At ten past ten there was a wrong number. At ten-fifteen she called.

'Hello . . . David?'

'Hello?'

'How are you?'

'All right.'

'I'm sorry I'm a little late in calling.'

'That's O.K.'

'Things are kinda complicated at home . . . I'm at home . . . Crimond home. It's funny, they kept my room the way it was, with my swim team pictures, my pom-poms, my Beatles posters, all that stuff. Sometimes it makes me feel around fifteen.'

That was unpromising. 'That sounds nice.'

'David, are you kinda down . . . ? Is it because I didn't call you?'

'Oh, no.'

'Have you had a bad day?'

'Sort of, at work. Somebody died.'

'Well, I guess maybe a Thanatology Program could get you down like that. What kind of patient?'

'A patient died, and . . .'

'A sad one? Young, maybe?'

'Mid fifties, maybe sixty.'

'Sudden?'

'Sort of. He had a big MI, but he was intubated, so he couldn't even say he was in pain.'

'How awful.'

'And somebody else died. A doctor.'

'A physician?'

'Yes.'

'Who, David? Who?'

167

'Don. You know, Don Kravitz, who was down there with you . . .'

'Don died?'

'Well, he was killed.'

'A wreck?'

'A what?'

'Like, was it an automobile accident?'

'No. He was working in an ER somewhere, and somebody shot him.'

'Oh, David, that's horrible . . . Did he just die straight away?'

'I really don't know.'

'Where was he shot?'

'In the head, Miz Jo said.'

'David, that's just horrible . . . An' he was workin' with you, wasn't he? In the Life Ending rotation?'

'We were supposed to be having a tutorial this afternoon.'

'Oh David. How awful for you . . . Is it still O.K. to come round?'

'Yes.'

'Maybe half an hour.'

'That'd be fine.'

'David, I'm real sorry I was late calling you. See you soon.'

'See you soon.'

'Thank you, Dr Campbell, uh, David, for coming here at such short notice. I appreciate you got a tight schedule over there, especially in the mornings, but I did feel it was important that you don't get to feel out of touch with us over here in Primary Care. I thought it was probably time we had a talk.'

'Thank you, sir.'

'From everything I hear, your contribution over there's esteemed very highly . . . It's not every physician can work in, uh, a mixed team like they got over there. Maybe you British make better team players than us, ah, Americans . . .' Dr Drucker had taken off his glasses and was polishing them on the hem of his white coat. 'Not that I'm criticizin' 'em . . . It's just a different tradition.'

It seemed highly unlikely that Campbell had been summoned to be told that. He sipped his coffee and waited. Dr Drucker put on his glasses again and said, 'That was a sad business about young Don Kravitz . . .' Campbell agreed. There was another pause.

'We know these things happen, but when one of our own young physicians . . .' Dr Drucker was not simply expressing formal regrets. His face was pale and his voice unsteady. He looked at Campbell across the desk. 'Again, a different way o' doin' things. A great loss to our residency program. I know he had problems, but he seemed to be gettin' over 'em and settlin' down. Did you know him well?'

Campbell wondered what version of Kravitz's 'problems' had reached Dr Drucker, and via whom. 'I spent quite a lot of time with him. He was on the rotation with me and he was, well, kind, and very helpful with all sorts of things, at work and outside.'

'We'll all miss him.'

'Yes.'

'Dr Campbell, I thought we might, uh, discuss the way things are goin' over at the Life Ending Americans Clinic . . . How things are . . . What you see yourself doing . . . How things might develop . . .'

'Develop, sir?'

'Yes . . . So to speak.'

'Oh.'

'You'll recall there were certain . . . interim arrangements. A few meetings we had, with various people there.'

'Yes,' said Campbell, still puzzled.

'Well, things are still sort of, uh, interim.'

'Oh.'

'Maybe less so, though.'

Campbell nodded.

'But not a whole lot less so.' Dr Drucker corrected himself very quickly. 'Still basically interim . . . Dr Campbell, the job you're doing over there is greatly appreciated . . .'

There was a pause. Campbell realized he was being told about things, not asked, and wondered now only how much he was going to be told. 'Thank you, Dr Drucker.'

'So, for the moment at least, while the interim arrangements persist, it'd be much appreciated if you could maintain your present commitment, uh, meantime . . . With of course the possibility, all things being equal and all parties agreeing, of some upward revision of your time commitment at some future date.'

'Upward?'

'Only if all parties, obviously including you, David, agree.'

'I see.'

'So what do you think?'

Campbell looked round the office then across at Dr Drucker. The head of Primary Care was a mild and rational man, discreetly uneasy about some of the more awful things around, and perhaps trying in his quiet, possibly ineffective way to improve them. Campbell thought about what he was asking and how he would feel about it if he were discussing it, say, with Dr Mikoyan rather than Dr Drucker. That made a difference. 'How about . . . downward, Dr Drucker?'

'I'm sorry?'

'Dr Drucker . . . Would it be possible to look again at my commitments, sir . . . ? I'm thinking mainly of the Family Practice end of things, which is what I came for . . . But I've been spending more and more . . .'

Dr Drucker shook his head. 'I'm sorry, David. We have a solemn obligation to maintain you at fifty percent commitment to LEAC. An' I really don't see any way out of that. Fact is, it's not negotiable.'

'Oh.'

'An' although I shouldn't be talking too much about things that are still under discussion elsewhere, I'd say that . . . well, the way things are goin', they're gonna need you over there at LEAC more rather than less.'

'I see . . . So the psychiatrists . . . ?'

'So you'll do it?'

Campbell sought a form of words free of any misleading taint of enthusiasm. 'If it's a commitment.'

'It's a commitment, David, a Divisional commitment, and I'm glad you see it that way . . . A substantial funding issue

170

is involved. Your cooperation will be greatly appreciated.'
Dr Drucker smiled and got up. Campbell went back to his
office at the Life Ending Americans Clinic and rang Stump.

'Sneed's problems . . . ?' Stump speared three olives at once
and slid the dish along the bar to Campbell. 'Sneed's problems are mainly to do with power and sex.' He took a long
swig of his beer and ate the olives. 'An', hell, whose aren't, if
you forget about money, which is boring anyway. Yup,
power 'n' sex, probably in that order, and getting more so.'
   Campbell drank his beer in silence, hoping Stump would
stick to the power aspects of the case, or at least prove not to
know sufficient about the rest to embarrass him.
   'Sneed's done real well,' Stump went on, 'for a fat kid from
nowhere in a cornfield. Her CV's unbelievable, a stack of
publications that'd make you lose track of the fact that basically she's a cow-college speech pathology graduate in search
of power, so she kicks off as Nebraska's cow-college speech
pathology graduate of the year the year she graduates.
Sixty-five, I guess. Then, zap, she's into research. Zap,
computer studies. Zap, communication. Zap, a doctorate in
some bullshit communication stuff. An' last year it turns out
that the Federal flavour of the month in Health Care is Life
Ending, so, zap, Life Ending Communication. So watch
out, everybody . . . Basically, she's into power.'
   'What's her future?'
   'Where the power is. So I guess administration. She could
start slidin' sideways anytime now . . . An' the sex thing,
that's more interestin' than you'd think.'
   Campbell reached for the olives again. 'Oh?'
   'Nobody's real sure, an' maybe there's more to this than
meets the eye, but that tail-crazy Edinburgh bastard last
year . . .'
   'Gus?'
   'Yeah, Gus . . . Well, maybe he did, maybe he didn't. No
way o' tellin' with Gus, but he could have. Hell, *you* could
have, you know the way she is . . . An' that's just the men.'
   'Really?'

171

'Yup . . . Well, you hear stories. You could say the breadth of her interests was . . . interesting.'

'Hm.' Campbell signalled for the bartender.

'But she'd never let the sex thing get in the way of the power thing. She's got it worked out . . . Enough intelligence to get by, plenty of energy an' pizzazz an' God alone knows how much ambition . . . You know she used to share a house with Amy?'

'She mentioned that.'

'After Amy an' Melvin separated and Melvin killed himself.'

'What?'

'Melvin, the shrink the lovely Miss Totenberg used to be married to. You didn't know that? I kinda thought . . .'

'I knew she had been married. I thought he just left her, with her jazz seventy-eights.'

'An' then he killed himself. Real soon.'

'Oh.'

'Blew his brains out. Messy, kinda redneck thing to do, 'specially for a shrink from the Northeast. But that's what he did.'

The bartender brought two more bottles of Heineken.

'Depressive?' Campbell asked.

'What?'

'The man who shot himself. Amy's ex-husband.'

'I guess so. Oddball anyway . . . Dr Totenberg's really had quite a hard life, bein' Teddy's daughter at MacHardy, then all that stuff. She didn't tell you?'

'I didn't know about that,' said Campbell. 'She seems fine now, though.'

Stump and Campbell were drinking at Leland's, an establishment near the center of Crimond patronized by MacHardy faculty and that fraction of the Southern town aspiring to the condition of hygienic bohemianism. Amid varnished pine and coach lamps, a bar staff said to be all graduate and mainly post-doctoral served foreign beer in clean glasses to the sound of muzak by J. S. Bach.

'Interesting lady, Miss Totenberg,' Stump said. Campbell, who felt he had heard enough to be going on with, agreed.

Three quarters of an hour and two or three beers later they had finished the olives. They crossed the street to a restaurant which, Stump thought, also stocked Heineken. They had a beer then ordered dinner. Campbell, who had arranged to meet Stump mainly in order to find out what was happening in the upper reaches of LEAPERS, eventually raised the topic.

'Administrators don't get told much,' Stump confided, 'but sometimes they hear li'l bits an' get to workin' things out for themselves. What kinda things had you in mind? The upcoming evaluation crisis in TC 206?'

'Only partly.'

'Current dilemmas in rural Life Ending?'

Càmpbell said nothing and drank his beer.

'What price nursing home Facilities for Life Ending Americans, now we're going broke? What to do now Mikoyan sees his chance, and even the terminal rodents are quitting?'

'More that sort of thing.'

'Well, it looked like it was going to be an interesting contest,' said Stump. 'I'm not so sure now.'

'Oh?'

'You can't have a jumping frog contest if one of the frogs won't jump . . . I don't often feel sorry for Teddy and his gang, but it looks like the contest's off because the internists brought along a frog that doesn't wanna jump now.'

'Oh.'

'Schlepp pulled out.'

'Did he?'

'What actually happened was, he couldn't be pushed in any more.'

'Oh?'

'A lot of the big guys in medicine leaned on him. "Abey," they said, "if you do this for us we'll treat you like a human being . . . Think of it, Abey," they said. "I'm thinkin'," said Abey. "Don't take too long," they said. "I'm thinkin' as fast as I can," he said.'

'What about the shrinks?'

'That's what the shrinks said. All of 'em. Mikoyan and his

li'l friend Nance, of course. An' Bottger, who said it loudest and to the most people.'

'The Dean?'

'I guess so. And to Phil. But mostly to the guys up in DC. In ALEA.'

'ALEA?'

'The Agency. For Life Ending Americans. Bottger knows people everywhere. Puts up the story that the internists wanna screw up everything good ole Cal worked for. Waved his bones around a good bit, and that sorta stuff works. Anyway, the word is Washington bought it. Phone calls were made. But, hell, I'm just a simple ole administrator . . .'

'So what's happening?'

'Nothing you'd notice. Jus' one or two things that'd make you think . . .'

'Think what?'

'That good ole Stef might be around for a while.'

'And Schlepp?'

'Dallas.'

'Dallas?'

'A full professor died there. And Dr Schlepp *likes* dermatology.'

They ordered wine: a bottle of red because Stump was having a steak and a bottle of white because Campbell wasn't. They talked of things other than the Program's leadership. Certain events of the last few days lingered in Campbell's mind. He told Stump about Mr Claypole.

'Yup, sounds like we did it again. A full court press with no expense spared. We got all the right people, and paid 'em plenty, an' still the customer ain't happy. Our Program ensures that the individual Life Ender has full access to the best of modern American medicine, delivered in the traditional free enterprise way, an' still the folks complain . . . Ole Mac's prices, an' a Federal program going broke? An' nobody's pleased?'

'Did it? Go broke? With Mr Claypole?'

'Hell, no. He got in early.'

'But if he hadn't . . . How much would all that have cost? Thousands?'

'Tens of thousands anyway. Hell, a code costs maybe a thousand.'

Campbell thought of the grinning man doing gymnastics on Mr Claypole's chest. 'Win or lose?'

'Win or lose.'

'Seems a lot.'

'It is a lot . . . For cracking ribs on a corpse.'

'The whole thing . . . seemed rather a lot.'

'Money?'

'Yes . . . Effort as well . . . For the quality of life.'

Stump laughed then puffed out his chest and bared his teeth in the manner of his late leader. 'Here at the Center . . . we cannot guarantee that the Federally funded and world-beating LEAPERS Phase Two Program will make your last hours on earth the most comfortable. But sure as hell they'll be your most expensive . . . That's what we call strategy.'

Campbell laughed and a silver-haired couple at the next table sent for their check and prepared to leave. Stump had been morose for most of the evening but looked now as if he might be beginning to enjoy himself. He swigged his wine as if it were beer. 'You know how I got into Health Care?' Campbell filled up his glass and sat back.

'Maybe ten years ago, hell, comin' up for eleven, I was sittin' in a real mean F-4 lookin' for some temples. The guys in the temples . . . I guess I should say the guys we thought were in the temples . . . were reckoned at that time to be a threat to the American way of life, at least in South East Asia. We had smart bombs. Like, the war was kinda dumb, but some of the bombs were smart, an' as soon as we'd found these li'l temples an' pacified 'em we could go straight back to base for a Coke and a steak . . . I shoulda explained, at that time I was a real simple American boy. Found 'em, flattened 'em, but on the way back to my steak I thought, jeeze, maybe there's more to life than creamin' little guys in temples with bombs you can't miss with. The hell with this, I thought. I wanna *help* people.

'It was nice an' sunny, flyin' home to Nang. Fuzzy fresh green jungle an' pretty mountains off west, a real nice after-noon in Viet Nam. Then it came to me. Health Care, I thought, get outa this and into Health Care. So I finished my tour, quit the service, went back to school an' did Health Administration. Wanna help people? Into Health Care. Easy. Why should I waste my life flattening little guys with high technology?' He paused. 'Like I said, I was just a simple American boy at the time.'

At the next table the old couple shuffled to their feet and made for the door. A waiter followed anxiously. The restaurant was now almost empty. Stump warmed to his theme.

'Some guys in Health Administration are in it because deep down they wanted to be the real thing, the sharp-eyed, steely-jawed whitecoat. An' some's in it because they hate 'em. Not me, either way. Bein' a physician just never came up, same as I never wanted to be a grunt. But I never *minded* grunts. Like a war, some guys fight it, some guys administrate it. I didn't want blood on my hands but I wanted to make it good for the guys who did. Mind the machine, do the books, sort out the hassles, write the summaries. In a war this size, I reckoned, they're gonna need people who like doin' that.

'So soon I'm learnin' the other war. We got objectives, we got resources. We got heroes and freeloaders, guys who love it an' guys who just do it. We got strokes an' hassles and a whole buncha other things I seen before. An' like before, we got wonderful technology an' a few billion dollars to play with. I tell you, the Health Care war is a big war.

'I graduate an' get a job. A coupla years at Podunk County Memorial an' I get time to think. That scares me, so I get this job with Cal, three years ago. Big deal Center, an' MacHardy's a place people talk about. But I get to startin' to think again. Whose war is this? Who's runnin' it? An' who for? An' how the hell did that get to happen . . . ? An' who's payin' anyway, an' did anyone ask them? An' like the other war, what about the technology? Like I seen before, has it got so big you just can't ask if maybe it's the wrong stuff?

'You know about Arclight? Arclight was SAC's dream plan for Nam. Guys in B-52s start in Guam, fly two thousand miles, flatten fifteen square miles of Nam an' fly back on home to Guam. You know MacHardy East?

MacHardy East has got just about as much to do with Health Care problems in West Carolina as a squadron of B-52s in Guam's got to do with the post-colonial politics of South East Asia. Costs as much, does as little of what you want. Like the kids in Podunk County didn't need more pediatricians or a noo CAT scanner at Memorial. They needed food, clothing, housing an' education. An' this guy Claypole didn't need Nance or a brain surgeon or those other guys you just said in MacHardy East. But that's what he got because that's what *we* got. We got B-52s an' MacHardy East, so that's the kind of war it's gonna be. See?'

Campbell was drunk enough to find Stump's analogy totally illuminating, though he had only sketchy ideas about the war in Viet Nam. 'I think I see what you mean.'

'But that's the American solution. There is no problem on earth that free enterprise technology and the almighty dollar can't between them solve. Except two. Viet Nam and Health Care Delivery.' He hiccoughed. 'Health Care,' he announced to the empty restaurant, 'is our domestic Viet Nam . . . It costs the earth and nobody's happy. It's run by crazy generals that'll believe anythin' with figures in, guys on a glassy-eyed technology trip who forgot the smell of shit. It's the way it is because basically it's out of control, but Uncle Sam an' the citizens keep on forkin' out because a mistake that big you just can't admit to. So you make it look good an' call some guys heroes, but for some other guys it's a nightmare you don't wake up from.'

Campbell thought about Mr Claypole's last hours. Stump looked round for the waiter and said, 'But you gotta admit our technology's wonderful.'

'Very impressive, as technology.'

'The thing I keep forgettin' is, the little guys on the bicycles won.'

They finished dinner, had a series of cups of coffee and made their way out into the night. It was warm and still. A crowd of black youths drifted by conversing in a language of their own. Campbell found his car parked just ahead of Stump's, and got in on the wrong side. Stump stood laughing as he got out and walked round. 'It ain't so much the side

you sit on that they bother about in this State . . . It's the
side you drive on. Take care, Dave.'

'Goodnight.'

'Goodnight.'

'So we got a forty-seven-year-old separated white male with a
hung transition from Bargaining an' a whole buncha
psychosexual stuff. Uh, an' he openly violates his diabetic
diet. So I guess he's a KR Two with a MILES of aroun'
seven. An' he jus' ain't even tryin', but Miz Love reckons I
should hang in there so's at least we can get to see what he
does with all this. But from the purely thanatologic
developmental point of view, he's a schmuck.'

'C'mon, Heidi, honey,' Miz Love spoke gently. 'We gotta
be more positive'n that. An' the whole point of the MILES
rating system is so's we don't have to guess. From all what
you say, Heidi, Mr Aycock comes to 'zackly an eight on the
MacHardy Index of Life Ending Satisfaction. It ain't much,
but it's Mr Aycock's an prob'ly he's doin' his best from a real
difficult place. MILES eight . . .' The student, a pale girl
with braces on her teeth, pouted. 'An' no guessin',' Miz Love
added with a winsome smile. 'Bob?'

Nance occupied the place at the centre of the powerful side
of the LEAC conference room table. His style was more
intimate than that of Dr Mikoyan. Throughout the case
presentation he had leaned forward and frowned like a TV
interviewer with a reputation for seriousness to maintain.
Now he smiled upon the pale student. 'Coupla questions,
Heidi . . . An' I'm sure you know the answer to both of 'em.
How does Hank Aycock *think* he's doin' . . . in his own
eyes? Huh?'

'Well,' said the girl. 'I never met a diabetic alcoholic
bankrupt car salesman whose wife just left an' who's dyin' of
a lung tumour before . . . So I cain't rightly tell, Dr Nance.
But . . .'

'I know Hank, from the Denial Counselling and Review
T-Group, an' insight's not one of his problems. Not for right
now anyway. Depression, Acceptance and all that stuff'll

come and maybe hurt him, but for right now we offer him the help we feel he needs, an' hope he takes it. More'n anybody I hope he progresses, but for now he is the way he is. An' the second question is, does he have any financial problems?'

'He's bankrupt again.'

'I meant with payin' us, Heidi, payin' all his doctors' bills. An' the answer's no. So with a guy like this we got limited goals, an' you gotta hang in there, like Miz Love says. Hank Aycock could still teach us a whole lot about his way of handling things.'

Nance lowered his voice and conversed with Miz Love. Campbell looked round the trainees. The youth on his right, to judge from his notes, was barely literate. Humbert, the black student with mirror glasses, was perhaps asleep. A thin redhead was entirely engrossed in pushing back the cuticle on her thumb, inspecting it so closely she squinted.

To judge from his behaviour at the Teaching Conference and before, Nance was somehow in the ascendant. He had been skipping round the Clinic with a smile and a word of encouragement for everyone, and had gradually infuriated Campbell with a series of little ploys designed to display successively Affability, Emergent Superiority and Being a Party to Important but Secret Information. Now after much grave muttering with Miz Love, he thanked the various contributors and drew proceedings to a close fully a quarter of an hour earlier than usual.

As Campbell left, he was summoned back by Miz Love because Dr Nance wanted a word with him.

'Dave, I know you gotta whole lotta issues to deal with right now, but I'd be real pleased if you could come along to my office for just a coupla minutes. We could take coffee in, if you'd like that. It's just there's a few things it'd be better if we could, you know, talk over . . . Is that O.K.? I mean, I know you gotta whole lotta things scheduled in for your clinic mornings, but when you know what it is we gotta discuss you'll appreciate why it was better we got together right now. Even though you're busy. Is that O.K. with you?'

He radiated a smile to Miz Love. 'Thanks, Patti . . . I'll be in my office for a few minutes . . . No calls, please . . .

Then I'll be over in conference with Dr Mikoyan. Definitely no calls, huh?'

Since Campbell had last been there, Nance's office had acquired some of the trappings of minor management. There was a four-decker system of wire trays only lightly garnished with letters and files, and a portentous leather-bound desk diary, open for that day but not particularly well filled. A brand new pocket dictaphone lay carelessly across it.

'Please take a seat, Dave . . . I don't know how you feel after these Teaching Conferences, but I'd rather do four hours of intensive personal therapy anytime . . . They just *drain* me . . . And now . . .' He sighed. '. . . administration. But it's gotta be done, even though frankly I hate it. Dave, you're probably wondering why I called you in here, when both of us have got just a stack of things to do and patients to see . . . Fact is, Dr Mikoyan asked me specially to get the two of us together so I could run some stuff by you about . . .' He leaned forward. '. . . the retreat. Oh, don't worry if it's somethin' you just heard about. Very few of us had anything at all on it before, well, say Friday. But Dr Mikoyan did want you to be, well, among the first to be . . . consulted, I guess.'

'Retreat?'

'For key faculty, major participants and senior staff. Only.'

'Oh.'

'So you're free for the second half of next week? Apart from LEAC commitments, of course.'

Campbell thought he was.

'Dr Mikoyan will be real pleased. You're key faculty, Dave. I'm sure you know that, and how much we appreciate it.'

'Here?'

Nance clutched his brow. 'Oh no! That's just not *possible*. No, it's gonna be up at Turkey Roost.'

'Turkey Roost?'

'Yeah, you know it? No? Well, the MacHardy family left one of their country properties to their University for the purposes of spiritual, cultural and academic recreation. So

we all go up there. It'll be three days, like, two nights there
and home on Friday. It's real pretty, Dave, you'll love it. A
gracious and stately old home, built maybe about nineteen-
thirty, and just a wonderful . . . a wonderful *experience*. Up
there away from all the pressures of Crimond and the Center.
It was Dr Mikoyan's idea, and Dr Sneed's real keen. Well,
really everybody is.'

'What's it for?'

'Like I said, spiritual, cultural and academic recreation.'

'No, the retreat.'

'That was Dr Mikoyan's idea mainly, with Dr Sneed,
who's real strong on brainstorming. The idea is we reshape
the Program.'

'Oh.'

'Dr Mikoyan thinks it real important that you come. In
fact you'll find a schedule in your box.'

'Thank you.'

Campbell got up to go. Nance walked round his desk.
'Dave, thanks for dropping by. I know you're real busy,
but with such a lot going on it's just *so* important we get to
talk.'

Back in his office, Campbell thought about what form an
attempt to 'reshape the Program' by means of 'brainstorming' might take, and tried to ring Stump. There was no reply
from his extension at the Thanatology Center, and before
Campbell had time to try anywhere else Ethelanne rang from
the front desk asking if he could see a patient. An elderly
white woman came in. She had a slow-growing scirrhous
carcinoma of the breast which appeared to be causing no
difficulties. She sat and talked at some length about her
husband's drinking habits then left after a quarter of an hour,
grateful and happy and apparently without noticing Campbell's hangover.

When she had gone he tried Stump's extension again, and
when there was no reply he tried his office over at the John
Sloop MacHardy Institute for Social Policy, where they had
once taken a mid-morning beer together. Again there was no
reply.

The next patient was an old black lady with end-stage

ischaemic heart disease. She was also an insulin dependent diabetic who had lost both legs and was blind. Despite her various misfortunes, or possibly because of them, she was simply and deeply religious. She had no quarrel with the inscrutable ways of her Maker, and explained to Campbell how life was a process of preparation for the hereafter, about which she talked with enthusiasm but not impatience. We should, she explained, expect a certain amount of hardship. 'Like gold, we all must pass through the refiner's fire, which makes us purer an' better, so then we can see the Lord face to face, an' look upon him, an' not be ashamed.'

Campbell listened politely and said very little. The lady asked him if his soul was troubled. There was a pause. She said she would pray for him, for the Lord to help him. Conversation moved to her angina, and how often she took her tablets. Later, as Campbell helped her turn her wheel-chair to go, she clasped his hand and said she would remember to pray for him, for the Lord to make him strong.

As there was no sign of the next patient, Campbell rang DeeAnn Plotkin, secretary to the late Dr Pulver and still in office at the Center, to find out if Stump was out of town, or working at home, as he said he sometimes did.

'Oh, Dr Campbell . . . You haven't heard?'

'What? Has something . . . ?'

'Dr Campbell, something terrible has happened . . . Last night, or maybe early this morning. Mr Stump was driving home from a meeting an' there was the most awful wreck . . . On sixty-five, by the intersection with two five one . . . They only identified him maybe two hours ago . . . It was apparently . . . real awful.'

'Where is he? I mean, is he . . . ?'

'I'm sorry, Dr Campbell, I shoulda said his *remains* gotten identified. Pore Mr Stump's dead . . . It's jus' terrible, an' so soon after pore Dr Pulver . . .'

That afternoon, as there was no tutorial with Kravitz, Campbell went once more to the lake near Pittsville and hired a boat. He rowed out heading for nowhere in particular and eventually found a sunny and deserted bay. He moored the boat and went ashore and walked around for a little, then sat on a rock thinking about Crimond, MacHardy, the Center and recent events there: in particular the deaths of the two people he knew best, apart of course from Amy.

After a while the silence of the bay was broken by two black youths who drifted past in a green hired boat, fishing and laughing. Soon after they had gone, the man Campbell had talked to the first time he had been at the lake appeared again, alone in a boat, working his way along the shore in the shade of the trees so slowly that the surface of the water was scarcely disturbed. He cast and waited and cast again, his line snaking out to the dark edge of the lake. He fished as though nothing else mattered until he reached the end of the shade, then rowed past Campbell, waving to him before disappearing beyond the next little headland.

Above the trees clouds gathered. Little clumps of white cumulus multiplied and rose higher, turning from white to grey and darkening the greater part of the western sky. With time to watch, Campbell did so, thinking sometimes about recent events and finding the free open-air symbol-show aspect of it not disagreeable, or at any rate not inappropriate. From being still and lifeless the air changed. A breeze stirred over the water, raising broad arcs of ripple that darted and faded. The clouds, still billowing upwards, reached the sun and the temperature dropped. Campbell's ordinary urban fatalism about weather gave way to a kind of observant interest, not unconnected with the chance of a soaking, and various schoolroom fragments concerning the mechanisms of afternoon thunderstorms reassembled in his mind.

He was, he thought, around a mile and a half from the boathouse: perhaps half an hour's rowing in still water. Another less certain calculation, about how long it might be before the rain started, also exercised his mind, as above the treetops to the west the cloud base assumed a solid lead grey. The breeze cooled and stiffened and the green boat began to nudge against the rocks with hollow, oil-drum noises. Pine trees began to rustle.

An outboard motor buzzed in the distance and then drew

closer. The two blacks passed again, heading back for the boathouse. Campbell got up, unhitched his boat, stepped in and pushed off with one oar until the water was deep enough for rowing. He swung round, heading back in the direction of the landing stage, and settled into the rhythm, pulling at a rate he could hope to keep up and which still might save him from a drenching.

Towards the middle of the lake the waves were larger. Heading into them, the light aluminium boat gave an impression of speed not confirmed by progress past fixed objects on shore. Campbell revised his calculations and, looking round to check his heading and seeing the clouds much darker and almost overheard, resigned himself to getting wet.

He was about half way back when the rain started. The wind had risen steadily and so had the waves, slowing him further even if he rowed harder than was comfortable. The first drops splashed down onto him and the boat, cooling him, darkening the powdery green paintwork and pricking the receding waves with rings and splashes that grew bigger as the rain became heavier. Campbell rowed on into it, and astern the last vestiges of blue were obliterated by clouds and grey steady sheets of rain. The wind dropped.

Ten minutes later he was soaked and uncomfortably cold. The rain poured steadily down, running from his hair and half blinding him, gathering in the flat bilges of the boat and hissing into the lake around, stilling the water and splashing a dim grey carpet of spray four or five inches from the surface. Away to the right, distant thunder rumbled, at first barely audible over the sound of the oars and the rain on the boat, but slowly getting closer and sharper as Campbell rowed on.

To the south lightning flickered, and from an almost lifelong habit instilled by a rural primary teacher intent on imparting some quantitative knowledge of the physical world on her charges while at the same time giving them something to distract their tiny minds from the traditional fear of electric storms, he began to count, in approximate seconds, the interval to the subsequent thunder.

Promptly on the sixth approximate second there was a loud crack. The formula for converting time to distance, however, for the moment escaped him. Before he could recall it another flash of lightning, much nearer and brighter and a vulgar shade of pink, occurred and Campbell began to count again, getting only as far as two before the thunder, also closer and crisper and originating somewhere above the shore on the right. Whatever the formula, two was close: a lot closer than six, and the distance was dropping fast.

Rowing a boat across a lake in what might turn out to be the middle of a thunderstorm was not, Campbell realized, the sort of thing that was recommended by such guardians of popular wisdom as scoutmasters and outdoor sports instructors. But he continued to do it, if only because the alternative was to sit there doing nothing. He rowed on and thought as he did so about the risks involved. They were not unduly perturbing. Kravitz and Stump had met their violent, young men's deaths, and if it was now his surreal fate to be swatted by electrical forces of natural origin while rowing for pleasure across an obscure lake in West Carolina, then so be it. The thought was even faintly liberating.

The next flash of lightning offered no opportunity to begin counting. It was close, very close indeed: an instantaneous and cataclysmic rending of the grey universe by a sheet of pink fire and a noise as sharp as a rifle shot and many hundreds of times louder, occurring, so far as Campbell could judge, at exactly the same time. He blinked, but was not blinded. He was deafened momentarily, but had not been hit. He took a deep breath and started to laugh, out of relief and at a sudden absurd image of huge, malign celestial target practice, hitherto unsuccessful. Laughing in the rain, he remembered the old black lady, blind and legless, and her intention to pray for him, for the Lord to make him strong. He rowed on. The next flash of lightning was disappointing: somewhere off to the left and followed by a muffled apologetic little thunderclap fully three seconds later. Turning round Campbell saw the boathouse and the landing stage only a few hundred yards away through the rain.

By the time he had moored the boat and carried the oars

and lifejacket up the landing stage the rain had eased to ordinariness and the sky had begun to brighten in the west. The lightning had ceased and the thunder faded to a demurely suppressed belching in the distance. There was no one about on the verandah of the boathouse, so Campbell splashed through its open door and found that the office section at the front was empty too.

'Come on in, Scotchman,' said a voice from the back. Campbell went on in, carrying his oars and lifejacket and leaving a trail of moist footprints behind him. At the back of the boathouse was a dimly lit workshop and storeroom. The man who hired boats and the lone fisherman sat facing each other across an upturned boat on which stood a half empty bottle of whisky and some glasses.

'We kep' some for you.'

'Thank you,' said Campbell, putting down his lifejacket and laying the oars against fifty or sixty others.

'An' if you hadn't turned up we was gonna drink yours an' wait for a while for the storm to pass then go out there an' look for yore body.'

'Thank you.'

'I'm black,' said the girl. She made it sound like a challenge.

Campbell smiled politely.

'I'm black, see?' She came closer, holding her glass at a threatening angle. There was a silence around them.

'Do you find that *embarrassing*?' She had raised her voice and one or two people were looking round at them. Campbell smiled again and said, 'No, not at all.'

'I'm *black*, and I'm a *woman*.' She had lowered her voice, but not by much, and several people around still appeared to be listening.

'Quite.'

'You're white.' She flared her nostrils in contempt. '*An*' you're a man.'

'Yes. Yes, I suppose so.' Campbell took a hearty gulp of gin and tonic. 'Where I come from,' he muttered brainlessly, 'most people are . . . Except of course the women.'

186

'An' bein' black *an*' bein' a woman I gotta take a whole lotta shit you guys never even have to think about.'

Campbell took another mouthful of gin and tonic, reflecting that he had not expected to find the pre-dinner drinks on the first evening of the Turkey Roost retreat either easy or enjoyable. His assailant was a bony girl of medium height in quite a pretty yellow dress. She was pale but faintly Mediterranean in colouring and feature, with soft wavy dark hair and pale blue eyes. Asked to speculate about her origins he might have guessed one-quarter Italian. Evidently he would have been wrong.

'An' black *women* have it tougher'n anybody.'

Another sip saw the end of his drink. Campbell decided that the best thing to do would be to go back to the beginning of the conversation and start again. 'I'm David Campbell,' he said mildly. 'I don't think I caught your name.'

'Mills.'

'Oh.'

'Magnolia Mills.'

'That's a pretty name.'

The girl looked at him with cold hatred. He stumbled on. 'I'm at MacHardy.' Hatred turned to contempt. 'But perhaps you are too . . . I mean, we could both be . . . and never have run into each other before . . .' The girl sipped her drink and distantly watched him squirm. An old, unequivocally black man in a white jacket was patrolling the edge of the gathering. Campbell willed him to notice his empty glass. In the event it was the girl who succeeded in attracting his attention.

'Martini, ma'am?'

'*Dry* Martini an' plenty ice.'

'Suhtainly, ma'am, an' fo' you, suh?'

'Gin and tonic, thank you . . . Not too much tonic, please.' Campbell had meant to say 'not too much gin', as the evening might turn out to be a long one. Before he could correct himself the old man had nodded understandingly and gone off with his glass.

'I'm with Black Life Ending.'

'Oh? In Washington?'

'Yeah.'

'With ALEA?'

'With A*B*LEA. We got a separate program within ALEA, an' I'm the Assistant Vice Chairperson with Special Responsibility for Program Coordination. But mainly I'm into Life Ending black women.'

'That must be very interesting.'

'I like it because it's something a black woman can put a lot of herself into.'

'I suppose so . . . One or two of our patients here . . .'

'You might think that it's sheer tokenism, an' maybe that's the way they were thinkin' when they hired me.' She snorted in private laughter. 'Like, the *men* they hired . . . Reverend this, Judge that . . . A buncha house niggers.'

The grave old waiter had returned with refills. Campbell thanked him for a drink in which there were only one or two bubbles to suggest the presence of even traces of tonic, and took a welcome gulp.

'So as a conscious black *and* a conscious woman, I . . .'

Campbell stopped listening and looked round. There were between twenty and thirty people in the room, mainly from MacHardy and for the most part familiar in appearance if not in name. Amy was there, talking to Dr Drucker and her father, who stood in a corner looking solemnly out over the crowd. The Dean was fully a head above everyone else, his huge ears and lugubrious manner giving him, in relation to the lesser creatures around him, the sad deracinated air of the only elephant in a small-town circus. In profile beside him, Amy, slender and tanned and with a fair amount of shoulder showing, looked less likely than ever as his daughter.

She had rung him that morning from 'Crimond home' before either of them were up. After an agreeable and quite encouraging exchange of sleepy intimacies sufficiently meaty to have Campbell wondering about the possibility of extensions and an elephantine ear applied somewhere, he had been made to understand the degree of discretion expected of him over the period of the retreat. Her preference for separate travel and no indication of anything between them other than a common interest in Life Ending in West Carolina had restored to the term 'retreat' much of its original monastic flavour. Then, only half an hour previously, while he had been unpacking two spare shirts and his current paperback, she had rung him in his room to tell him she was in room eight, upstairs and in the middle at the front, and that she might see him later.

'. . . not an ideological issue if you're white and a man, huh?'

'Quite.'

'Magnolia! Why, *hi*! Gee, it's just *great* to *see* you. How was the trip down from Washington, huh? Isn't Atlanta just *awful*. An' I just *loved* that thing you wrote in the Life Ender about the problems of the minority woman in the Life Ending situation.'

'Why, thank you, Sharron . . .'

'Great title too . . . "Black, a Woman and Now This". I loved it.'

'I hated it. Some honky chauvinist subeditor did that.'

'Oh . . . But it was a *wonderful* article . . .'

'I wanted to call it "Dying is a Black Feminist Issue".'

'But you said it all in the article, Magnolia, you said it all *wonderfully*. Minority women Life Enders have it tougher than anybody.'

'You don't have to tell an ABLEA chairperson that, but thanks, Sharron.'

'An' how *are* things in ABLEA, huh? Uh, David . . . Would you excuse us? Magnolia and I have some things we have to talk about right now . . . Great . . .'

Miss Sneed, in manic pink, took Miss Mills by the elbow and steered her to a corner. Campbell was dimly aware that he might just have been put down by Miss Sneed, but was not, in the particular circumstances, too bothered about it. He sipped his gin and reached for some peanuts. The old black man looked inquiringly at his glass and caught his eye. Campbell smiled and declined a top-up.

They adjourned to dinner and Campbell found himself at a table with Miz Love and the blond psychologist and tackling a small whole roast chicken which reminded him of the late Dr Pulver and the pleasures of vegetarianism. Miz Love ate hers in tiny ladylike mouthfuls; the psychologist cracked bones with his teeth and licked his fingers a lot. Conversation was general.

'Dr Mikoyan's right,' said Miz Love. 'It's a time to look forward . . . A pity about poor Candy, but at least she didn't suffer long.'

'Ethelanne's O.K.,' said the psychologist. 'An' in a town like Crimond a bit of minority visibility right there at the front desk does a whole lotta good.'

'I unnerstan' a black girl was s'posed to be comin' down from Washington.' Miz Love looked round the dining room. 'A girl from the minority group at ALEA . . . Seems she never showed up.'

The psychologist lowered his voice. 'You know how they are.'

Miz Love reproached him with a soulful pause then smiled and said, 'But our Ethelanne's real reliable . . . You can *depend* on her . . . At least so far. An' you can always *unnerstan'* the way she spells.'

Miss Sneed and the not very black girl from Washington were at the next table, but too engrossed in each other and the things they had to talk about to notice casual conversation around them. At the same table Nance twinkled in vain at a wiry man with a crew cut, possibly also from Washington, but too engrossed in his chicken to respond. On the other side of the room, at the only table with place cards and a service of wine, Amy shared a joke with Dr Mikoyan, Dr Bottger, Dr Drucker and her father.

'Everybody admired pore Mr Stump's energy . . . *but* . . .' Miz Love was looking on the bright side of things again. 'You know what I mean? The Administrative Director of a LEAPERS Program just has to be *good with people*. Of course nobody likes change just for the sake of it, but when something like that happens and there have to be changes, like, they're *forced* upon you, it's important to get somebody who's *good with people*.' From the psychologist, nodding and the continued crunch of bones signified agreement. Campbell, who had not been paying much attention, wondered without enthusiasm who the new appointee, Stump's successor, might be.

It did not, he decided, matter much to him now. For the second or third time in the evening he thought how easy and pleasant it would be to have a quick word with Dr Drucker, and resign. What he was doing bore less and less relationship to what he had been appointed to do. Recent developments would undoubtedly continue that trend. The whole LEAPERS scene was distasteful and unreal and, from what Dr Drucker had said, his prospects of any escape short of resignation were nil. He turned his chicken over, wishing he had resigned there and then in Dr Drucker's office.

After dinner they went downstairs for the first working session. It was billed in the schedule as 'Looking Forward' and featured Dr Mikoyan and Miss Sneed under the chairmanship of Dr Teddy Totenberg. In a long low room hung with the hunting trophies of a turn-of-the-century MacHardy, Campbell sat fighting off the combined effects of gin and the Dean's rhetoric, while the assembled 'key faculty, major participants and senior staff' variously listened and took notes.

'. . . an' so, I have much pleasure, without further delay or formality, in handing over this, uh, important, exciting and forward-looking meeting to a man who has long enjoyed mah full confidence and highest professional respect . . . A pioneer in this important field, in which MacHardy, as we all know, has long been a world leader, largely thanks to the efforts of men like him . . . Uh . . . I give you Stef Mikoyan, our new an' may I say very worthy Director of the MacHardy LEAPERS Program. . . . Stef . . .'

Mikoyan, gleaming with smugness, advanced on the little lectern. 'Thanks, Teddy . . . Uh, I didn't bring no slides, so I guess this is gonna be . . . philosophy, mainly, I guess. I wanna say first how glad I am to have been given this opportunity to serve you, an' MacHardy, an' our friends in Washington in this way . . . So I thought . . . I wanna share some ideas with you, in a kinda exploratory way . . . This is nothin' heavy, jus' some ideas that've been goin' aroun', to do with the way we see ourselves and our relationships in the Program . . . our roles, our duties, like, to our research goals, our Center, our Agency in Washington . . . An' may I

say how glad I am to see here both Jerry an' Magnolia . . .
Yeah, give 'em a big hand, they came a long way . . . both
Jerry an' Magnolia, from ALEA . . . oh, an' ABLEA. Those
of you who've worked with me know I'm fairly non-directive,
even for a shrink, an' I wanna emphasize that we're here to,
uh, look at problems, an' find answers, like, together . . .'

Above him, the dull eyes of a stuffed moose looked out.
Beside him the Dean settled into his chair with the air of one
who has attended far too many such occasions. On the other
side of the Dean, and also facing the audience, Miss Sneed,
with a muscular unfading directionless smile, fingered notes
which looked as if they might form the basis of a very long
talk. Campbell switched off and thought of home.

A change of speaker roused him. Miss Sneed, undis-
guisably pudgy under her little-girl pink frock, simpered
before her audience. 'Thanks, Stef . . . Labels as such have
never meant a lot to me, an' for really important things I've
often found they just get in the way, but . . .' She smiled
glassily round at Mikoyan, '. . . as your new Administrative
Director . . .'

The session ended around half past ten. By that time Miss
Sneed had defined in some detail her interests and her new
role, using a series of slides to show, by means of flow
diagrams and organizational charts, how all those aspects of
the work of the Program concerned with Education, Evaluation, Communication and Administration fell neatly into her
area of responsibility, to the advantage of all concerned. One
slide only, a feebly branching thing headed 'Psychiatric and
Medical-model Activities', failed to culminate in a little box
labelled 'Administrative Director'. Dr Mikoyan leaned back
in his chair, giving every appearance of finding the proposed
arrangements to his liking. No one else seemed to care very
much. There were few questions, and the session closed with
some clichés from the Dean.

In the general drift to the bar it became apparent that not
all present were staying the night. The Dean, Dr Bottger, Dr
Drucker and the two visitors from Washington made their
farewells, and a clutch of the resident contingent went down
with them to the vestibule, like children left at camp. Camp-

bell realized he had missed an opportunity to resign and decided to have a drink instead, with the vague intention that he might also find a chance to talk to Amy about the possibility of a suitably discreet get-together in the near future.

An opportunity for that did not arise. He saw her briefly across the room, socializing conscientiously with people of whom she had previously spoken with distaste. Spurred by her example he did the same, but was distressed to find, a couple of whiskies later, that she had gone. He decided to take the night air by himself.

The house, a rambling two-storey wooden affair midway between shooting-lodge and country mansion, was set on a hillside and surrounded by trees. Half a moon, high in the sky, made occasional pools of light on the ground and there were well-marked paths of beaten earth leading to various huts and farm buildings. The night was still and clear and the silence, after two and a half hours of Mikoyan and Sneed, welcome. Campbell walked for ten minutes or so, stopping to watch an owl glide in a moonlit clearing, and to listen to various dry mysterious small-animal noises in the undergrowth. At around eleven-fifteen he went back to the house, noting as he approached it that in the room best answering the description 'upstairs and in the middle at the front' the light was on.

There was still a fair amount of jolly noise coming from the bar. Campbell avoided it and went straight upstairs to his own room and cleaned his teeth then, after a moment's thought to confirm that it was a reasonable if not an excellent idea, quietly walked the few yards along the corridor to room eight.

At the door he paused, his hand raised to knock softly. From inside came a sound he had not expected to hear, or at least not just then. It was familiar and, in other circumstances, welcome: the happy throaty giggling noise that Amy made when they were in bed together and she was enjoying herself.

He did not knock, but walked quietly away and went downstairs to rejoin those members of the retreat remaining in the bar. He had two more whiskies and a long conversation with Nance, who was drinking orange juice. Things could have become quite unpleasant had not Ben Benvenuto, the data man, joined them. Nance took the opportunity to leave to refill his glass and did not come back.

Benvenuto turned out to be literate, articulate and, for an ex-priest now employed collecting data about death and dying, a remarkably jolly man. Campbell, who had been vaguely trying to work out which members of the original group from dinner could no longer be accounted for, gave up his attempt in favour of a splendidly ranging philosophical and occasionally religious dialogue which went quite excellently with the whisky, and lasted until midnight, when the black waiter closed the bar.

Alone and drunk, Campbell went to bed and fell asleep quickly. He was wakened by a loud noise. As he reached for the bedlight he heard a scream, loud and long, then a shot then, after a pause, another shot. They were very close, not outside in the woods but near enough to make the walls shake. As the echo faded there was another scream, this time a long hysterical shriek, also very close.

He got up and pulled on slacks and a shirt and went barefoot into the corridor. It was dimly lit and empty, so ordinary that for a strange, suspended moment he wondered if he had simply had a nightmare of unusual vividness, but a fierce whiff of gunsmoke made it real.

With a sick, hollow feeling he went straight to Amy's room and opened the door. The light was on and she was sitting stiffly on the edge of the bed, naked and holding both hands to her face. Behind her, lying on the bed, was the naked body of a white female, youngish and overweight. Blood was spattered on the wall by the bedlight and a pool of blood spread over the pillow. On it, curly off-blonde hair drenched in blood half hid the face of the new Administrative Director of the MacHardy University Medical Center LEAPERS Project.

Amy still clasped her hands to her face. Campbell took a step towards her and was startled by a third presence in the room. Behind the door, and slumped against the wall with legs splayed, was the clothed corpse of a lean, middle-aged

white male. On the wall above was a star-shaped red mess.
The face hung low over the chest and Campbell stooped to
confirm a suspicion. The features, now pale and bloodstained, were those he had last seen in the photograph on
Amy's dressing table down in Split Rock. The rest of the
head hardly existed, except as the red mass on the wall. The
corpse held in its right hand a large automatic pistol.

'Amy.'

'Who is it?'

'David . . . David Campbell.'

'Oh.' She took her hands from her face and looked up.
There was a noise behind Campbell. He whirled round.
Benvenuto, the data man, stood in the doorway in a brown
dressing gown.

'Sorry, David. Some trouble, huh? Hello, Amy. You all
right? Good. Well, I guess it'd be smart to let the police
know . . . I can do that for you if you want. Are you sure
you're all right?'

In an hour it was all over. Two patrolmen came and took
photographs and made notes, taking names and addresses
and generally behaving as though recent events at Turkey
Roost amounted to no more than, say, a traffic incident.
Campbell began to wonder if this sort of thing happened all
the time in West Carolina, then he remembered that it did.
There was no mystery and no surviving suspect. The police
went away. The two corpses were removed in a van, people
in dressing gowns stood around talking for a while, the black
servant found another room for Dr Totenberg and at about
three in the morning everyone went back to bed.

Campbell was almost asleep when he heard a faint knock-
ing at his door. He ignored it and eventually it stopped.

On the following pages are details of Arrow books that will be of interest.

DR GORDON'S CASEBOOK

Richard Gordon

'Well, I see no reason why anyone should expect a doctor to be on call seven days a week, twenty-four hours a day. Considering the sort of risky life your average GP leads, it's not only inhuman but simple-minded to think that a doctor could stay sober that long . . .'

Following in the ink marks of Samuel Pepys, Mr Pooter and Simon Crisp, comes Dr Richard Gordon, intent on chronicling the life of your average absent-minded, hard-pressed and all-too-human, middle-aged GP. His daughter claims he can't tell his Horner's Syndrome from his Turner's, his houseman son scoffs at his old-fashioned ideas.

Plagued by lost swabs, loose female patients and dreams of Sigmund Freud, Dr Gordon battles on against an ungrateful world and the eccentricities of a health system that seems determined to ignore him.

THE OFFICIAL RULES

Paul Dickson

Bringing hope, comfort and comic relief to the countless thousands of people who feel baffled by the bizarre behaviour of the universe and by the generally bad behaviour of inanimate objects comes Paul Dickson's THE OFFICIAL RULES.

From Murphy to Morley, from Mother Sigafoo to Dean Martin, this is the most hilarious and most comprehensive collection of rules to live by that anyone has ever dared to attempt.

From food (*no man is lonely eating spaghetti*) to sex (*a man should be greater than some of his parts*), from drink (*you're not drunk if you can lie on the floor without holding on*) to health (*never go to a doctor whose office plants have died*), it offers the weary life-traveller the sort of realistic advice that Aunt Amanda never even considered.

A NURSE IN PARTS

Evelyn Prentis

'At the end of all our adding and subtracting and tedious manipulation of the household accounts, we would have been bankrupt but for the fact that we had never had any money in the bank. I prayed long and earnestly for something to turn up, and when it didn't I did the only thing I could do. I went back to hospital and became a part-time nurse.'

And so Evelyn Prentis became a woman living in two worlds. When she waved good-bye to the family and pedalled to work, she became a nurse; when she came off duty and pedalled back home she forgot she was a nurse and became, once more, a wife and a mother. She was, in fact, *A Nurse in Parts*.

You met her first in *A Nurse in Time* and *A Nurse in Action*. Now she is back once more, with adventures as chaotic, delightful and entertaining as ever.

DIARY OF A SOMEBODY
Christopher Matthew

'Quite definitely the funniest book I've had the pleasure of reading.' *Tribune*

At weekend houseparties and the elegant gatherings of the London season, at trendy Workers' Workshops and in the expectant crowds at the new National, Simon Crisp is always noticed. He's the one with the coffee stains on his trousers, the air of punctured dignity and educated worry. Humiliated by hurled apple cores and exploding plastic pants, by practical jokes in the office and in his West London flat, he's a fall-guy for our times.

This is his diary. It curiously resembles that classic of ninety years ago, *The Diary of a Nobody*. Especially in one respect: Simon never sees the joke.

But we do. And deliciously so.

'A genuinely funny book.' *Benny Green, Spectator*

'Spellbinding. I read the diary in one sitting.' *The Times*

THE RUNNING YEARS

Claire Rayner

She was born in 1893, in the slums of London. The daughter of immigrants, the descendants of exiles, she was part of a people doomed to wander, forever strangers in the lands they had chosen as home.

But Hannah Lazar was different. She was born and bred a Londoner, and London was where she belonged. As Strongwilled as she was beautiful, Hannah would uproot herself from the gloomy poverty of her parents' lives to enter a world of elegance and wealth. As her ancestors had journeyed from land to land, with only their own resilience and determination to help them survive, Hannah would move from the slums of the East End to the salons of Mayfair, to a life that she could call her own.

The Running Years is Claire Rayner's most powerful and spectacular novel to date, a breathtaking testament to the human spirit – a richly dramatic and intricately woven story that traces the fortunes of two Jewish families from the razing of Jerusalem in 70 AD through two thousand years of violence, love and change.

'A huge canvas, this, with powerful characters and a gripping story' *Woman's own*

'A feast' *Yorkshire Post*

BESTSELLING HUMOUR BOOKS FROM ARROW

All these books are available from your bookshop or news-agent or you can order them direct. Just tick the titles you require and complete the form below.

☐	THE ASCENT OF RUM DOODLE	W. E. Bowman	£1.75
☐	THE COMPLETE NAFF GUIDE	Bryson, Fitzherbert and Legris	£2.50
☐	SWEET AND SOUR LABRADOR	Jasper Carrott	£1.50
☐	GULLIBLE'S TRAVELS	Billy Connolly	£1.75
☐	THE MALADY LINGERS ON	Les Dawson	£1.25
☐	A. J. WENTWORTH	H. F. Ellis	£1.60
☐	THE CUSTARD STOPS AT HATFIELD	Kenny Everett	£1.75
☐	BUREAUCRATS — HOW TO ANNOY THEM	R. T. Fishall	£1.25
☐	THE ART OF COARSE RUGBY	Michael Green	£1.75
☐	THE ARMCHAIR ANARCHIST'S ALMANAC	Mike Harding	£1.60
☐	CHRISTMAS ALREADY?	Gray Jolliffe	£1.25
☐	THE JUNKET MAN	Christopher Matthew	£1.75
☐	FLASH FILSTRUP	Peter Plant	£1.00
☐	A LEG IN THE WIND	Ralph Steadman	£1.75
☐	POSITIVELY VETTED	Eddie Straiton	£1.75
☐	TALES FROM A LONG ROOM	Peter Tinniswood	£1.75

Postage _____

Total _____

ARROW BOOKS, BOOKSERVICE BY POST, PO BOX 29, DOUGLAS, ISLE OF MAN, BRITISH ISLES

Please enclose a cheque or postal order made out to Arrow Books Ltd for the amount due including 15p per book for postage and packing both for orders within the UK and for overseas orders.

Please print clearly

NAME ....

ADDRESS ....

....

Whilst every effort is made to keep prices down and to keep popular books in print, Arrow Books cannot guarantee that prices will be the same as those advertised here or that the books will be available.